Robert G. Barrett was raised in Bondi where he has worked mainly as a butcher. After thirty years he moved to Terrigal on the Central Coast of New South Wales. Robert has appeared in a number of films and TV commercials but prefers to concentrate on a career as a writer.

ROBERT G. BARRETT

Guns 'n' Rosé

PAN
Pan Macmillan Australia

First published 1996 in Pan by Pan Macmillan
Australia Pty Limited
1 Market Street, Sydney

Reprinted 1997, 2002, 2005, 2008

National Library of Australia
cataloguing-in-publication data:

Barrett, Robert G.

Guns 'n' rosé.

ISBN 9780330358514

I. Title.

A823.3

Typeset in 11/13.5pt Times by Post Typesetters, Brisbane
Printed by IVE

MIX
Paper from
responsible sources
FSC® C018183
www.fsc.org

A MESSAGE FROM THE AUTHOR

Firstly, I have to thank everyone for buying the books and making them the success they are. You've been more than kind. And the possum lady thanks you for buying the T-shirts too; she can now afford to feed her two kids and she's bought herself some teeth as well. Also, thanks for all the letters. I'm getting heaps of them and they're all great; some are even better than others. I'm doing my best to answer all of them, but at the moment I've been flat out, so if a reply is a bit late in coming, I'm sorry, but you should get one eventually.

Secondly, people are always asking what's going on with Les Norton on the screen. Well, I've done it. I have finally sold my soul to the devil. The devil in this case being a company in Sydney called Radio Super-highway owned by a person called John Singleton. Radio Superhighway has bought the rights off me to make a Les Norton TV series. When I say 'bought', obtained a hire-purchase would be a better description. I don't get a zac until when, and if, the series goes to air. So don't stop buying the books and T-shirts in the meantime. I have to eat and the possum lady has to feed her kids and she still needs more teeth. I also have to stress that, along with selling my soul to the devil, I also had to sell him a thing called creative control, which means they can virtually do what they like with my books. So if you turn on the TV and Carlotta comes out playing Les Norton and Joh Bjelke-Petersen shows up playing Price Galese: don't blame me. However, I'm sure John Singleton and Radio Superhighway want this to be a success just as much as I and my readers do, so I don't think they'll murder it too much. Anyway, they've only obtained the TV rights from me. I can still make a Les Norton movie — which I will do one day and I can assure you it will be done properly. So that's what's going on.

Finally, the possum lady said that along with the TEAM NORTON caps in either black or green with gold lettering, there's another two T-shirts available — GUNS 'N' ROSÉ and DAVO'S LITTLE SOMETHING. Still only $32 for a T-shirt and $28 for a cap. Just send a cheque, along with your size (M, L, XL), choice of T-shirt or cap and address it to Psycho Possum Productions, PO Box 3348, Tamarama, Sydney NSW, 2026. The possum lady also said if people come up and ask you where you got your T-shirt or cap, don't tell them. Talk to them if you want to, but don't tell them anything. Okay? As for me, I'll see you in the next book. Thanks again.

Robert G. Barrett
Terrigal, 1996

Despite all his ill-gotten gains and everything he had going for him, Les Norton was by no means the happiest man in the world at the moment. By no means. Certainly he wasn't short of a dollar and he owned his house at Bondi with stuff planted all over the place that he could sell if he wanted to and he had a fairly steady job amongst friends that paid him a substantial income for what little work he did a few nights a week, not counting the fringe benefits. Not a bad start in life. Yet on the other hand, Les couldn't seem to take a trick and sometimes wondered just where life was leading him.

After the Bondi Baths caper, Norton split from Side Valve Susie's unit, and so did Susie; along with the good-looking lawyer who handled all the business in Melbourne. Which effectively ended any ideas he had for a bit of steady porking with an old friend he fancied just round the corner. Goodbye, Les, and thanks for your help. And since then Norton's love life had been more or less batting zero. Around this time he loaned a bloke he knew and trusted a thousand dollars. The bloke was all right, except he had a heart attack and died at forty-one; and in the surf at Coogee of all places. So he got buried along with Norton's thousand bucks. Then Les' car was stolen. The old, white Ford ute he never washed. Some young hoons nicked it up the Cross one night and used it in a ram-raid on an appliance store in Kensington, getting away all right and leaving what was left of Norton's old ute down a back alley in Alexandria.

Norton was pissed off, but he wasn't worried all that much as the ute was fast becoming a heap of shit and he was almost glad to get rid of it. But because Les was a bit slack in getting off his arse and reporting it, the police traced the car and took him in for questioning. Les had a solid alibi and could prove there was no way he had anything to do with it. But Les was still a bit edgy after the Bondi Baths caper. Although they appeared to have got away with it, it still unnerved him the whole time he was being questioned in Maroubra police station. He kept thinking any minute some detective was going to say, 'Oh, and by the way, Les, just exactly where were you on Friday night the such-and-such of the so-and-so?' Which was just one of several things unnerving Norton at the present time.

All the old members of the Icebergs were now drinking at the Bondi Diggers, where Les used to enjoy a cool one now and again. Every time he'd arrive there always seemed to be a bunch of them hanging around, clutching their schooners and staring sad-faced out the windows across Bondi Bay to the charred rubble of where their clubhouse used to be and shaking their heads and moaning about how it was the end of an era along with all the trophies and mementos they'd gathered over the years and how Bondi just wasn't the same without the baths. Les had to agree with them. It was a bummer all right. A dead-set, crying bloody shame. And sometimes, with a few beers under his belt, Les would have liked to have told them the truth and got it all off his chest. And they weren't the only ones complaining. It seemed everywhere Les went he'd bump into people and the first thing they seemed to say was, 'Bondi just doesn't seem the same without the baths'. Like several mothers he knew down at North Bondi with their children, lamenting the fact that they couldn't take their children to the big pool where they could learn to swim properly.

On top of that, Bondi seemed to be turning into a bigger shitfight than ever. Gangs of hoons coming in from the suburbs, fighting with the police while they rioted and did their best to wreck everything along Campbell Parade. Hordes of soapy backpackers trashing the entire beach while they got pissed out of their brains, leaving it to the council to clean up and the poor, long-suffering local lifesavers to drag their smelly European or pommy bodies out of the surf when they went for a drunken swim and started to drown. A lot of locals reckoned, instead of pulling them out of the water when they started drowning, the lifesavers should put a hose on them and finish the job off. Though this gave Norton the shits as much as it got on his nerves. And talking about backpackers—there was Warren.

Warren's mental condition seemed to have deteriorated since Isola left and it wasn't from a broken heart. She left a day earlier than she intended, along with what money Warren had left lying around, and his VISA card. Isola might have only had a backpack, but somehow she managed to stuff three pairs of R. M. Williams jeans, several bottles of Estee Lauder perfume, four large bottles of Jack Daniels and a number of Ken Done outfits into it before she brushed the trip to Bali and jetted straight back to Holland; after flushing Warren's VISA card down the can at Kingsford Smith Airport. And there was SFA Warren could do about it; Isola could sign his name better than Warren could. As Norton lamented to Warren in the kitchen one morning just after he got his car stolen, shit certainly happens, doesn't it? Now Warren was getting his rocks off in a strange way; growing pot in the backyard, getting stoned, then going up to Bondi Junction where the nice ladies from the church sold secondhand clothes, magazines and other bric-a-brac for charity in the plaza near the ANZ bank and trying to freak the poor old dears out of their minds. Somehow Warren had got hold of a box of pornographic magazines that were supposed to have been pulped. He'd take a few up the plaza, slip them in amongst the *National Geographics*, *New Idea*, *House and Garden* or whatever, then stand back with a telephoto-lens camera and take shots of the good, God-fearing Christian ladies when either they or a customer would come across WILD LESBIAN LEATHER LICK FEST. YOUNG FOXES WITH SHAVED BOXES. SCHOOL GIRL BONDAGE GANG BANG. WILHELMINA'S WILD WET WHIPS.

Norton thought this a bit sick on Warren's part, though he had to admit his flatmate did have a flair for photography; some of his candid snaps of the old dears' faces were unbelievable. However, Les declined Warren's offer of a hot one and then joining him one Saturday. Les, however, didn't mind a hot one courtesy of Warren down the backyard with the music going on his days off. It was laid back and secluded and seemed better than going down the beach and bumping into old Icebergs and other people all parroting the same line— 'Bondi just isn't the same without the baths'. But staying home stoned only seemed to add a sense of paranoia to Norton's nagging guilt complex and increasing nervousness, as if he was trapped in his own home and mind with all that other rattle still swirling around outside like some invisible dust storm. There was only one answer—Norton needed a holiday. Only for about a week or so and not too far away, but where no one knew him. Just sitting around some hotel or resort, eating good food, drinking piss, reading, doing bugger all. Maybe go for a swim or something. The ute was gone. But it wouldn't cost much to hire an el cheapo one and just hit the road. Port Stephens sounded all right. Or maybe Mollymook or Ulladulla. Les had never been to the South Coast.

And that's exactly what Les was thinking as he stood in front of his bedroom mirror, wearing his best Levi's, a brown collarless shirt and brown grunge boots, on a balmy Tuesday night in early autumn getting ready for a shift at the Kelly Club. I'll tell Price after work tonight I'm pissing off for a week, he thought. Get someone else. And if you don't like the idea. Stiff shit!

Warren hadn't come home from the advertising agency yet and Billy had started work an hour earlier, so he missed a lift with his good mate and offsider. But the taxi he'd rung for would be out the front in a couple of minutes. He gave himself a last detail then got a brown cotton jacket out of his wardrobe and picked up a novel he was reading just as a pair of headlights washed across the front windows and a horn tooted out in the street. Les tossed his jacket over his shoulder and locked the front door behind him. It's funny, he thought as the driver did a U-turn back up Cox Avenue towards Lamrock after Les told him where they were going, going away on your own's okay, but it'd be nice to have a mate along with you. Someone to have a mag with, crack a few jokes, get some laughs going. Talk things over. Maybe get things off your chest. Norton chuckled to himself. Yeah, that's it, a bit of male bonding. The taxi stopped for the lights at O'Brien and Old South Head Road and a tall, sinewy girl with scraggly brown hair, wearing jeans and a black top that made her tits looks like two choice, ripe honeydew melons, crossed with the lights and sauntered into the store on the O'Brien Street corner. Norton's eyes never left her for a moment. Yeah, so much for bloody male bonding. I think I'd rather take that with me. For about six months.

Billy was inside the door at the club dressed much like Norton and all smiles when he opened it after Les knocked.

'Hello, Billy. How's things, mate?'

'Not too bad, Les,' replied Billy. 'Can't complain. What about yourself?'

'Oh, pretty good. Sort of.'

'Pretty good, sort of?'

'Yeah,' nodded Les, as Billy closed the door. 'I'll tell

you about it later. I'll just duck up and let Don Corleone and the rest of them know I'm here.'

'Righto. I won't be going far.'

There were about fifty or so punters spread around the green felt tables playing mainly Euchre or German Whist for hundreds of dollars a point on credit; no money changed hands. Although the place was unofficially a club, Price now charged everyone that came in five dollars. He paid tax on this, which made for a legal income and the money over that more than paid for Les' and Billy's wages with a bonus now and again. For their five dollars the punters, as well as being able to play cards in peace, were able to eat fresh, tasty sandwiches and drink tea or coffee till it was coming out their ears. Billy reckoned it was worth five dollars just for the smoked salmon sandwiches alone. So between this and the points he creamed off the punters, plus his own winnings and the winnings from his string of champion racehorses Price was making just as much money as ever and doing it cosier and that close to legitimately it didn't make any difference. For the dapper, silver-haired, ex-casino owner, it was a nice little vibe all round. He was standing at the back wearing an immaculate grey suit and green tie talking to George Brennan, who was wearing a Bermuda jacket and dark tie. They both stopped their conversation and smiled when they saw Norton approaching.

'Hello, Price. George. How's things?'

'Good,' answered George. 'Couldn't be creamier.'

'Sensaish,' said Price, feinting a left rip to Norton's ribs. 'If I was any fitter I'd be dangerous. What about you, Les, me old mate?'

'Ohh, all right. Sort of.'

'All right, sort of?' said Price.

'Yeah,' nodded Les. 'I'll tell you about it after work.'

'You know what you need?' said George.

'Yeah, what, George?' replied Norton, expecting some half-arsed remark.

'A holiday.'

'A what?' Les gave George a double blink.

'A holiday. You need a break.'

'George is right,' nodded Price. 'You've been looking a bit jaded lately, old fellah. A few days off would do you the world of good.'

'It would?' Norton couldn't quite believe what he was hearing.

'Yeah. A hundred per cent.' Price gave Les a friendly slap on the shoulder. 'Anyway, we'll talk about it after we knock off tonight.'

'Yeah, right,' Les nodded slowly. 'We'll talk about it then.' Slightly puzzled and at the same time pleasantly surprised at how this all fell into place so easily, Norton left Price and George to whatever it was they were talking about, had a quick look round the club then joined Billy inside the front door.

'So how's things?' said Billy, glancing up from the latest Frederick Forsyth paperback he was reading.

'Terrific,' answered Les. 'Good. Even better than I thought.'

'How do you mean?'

'Well, I was gonna tell Price I wanted to take a few days off. But before I got a chance, he told me I looked like I needed a holiday and to take a break.'

'Sounds pretty good to me,' replied Billy, going back to his novel and turning the page.

'Yeah, pretty good,' agreed Les. He took a copy of *The Hand that Signed the Paper* from his jacket, thumbed to the page he was reading, then looked back up in the direction of the office, his eyes slightly narrowed. 'Maybe a bit too good.'

Billy disregarded Norton's last comment, went back to his book and the night went accordingly. Members and their guests came and went, having a punt or a feed or whatever. Eddie arrived late in his black leather jacket and jeans, had a talk and a joke for a while, then went upstairs and stayed there. Before they knew it the night was over; the last punter was gone, along with the staff, the place was tidied up waiting for the cleaners and they were settled quietly in Price's office having a drink. Price was at his desk, Les in front to his right, George next to him with Eddie and Billy on the other side. Les and Billy were drinking Eumundi Lager, George a Stolly and cranberry juice, Eddie a Light and Price had a tall Glenfiddich and soda.

Price raised his glass. 'Well, here's cheers, boys. All the best.'

'Yeah, not a bad night,' said Billy.

'Yep, it was all right,' agreed Les.

They all took a sip of their respective drinks and settled a little further into their seats. Before anyone got too comfortable, Price turned to George.

'Now, George, what was that we were saying to Les earlier?'

'About how we reckoned the big sheila needed a holiday.' George gave Les a brief once-up-and-down.

9

'Yeah, he sure does. Have a look at him—he's a fucked unit.'

'Well, there you go, Les,' said Price. 'Words of wisdom from a man who should know.' Price took another sip of Scotch. 'You have been looking a bit tired lately, Les. That baths things did turn out a bit how's your father. I wouldn't blame you if you wanted to take a break.'

Norton laughed quietly and shook his head. 'You know, it's funny, Price, but that's exactly what I was thinking earlier. I wouldn't mind going away for a while. Bondi's giving me the shits at the moment.'

'Then that's it.' Price raised his glass towards Norton. 'Our boy Les is taking a week off.'

There was a general hub-hub of compliments and laughter; Les almost felt like it was his birthday. When it settled down George was the first to speak.

'So, ah . . . where were you thinking of going, Les?'

Norton shrugged. 'I don't know, George. I was thinking of going down the South Coast. I've never been there. I don't want to go too far away.'

'The South Coast, eh,' nodded George.

There was a brief silence. Price tinkled the ice round his glass then looked at Les. 'How would you like a week up in my place at Terrigal. That's not far away.'

'Terrigal?'

'Yeah, you were up there not that long ago. You reckon you had a top time.'

'Yeah, terrific,' said Les.

'And I stuffed things up by making you come back early. So this time I'll make it up to you. You can have my joint for a week. And seeing as those low-lifes stole

10

that immaculate ute of yours, I'll let you hire a car on me, too.' Price looked around the room. 'Fair dinkum. Am I a good boss or what?'

'The best,' agreed Billy.

'Heart as big as Phar Lap's and made of twenty-four carat gold,' said Eddie.

'Well, what do you reckon, Les?' beamed Price.

Norton shook his head almost in disbelief. He felt that good he was almost embarrassed. 'Shit! I don't know what to say, Price. Thanks a lot, mate. I really appreciate it.'

Price waved a hand dismissively. 'Think nothing of it, Les. You're family to us. And you'll like the place now, too. I've had it all done up. I rent it to these corporate cowboys and rich dudes. You'll love it.'

'Thanks, Price,' repeated Les. 'That's terrific of you.' Norton felt happy, relieved and glad to be amongst friends who appreciated the fact that he was feeling a bit down at the moment. It was like Price said—almost as if he was family.

'And, ah, while you're up there, Les,' said Price. 'I might get you to do me a bit of a favour.'

'A favour?' Norton sat up a little in his seat, his eyes narrowed slightly and he stared directly at Price.

Price moved his gaze across to George Brennan. 'George'll tell you all about it, Les.'

Norton zeroed his eyes in on George like two laser beams. 'So, go ahead, George . . . old mate. Tell me, what's this favour? I'm all ears.'

George lifted his chin a little and the look he gave Norton was almost saintly. 'While you're up there, Les, I'd like you to look after my young nephew,

11

Jimmy . . . James. He's my favourite nephew and I love him dearly. And that's the truth, Les.'

'The truth, eh? Okay, George, what about some more truth? How old's this James? And what's he doing up there?'

'He's . . . nineteen. And at the present time young James is in Kurrirong Juvenile Justice Centre doing a year . . . sort of.'

'Doing a year . . . sort of?' repeated Les.

'Well, he's doing his time at Mount Narang. But we got him transferred to Kurrirong because some nutter in the other nick is convinced James gave him up and wants to kill him . . . blade him. We're still not sure if he's safe in Kurrirong. But we got him five days' compassionate leave while we sort the rattle out with this other Elliott and either get him necked or his legs broken or transferred to Goulburn or something. That's all.'

'That's all?' said Les.

'Yeah,' nodded George. 'That's it. Just look after my young nephew for five days in Terrigal. Take him out, have a good time, do what you like. You'll like him, though. He's a top bloke.'

'A top bloke, eh? Well, if he's such a top bloke, what's he doing in the nick?'

'Ahh, some rotten cops up there who don't like him set him up on a pot charge.'

'Pot? Shit, that's bugger all. Especially if he was set up.'

'And now he's got some nutter wanting to kill him for nothing.'

'Yeah, well he sure doesn't need that, the poor cunt.'

12

'So, Les,' said Price, 'in a way you'd be doing both yourself and the kid a favour if you go up there. And George, of course—the kid's uncle.'

'That's right, Les,' said George, 'a big favour.'

Les stared into his bottle of beer for a moment. He knew almost from the word go that it was too good to be true. But on the other hand, it did save a lot of stuffing around and he was muttering something to himself earlier about having a bit of company. And besides that, if James turned out to be a flip, it was only an hour and a half back to Sydney and he could piss off somewhere else. Les took a mouthful of beer then shrugged a look across to George. 'Yeah, why not? Why bloody not? So what's this nephew of yours' surname, George?'

'Rosewater,' replied George.

'Rosewater?' Norton closed his eyes, shook his head and laughed. 'Jimmy Rosewater. Doing a lag at Kurrirong Juvenile Justice Centre.' Norton tossed back his head and laughed again. 'I like it. Oh yes, I like it.'

By the time everybody except Eddie was half drunk, Les knew what he had to do, where he had to go, and had a road map and the directions on a piece of paper showing him how to get there. He also had the keys to the house and $3000 in cash. All he had to do was pick up a hire car the next morning, take a relaxing drive to Terrigal and collect young James on Thursday morning. Les also had this feeling of deja vu or as if his life at times was like an episode of 'Minder' running over and over, and like poor, suffering Terry, he was always doing the right thing by people and getting shafted for his trouble. But by the time George and Price plied him with copious quantities of cold beer and choice bourbon, Les would have agreed to anything just to get out of Bondi for a while. In fact, when Eddie dropped him home on the way to Price's house at Vaucluse, Les was rolling around in the back of the Rolls-Royce with Price singing 'New York, New York' and 'If You're Going to San Francisco'. And when he almost fell out the door of the Roller, Les felt like he didn't have an enemy in the world and he was looking forward to getting away in the morning.

Warren was in bed asleep, so Les did his best not to wake him while he had a glass of filtered water from the fridge and an Ovaltine from the microwave oven, which he sipped on the back verandah as he gazed into the garden. Before Les knew it, he was yawning away and not thinking about much except getting to bed. Terrigal did play briefly on his mind, however. It's funny, he mused as he sipped the last of his Ovaltine, it doesn't seem like that long since I was up there. Not that I saw much the last time. All I seemed to see was that ratbag sheila's ted. I wonder if I'll bump into the beautiful Sophia again? Norton drained the last of his Ovaltine and walked towards the kitchen. Bloody hope not. He rinsed his mug then hit the sack and crashed out like a light.

Les wasn't feeling all that bad when he rose around eight, climbed into a pair of shorts and a T-shirt, had a horrible boozy dump, cleaned his teeth and found Warren sitting at the kitchen table wearing Levi's and a matching denim shirt.

'G'day, Woz,' said Norton. 'How's things?'

'All right,' replied Warren, taking a glance at his watch. 'Except I'm just about to hit the toe for the pickle factory.' He took a sip of coffee and looked up at Les. 'So what's your story, homeboy? How was work last night? Any murders? Bashings?'

'No, it was pretty quiet, to tell you the truth.' Norton opened a cupboard and started getting some cereal and coffee together. 'I keep telling you, Woz, nothing happens up there now. It's like an old folks' home. In fact, it's that quiet I've been laid off for a week.'

'Laid off?'

'Yep. Downsized. It's a proper bastard.'

'Shit! I thought you were pretty sweet up there.'

'So did I. Instead, Price has turned out to be nothing but a rotten cunt.'

15

'So what are you going to do?'

'I'm staying at his place in Terrigal for a week.'

'You're what?'

Without mentioning George's nephew, Les told Warren pretty much the truth about Price giving him a week off and the use of the house. Warren was impressed.

'So that's the story, Woz. Don't wreck the joint while I'm away, and I'll see you next Wednesday.'

'Fair enough. Have a good time up there.' Warren drained the last of his coffee and rinsed the mug. 'Well, I'm gonna clean my teeth and piss off.'

'Yeah, you're up earlier than usual. Got a big day on with the other rocket scientists in the ad agency, have you?'

'Yep. In fact there's a board meeting straight up where I will have to fight to get my point across. Which, if I do, could mean mucho extra dinero for yours truly. And, Les, if something's worth fighting for, it's worth fighting dirty for. They won't know what hit them when big Woz walks in the room.'

'Go get 'em, Woz. But just remember what my old grandma used to say.'

'What's that, Les?'

'Never get in a fight with a pig. You both finish up covered in shit and the pig likes it.'

'True, Les, but the mugs I'm dealing with think the truth is very interesting but entirely irrelevant. And mugs that think logically, captain, are completely out of touch with the real world.'

'Exactly, Spock. The more you run over a dead cane toad, the flatter it gets. And all things being equal, fat people use more soap.'

'I'm going to clean my teeth.'

Warren left for the bathroom, leaving Les to potter around getting himself some breakfast. He was back within seconds, standing in front of Les holding his toothbrush.

'I'll tell you something, Les,' said Warren. 'You're a reasonably articulate bloke, you own a nice house in Bondi worth quite a bit of money, you're fit, you can fight, and you're not bad with the sheilas. But one thing, Les, don't ever get around thinking your shit doesn't stink. Christ!'

Norton moved aside to let Warren clean his teeth in the kitchen sink. 'I never have,' he replied. 'I reckon my farts are okay. But my craps? Never. Though I will say one thing, Woz. I reckon my craps are more like they are today than they ever were before.'

After Warren left for work, Norton sat alone in the kitchen finishing his coffee, with some FM radio drifting in from the loungeroom. He stuffed around, taking his time, then looked at his watch and decided he might as well get his arse into gear. The sooner he packed his gear, the sooner he'd be out of beautiful, downtown Bondi. He ratted through his room picking out what he thought he'd need for a week away; clothes, cassettes and his VISA cards mainly. Plus a few other odds and ends. He wouldn't need any cash because Price had given him more than he could possibly spend. After he packed two bags plus his overnight one, Les changed into a pair of jeans and a clean Hahn-Ice T-shirt, walked down to Six Ways and got a taxi to the car rental office in Bondi Junction.

The girl there was polite but terribly sorry that all

17

the BMWs and LTDs were gone. However, there was a near new, dark blue Holden Berlina tanked up and ready to go. And yes, Mr Norton, it did have a good stereo system. Norton signed the necessary papers, returned the young lady's smile and drove off.

Well, nothing wrong with this, thought Les, as he cruised down the back of Bondi Junction towards Old South Head Road. The Berlina went like a dream, so did the stereo, the air-conditioning and the power steering. And a ton of guts too, Les smiled to himself, as he tromped it and left a mini-van in his wake. Wasn't it P. J. O'Rourke who said that the best cars to drive are hire cars? They always seem to perform better than your own and they're indestructible. After his old Ford ute it was like driving a Dino Ferrari.

Les screeched to a halt outside Chez Norton and wasn't there twenty minutes before he had his bags in the car, the house locked and a note left for Warren to tell the neighbours to keep an eye on the house. Well, goodbye Bondi. Norton smiled and rubbed his hands together for an instant as he cruised comfortably and effortlessly back up Lamrock Avenue. I'll see you next week. And if it's any good up there it might just be another week.

Les didn't bother with the stereo till he was well over the bridge and going past Gordon. The traffic seemed a little heavier than normal with quite a few big trucks rumbling along, so he concentrated on that and one or two other things that were on his mind. He was getting a pretty good deal, there were no two ways about that, and it didn't worry him one way or the other whether Jimmy turned out to be okay or a complete dill. But George had never spoken of him before and Les had met just about all of George's family since he'd been at the club. And Price seemed to have an unusually avid interest in all this, seeing it was only one of George's nephews—telling Les to look after him, see he didn't get into any trouble and if he needed help with anything to give him a hand. The spiel about how Jimmy happened to be in the nick and the trouble was probably fair dinkum. But if you got a prisoner out on compassionate leave, wasn't he supposed to have a guard with him at all times? Though you could expect Price and George would have pulled every string in the book to get around that. Maybe Les had been slotted in as Jimmy's guard for the week or whatever. There were a couple of things that seemed a bit strange. Still, if Jimmy was George's nephew, he should know how to do the right thing because the Brennans were all pretty staunch and well known around Balmain. No matter what, he'd still be someone to talk to and have a drink with.

Before Les knew it, the traffic had eased and he was almost at the turn-off before Hornsby. He stopped for the lights, fiddled in his overnight bag for a cassette and slipped it into the stereo. The lights turned green and as Les drove down onto the F3 Gina Jeffreys started banging out the old Janis Joplin song, 'Mercedes Benz'. By the time this cut into The Fabulous Thunderbirds' 'We Got To Stick Together', Les was having the time of his life cruising along in the powerful new car. It seemed to eat up the miles and he'd gone over the Hawkesbury River with its beautiful view of Brooklyn and the water, up Jolls Bridge and was cruising up and over Mooney Mooney Bridge towards the Gosford turn-off. A big Shell truck stop zoomed up on his right a few kilometres further on and Les reflected on the map they gave him and knew that the gaol he was supposed to pick Jimmy up at was round here somewhere. The lights turned green, Brisbane Water and Gosford loomed up in the distance at the bottom of the hill and Les wound down the winding road, past the Woy Woy turn-off and over the Brian McGowan Bridge onto The Entrance Road past the furniture showrooms and other small shopping complexes. Next thing he'd reached the big roundabout and had turned right into Terrigal Drive past Erina Fair, the gardening centres, and the houses on either side of the road nestled amongst the trees. Maybe it was the car, all the trees around him or just the fresh air, but Les suddenly felt relaxed and happy again. Like a weight had been lifted from him. A few kilometres on, he turned right near a hotel and a small bridge. There was a huge expanse of ocean and just over the rise was the popular seaside town of Terrigal.

The first thing Les noticed as he cruised into Terrigal was a colourful fish and chip shop opposite the parking area next to the surf club, with white chairs and tables out front called the Flathead Spot, which for some reason looked like it would just have to sell beautiful, fresh seafood. There were surf shops, restaurants and the ubiquitous real-estate agencies and the next thing Les noticed was the main drag running through Terrigal was now a one-way street. He stopped for a pedestrian crossing on the corner, then drove past a row of towering pine trees that ran alongside the beach and more shops and restaurants opposite; the one that stood out was a brightly lit and labelled bottle shop next to a newsagency. Mmmhh, mused Les, I reckon I'll be in to see you before the week is up.

It was still sunny and warm with a few clouds around and a constant sea breeze was feathering the ocean with white horses and rocking the boats anchored in the Haven. There were people lying on the beach or swimming, strolling around casually or seated in the cafes. But compared to Bondi it was Sleepy Hollow.

Les drove past the shops then stopped at the next corner for another pedestrian crossing and the next thing he noticed was the old Florida Hotel was gone. In its place was a huge, spacious resort. It was all pinky browns, mustard and ochre colours, about six or more storeys high and appeared to take up the entire block. A wooden pergola holding a canopy of vines hung over rows of flowerbeds angled round the front and a sign on the corner said TERRIGAL PINES HOLIDAY RESORT. A set of steps led into a roomy beer garden and there appeared to be rows of shops running off and around that. It was all terraces and huge, rounded glass windows with an angled roof above and seemed to give the appearance someone had taken a ritzy chalet out of the Swiss Alps and placed it next to a beach. It looked pretty good to Les. Yes, he smiled to himself again, I reckon I might be calling in to see you as well in the next few days. The road ahead became two-way and led up another hill past the Haven. Les turned right at the pedestrian crossing and thought he might do a quick victory lap of the block and see what else there was.

After driving past a hot bread shop, a butcher, and a fruit shop next to a lane, Les then turned right again at a couple of banks opposite the resort. There was a church on the corner, a medical centre next to the local wallopers, then it was more shops, mainly boutiques and cafes with chairs out the front and no shortage of punters sitting in the sun enjoying their cafe lattes, cappuccinos or whatever. The road turned right again into a one-way street with even more shops, including a video store, a TAB and an original barber shop with a bloke standing out the front with a grey beard wearing a blue coat; you could almost smell the Spruso, Bay Rum and Yardleys Brilliantine from the car.

Turning right again at the pedestrian crossing, Les found himself back where he started. Well, how good's this? thought Les, feeling even happier than he did before. This place looks grouse. I never even got much of a chance to notice it last time. Now I'm here for a week with three big ones burning a hole in my kick. How absolutely sweet it is. Now let's go and find The Don's place and get unpacked. At a leisurely, unhurried pace Les drove ahead, this time up a hill past the boats in the Haven and the steep rise of the Skillion and past the turn-off to North Avoca. There was a lone restaurant on the right called the Silver Conche that looked pretty good, then Price's street a bit further along on the left; only it had been re-zoned for some reason and was now called Mill Hill Road. Price's house was just down on the left, exactly as Les had left it last time. The only difference was it appeared to have been given a classier landscape job out the front and the block of land on the right was gone and somebody had built a two-storey home there. Norton eased the Berlina up in front of the double garage and cut the engine.

Three small Japanese cars were parked outside the new home on the right; Les gave them a cursory glance as he got his bags from the car and carried them up the short side passage to the front door. There was no one around, the only street noise was the wind gently tossing the branches in the surrounding trees and several magpies, kookaburras and wattle birds singing to each from somewhere amongst the leaves. Norton let his eyes run over the neatly trimmed flowerbeds, colourful indoor plants and ferns, then opened the front door and stepped inside, closing it behind him. Yes, he smiled to himself, just as I remember the place. A bedroom, study and kitchen on the left and a short hallway to the sunken lounge. A passageway with bedrooms running off it to the right, the bathroom and the larger bedroom he was in before next to the double garage facing the street. Les dropped his bags for a moment, walked down into the loungeroom and over to the electric curtain which was now a pink and brown floral design. He pressed the button and it swished back to reveal the swimming pool, sparkling in the sun and sheltered from the breeze by the surrounding cabana set amongst more fresh landscaping, flowerbeds and mini-date palms. The house had been recarpeted in swirls of thick, brown axminster, the furniture was all soft, cream velvet and plenty of it. Bird and flower prints hung on the walls, a chandelier hung from the ceiling and on a small oak cabinet near a smoked-glass coffee table sat a combined fax, telephone and answering service.

Norton left the curtains drawn and walked down-stairs to the bottom half of the house and the other bed-rooms, opened the back door next to the laundry and stepped out into the pool area. He had a quick stroll around, tried not to burst out laughing, he was that happy, and went back inside. S'pose I may as well have my old bedroom facing the street, he thought, tossing his bags on the double bed then flicking on the light. The old bedroom had been repainted and car-peted too. A teak dressing table sat near the built-in wardrobes and thick, dark green curtains hung across the window. Les drew them back to let some more light in and started unpacking, all the time thinking about the pool out the back. In near record time, Les had everything sorted out, his Speedos on, a towel round his neck and was almost sprinting downstairs and out the back door. Without further to-do, he dropped his towel on the nearest stretch of landscaped turf and barrel-rolled into the pool like a leaping killer whale.

The water was absolutely glorious; cool, refreshing and not over-chlorinated. Les swam, wallowed, duck-dived and flopped around in general, not believing the change in fortune that had come over him. One minute he was in the middle of the city feeling like he was being slowly choked to death and wondering where it was all going to finish. Now he was totally relaxed. The water in the pool felt like it was cleansing him of all his sins and worries, the sun beaming down from above seemed to be putting the charge back into his life batteries already. Norton floated on his back, spurted out a jet of water, then looked up into the sky with the odd tuft of white cloud scudding around and

24

winked into the blue cosmos. And when did I ever doubt you, old mate, he smiled. Les flopped around a while longer then got out, put his sunglasses on and with his towel round his waist thought he might check out the surroundings.

The house on the left was brown brick, with white lattice at the back full of healthy green vines and red bougainvillea. A brick and concrete patio dotted with more vines and pots of flowers overlooked a sloping, neatly trimmed backyard that led to what appeared to be a reserve full of towering gum trees and native shrubs. A slim woman, possibly in her sixties, with straight, greyish blonde hair, wearing white shorts and a white top, sat at a wrought-iron table writing a letter. Near her stood a man about the same age with a salt 'n' pepper beard and glasses. He was wearing a striped T-shirt and blue shorts and he had a stick in his hand. He was talking to someone or something at his feet. Les had a closer look and saw it was two agitated magpies, whistling, squawking and preening their chests.

'All right, all right, don't shit yourselves,' said the man. 'I'm coming.'

The magpies started walking and the man with the stick followed them down from the patio to some shrubs near the start of the backyard. On the way, two beautifully marked dragon lizards sitting on two rocks took no notice of him till the man fed each of them a grape which they both immediately started chewing. The man stopped at the shrubs, poked the stick in and pulled out half a dead snake, which sent the two magpies into even more of a squawking, flapping, whistling frenzy.

'Look,' said the man, 'it's dead. The kookaburras have been eating it.' The man flicked the dead snake from the stick and gave it a couple of healthy belts with the stick for their benefit.

The two magpies had a look, then settled down and followed the man as he started walking back to the patio. On the way he stopped to give the two dragon lizards a quick pat and say something, then joined his wife back on the patio. The two magpies stayed with him for a moment before flying up onto the fence where they started whistling happily now that the drama was all over.

Well, don't that beat it all, Norton smiled to himself. I wonder who that mysterious, bearded man was? Doctor Dolittle? The man and his wife didn't seem to notice Les, so he left them and strolled between the pool and the cabana to where the fence ran opposite the house on the right.

It was a two-storey, brick job, painted white and blue with a blue roof. A wooden sundeck dotted with flowers and trees in ceramic pots, faced the ocean above Les and below it was another wooden sundeck strung with clotheslines and hanging plants. A set of steps ran down to a backyard that was fenced off above another, sloping yard that had been cleared except for several tall trees and a smattering of lumpy, sandstone boulders. A children's slippery dip and swing stood in the yard near a cubbyhouse built out from the fence and next to it was a rotary clothesline. Not far from the clothesline, a girl in a white two-piece was sunbaking face up on a banana-lounge. She had nice legs, solid boobs with a soft roll of fat round her tummy and her dark hair was bobbed 'Melrose Place' style around her eyes and neck. Les couldn't make out her face because she was wearing dark sunglasses, but he could see it was a bit plump with a double chin and full lips. Whip a few kilos off her, mused Les, and she might be half a good sort.

Just as Norton started looking at her a phone rang from under the house. The girl seemed to come to life, sat up and slid her sunglasses on top of her head and noticed Les. Norton was tempted to smile down and give her a wave. But feeling she'd probably think he was perving on her, he turned away and started picking at nothing on a small window ledge on the cabana while he watched her reflection in the glass. She got to her feet and went up the stairs to the lower part of the house. However, before she went inside she turned around and gave Norton a couple of very heavy, long-distance once-up-and-downs, then the screen door shut behind her. Norton turned around and snapped his fingers at something Price had mentioned in the office when they were all drunk on Tuesday night. Price had owned the vacant block next door which he sold privately to the bloke who had built the house. He lived upstairs and rented out underneath.

So that's who lives there, mused Norton. I'll bet she shares with someone. Probably a boyfriend. I wonder what the owner's like? Not that it's any of my business, but going by the swings and things and all those toys lying around, I reckon he likes kids. Les wandered back alongside the pool, stooped down and absently plucked out a couple of leaves, then went inside.

The kitchen was tiled white and modern with a

porta-gas stove, plenty of kitchenware and a top-of-the-line double fridge with an ice-making machine in the front. Inside was spotlessly clean, but totally empty except for a water jug and a tub of ice-blocks in the deep freeze. Les closed the doors then drummed his fingers on the top and looked thoughtful. Well, if I'm going to stay here for a week, I'm going to need provisions, and plenty of them. I don't know what young James is like on the tooth or whether he likes a drink, but I know I do. Les climbed into a pair of Levi shorts and his old, blue Surfer HQ T-shirt then drove down to Terrigal shopping centre.

There was a parking spot just in front of the taxi rank beneath the pine trees; Norton got out of the car and decided he might have a quick look around the beach before he did his shopping. He zapped the car doors, strolled across the park past the picnic sheds and started walking along the promenade. It was a little different to the last time he saw it. Part of the promenade had collapsed and was fenced off with pine logs and a sign saying KEEP CLEAR. STORM DAMAGE. Les wasn't sure what the tide was doing, but where there was once nothing but beautiful beach, there were now rocks and boulders dumped up against the seawall by the council. There were more scattered rocks as Les walked along, the blackened remains of an old wooden fence and a jumble of old, concrete steps. At the end, a pathway led to a small, open-air pool beneath the cliffs, which was half full of sand and looking a bit neglected. Les had seen better sights. But, he mused, like most beaches it would all probably come back in time. Though you'd think the local council would put a decent open-air pool in there. It's such a nice spot under those cliffs and little trees. He had another look around and watched some people fishing off the point then walked back along the promenade.

There were half-a-dozen or so men in Speedos sitting out the front of the surf club, talking and listening to a radio in the first-aid room tuned to some station cranking out old baby boomer ballads. The surf club had a canteen open and Norton arrived just as a bloke in horn-rimmed glasses and shorts got hold of a microphone hooked to the club's PA system and let go a spiel in word-perfect 'Strine'.

'G'dayagenladeezngenilmen. Juzleddinyknowthe-zerfglubgandeenstilloben. Wegodizygoldjogwedgesn-baddlebobs. Gogagolajipsnoddogz. Odbies zozich-rollszundanoylenlibblog. Angewagenladezangenil-menanavanizday.'

Well, there you go, Les smiled to himself. Who says Australia is losing its cultural identity? That man just raised it to new heights with barely a few words from an ancient dialect. Let's hope he lives long enough to pass it on down to the young ones. Norton watched absently as a couple of punters came up and bought some 'odogzngoke', then he crossed over to the bottle shop.

The bottle shop was clean, modern and bright with a yellow paper parrot hanging from the ceiling and almost the best selection of booze Les had ever seen. Coolers brimming with designer and local beers, shelves groaning with exotic spirits and a wine selection that would have sent Len Evans into hog heaven. A tall man in a Grolsch T-shirt was behind the counter adding up something on a calculator. He looked up as a woman in shorts with thick, dark hair going grey burst through the door covered in sweat from a power walk. She said something, then disappeared out the back, leaving a dotted trail of sweat on the polished wooden floor while the man went back to his calculator. Les perused the selection and bought a dozen mixed beers, three bottles of Bacardi and two bottles of flavoured Liudka vodka—strawberry and rock-melon—which he placed straight in the car. A small supermarket was almost next door; Les hit that and came out with milk, bread, butter and whatever which he placed in the car also. There was a butcher shop in the main drag. But Norton thought he might check out the one round the corner as it was next to the fruit shop.

It was one of those small, quality shops with a window display of choice cuts of meat that made your mouth water just looking at them. There was no one inside the shop except for a tall, brown-haired butcher nattering happily away to his shorter, dark-haired workmate while they trimmed stuff on the block. They were even happier when Les walked in with a roll of notes and happier again when he walked out with an armful of steaks, chops, bacon and sausages.

The fruit shop next door was another eye opener and, to Norton, shopping at Terrigal just seemed to get better and better. The roomy store was chock full of fruit and vegetables of every size, shape and variety. Salad mixes, Roma tomatoes, kumeras, papayas, all kinds of grapes and everything as fresh as it comes. Plus bottles of balsamic vinegar, virgin olive oil, jars of crushed garlic and ginger; you name it, they had it. But best of all was a machine they rolled fresh, local oranges into and out came sparkling fresh orange juice. There were a couple of young blokes out the back packing trays near a ghetto-blaster tuned to 2JJJ. An attractive woman in white jeans with a lovely smile and dark, Spanish-looking eyes served Les, wishing him a happy day as he walked out with a carton of fruit and vegetables and three two-litre containers of fresh orange juice. Les put all this in the car, then looked at his watch. The sun was well over the yardarm, so he thought he might check out the hotel and have a cool one.

Les missed it before, but as he walked up the steps into the beer garden he noticed a sign strung above, white on black, saying CLUB ALGIERS OVER-30S DISCO. FRIDAY NIGHT. QUAY WEST DISCO. An over-30s disco, Norton smiled to himself. That could be all right. And I can just squeeze in there. I might come down and have a look. There were a few people scattered around the beer garden; Les strolled through the chairs and tables into the bar which was next to the food area. It had more chairs and tables, a jukebox, Sky TV near an open fireplace and another area to the right full of card machines. He ordered a schooner of New and, being a mug tourist, made a few enquiries from a tall, young barman in black. Yes, Club Algiers was on in the disco on Fridays and it wasn't a bad night; lots of people. The disco was also open tonight and this would be the last Wednesday of the summer season. There was another bar upstairs—The Baron Riley. It was a piano bar and named after a ship that sank off Terrigal in 1860, and sold the best cocktails on the Central Coast.

Les thanked the barman then walked outside and drank his schooner at a table under the vines overlooking the ocean.

The sea breeze had picked up slightly, flicking even more white caps across the blue of the ocean, but it was still a treat sitting there 'far from the madding crowd' in Bondi. The south end of Terrigal might have been a bit knocked around from the storm, however there was still a long, beautiful expanse of golden sand running all the way to Wamberal Lagoon and Forrester's Beach beyond and the surrounding trees made the low, mountain range in from the sea a carpet of deep, mist-covered green. Les could have sat there and had another five schooners easily; it was peaceful, relaxed and the sound of the waves softly and rhythmically washing over the sand and rocks below was almost hypnotic. But all the food in the car, especially the steaks, was calling and Norton's mouth was watering worse than his stomach was rumbling. He drained his schooner to the last drop of froth and this time drove home via the church on the corner.

It took Les roughly an hour to stow away all the food and booze, organise some more ice and work out the microwave oven, along with everything else in the kitchen, sip a Eumundi and feed himself. He made a rocket salad with balsamic vinegar and olive oil, baked half a kumera smothered with cottage cheese and herb dressing and grilled two of the choicest, boneless sirloins and two sausages which he washed down with fresh orange juice, bread rolls and a small plunger of coffee while he read the paper. The solid feed didn't slow Les down; if anything it seemed to liven him up.

I don't know whether it was that orange juice or the air up here, he mused as he finished the paper, but I feel like I could go ten rounds with Mike Tyson. Well, five anyway. After burping and farting around while he cleaned up the mess, Norton now decided it was time for drinky-poohs at Price's.

Cooking a meal wasn't much trouble, and this was easier again by ten. He found a large, high-ball glass, half filled it with ice, added a liberal splash of Bacardi, a moderately liberal splash of strawberry vodka and topped it up with fresh orange juice. The first mouthful nearly sent shivers up Norton's spine. Oh yes, oh yes indeed. He rummaged through his tapes, dropped one into the stereo and settled back on the lounge. Lee Kernaghan slipped into 'Skinny Dippin'', Les gargled some more Bacardi, vodka and OJ and started to wonder if it got any better than this.

After about ten drinks Les lost count. He was getting nice and drunk. But not bloated or mindless; just in a roaring good mood. He'd switched the outside lights on and decided if he did start to get his wobbly boot on a bit, he could simply take his drink down to the pool, dive in and freshen up again. It was a mild, still night outside with plenty of stars around and things were more than pleasant hanging around by the pool. The only trouble was that about a hundred mosquitoes had the same idea too. I know what I'll be getting tomorrow, grimaced Norton, as he squashed one about the same size as a Cape Barren goose that settled on his forearm. About ten gallons of Aeroguard and a dozen stainless steel fly swats. He went inside for the last time and left the mozzies to it.

Les kept drinking, one cassette went into another and before he realised it the night wasn't getting any younger. But for some reason Les didn't feel at all like going to bed or watching TV. He felt like kicking on. Then he suddenly thought of something the barman at the resort had said to him. Tonight was the last time the disco was open on Wednesday and there was another bar upstairs which sold grouse cocktails. Ooh! What's that you say, Shintaro? Les smiled boozily at his reflection in one of the windows. Disco. Cocktails. It's only about a ten-minute walk down the road. Why not go and have a look? Les finished his drink, made another and drank that while he showered, shaved, shampooed and conditioned and hit himself with a bit of deodorant and a dab or two of Calvin Klein's Obsession. Whistling happily he climbed into the same jeans he wore earlier, his brown grunge boots and a two-tone brown, collarless shirt, gave himself a last detail and started walking down to the hotel.

There were plenty of trees and streetlights, but no footpaths. However, the walk down was virtually turn right a couple of hundred metres up from Price's house, turn left, then right again; except the last turn right went down a hill that would challenge a mountain goat. It was shorter than the other road that went past the North Avoca turn-off and Les had zoomed up it earlier in the Berlina. But coming back later with a further gutful of booze wouldn't be a great deal of fun if there were no taxis around. Ahh, who gives a stuff? thought Les. The exercise'll work some of the piss out of me and how good's this fresh air, and what about the view from up here? Ambling down the hill, Les could see the lights of the hotel and parts of Terrigal village, lights from the houses all along Wamberal Beach, the vast, inky expanse of the ocean, the forested darkness of the surrounding hills and the steep, rugged headlands around Forrester's Beach further along the coast. The sky was still full of stars, there was hardly any traffic and the breeze coming in from the ocean was sweet and clean. A dog gave a couple of barks from some house as Norton proceeded down the hill. He passed a grove of trees on his left, the church, some shops and a hardware store that was closing down on his right and next thing Terrigal Pines Resort loomed up in front of him. Will I have a look in the beer garden? mused Les. No, bugger it. Straight up to this Baron Riley Bar for a cocktail. Like he still had the momentum of the hill behind him, Les angled right at the hardware store, zoomed directly across the road from the post office, past the flowerbeds and pine trees around the driveway, straight through the revolving door into the foyer.

Inside was all bright and roomy with a high ceiling, plush leather lounges, Chinese motifs on the wall and various other prints and paintings. A bank of lifts sat next to the revolving door and across the foyer a wide set of green carpeted stairs half spiralled to the next floor. Les took the stairs and came out near some marble columns and two restaurants. Between them a pair of high, wooden, inlaid-glass doors opened to the Baron Riley Bar; Les walked straight in again. It, too, was bright with high ceilings, polished wooden floors and more thick columns as you entered surrounded by indoor palms. Round tables with wicker chairs separated the bar on your left and a piano on the right with another restaurant glassed off below that. Another lounge squared off with a wood-topped green railing, full of comfortable sofas and small tables with a bookcase and paintings on the walls was set above the piano in front of a passageway with a long, wooden table and prints of old sailing ships on the wall that ran along to another lounge area at the back. The whole place was very elegant and swish and built to take advantage of the beautiful ocean view outside and more than likely boomed on the weekends and the tourist season. Tonight, however, there was about a dozen or so people in there counting Les, the piano player and the three girls in dark green trousers and red paisley vests working the bar. Oh well, thought Norton, it's only a Wednesday night. And there might be some punters in the disco. Right now, after that back-breaking walk down, I'm in dire need of a cocktail. The bar was in three sections. One faced the piano, another the door and the other the swimming pool outside shining in the moonlight. Les chose a bar stool facing the doorway and picked up the cocktail list. A minute or two later a young girl with neat, dark hair and a pretty, almost pixie kind of face came over.

'Yes, sir. What can I get you?' she smiled.

Norton perused the cocktail list again then placed it on the bar. 'Yeah, I'll have a Chocolate Surprise, please.'

'Certainly, sir.'

The girl shuffled around behind the bar, a blender whirled and before he knew it, Norton had what looked like a chocolate milkshake spliced with strawberries sitting in front of him, only with a lot more kick. After paying the girl, Les took another mouthful and checked out the punters. There was a skinny girl in a white shirt and black vest seated round the corner who looked like kd lang, a couple two stools up staring into each other's eyes while they smoked their heads off, one or two more couples and half-a-dozen mixed shapes and sizes at a table near the piano player who could have been his friends. The piano player had thick brown hair over a salt-and-pepper beard and was crooning old Cole Porter and Ira Gershwin classics in a white tuxedo. He had a good voice and was an excellent pianist, but every now and again he'd slip in his own version of the lyrics. At the moment he was singing 'Don't Get Around Much Any More', only it was coming out:

'Bonked my girlfriend last night
Shot all over the floor
Cleaned it up with my toothbrush
Don't clean my teeth much any more.'

It went over kd lang's and the couple's heads. But the mixed shapes lapped it up, along with the staff and Norton. That finished, then it was 'These Foolish Things'.

'Two shades of lipstick on an old French letter
A case of syphilis that just won't get better
And when I piss it stings
These foolish things
Remind me of you.'

37

Norton chortled away and finished his milkshake. It was lovely and tasty, but all the cream and liqueurs made you thirsty. He caught the same girl's eye and she came over.

Les looked at her for a moment and thought; why not? I'm just a tourist in town. 'I'll have a bottle of Corona and a stinger, thanks.'

'Certainly, sir. Lime in the Corona?'

'Yes, please.'

Norton hoofed the stinger down in two belts followed by a third of the Corona. Bloody hell, he grimaced, when his eyes stopped spinning and the beer washed away the taste of creme de menthe. No wonder bloody Mitzi date-raped me back in Hawaii. She had about fifty of those rotten things. He took another sip of beer and decided to have a look out the back; there wasn't much chance of him losing his stool.

It was more comfortable lounges and colonial furniture. There was a large fireplace, a bookcase, more paintings on the walls and long high windows overlooking the beer garden and the ocean. There weren't many people in the beer garden and only about eight in the lounge counting Les; four young girls and over to his right, two po-faced women about fifty were talking to a dark-haired girl facing them, who was wearing a denim jacket. Les couldn't see her face, but for some reason the hair looked familiar. He stood there for a minute or two sipping his beer and while he checked out one of the paintings he seemed to get this feeling of eyes watching him from a reflection in a window. Well, this is all very nice, but I want some ak-shun-I-wanna-live. Norton finished his beer, placed the bottle on the nearest table and left down the stairs, the same way he came in.

The disco was round the corner from the revolving door, past a brass railing and some shops. It was a black-and-silver door and windows and a black-and-silver sign saying QUAY WEST NITE CLUB. Standing just inside the door near the counter, a lounge and some potted palms was a tired-looking doorman in black and white who looked more pudding than condition. It was five bucks entry. Les pulled out some money and went to pay the equally tired-looking girl at the counter when the doorman came over.

'Sorry, mate. I can't let you in.'

'Can't let me in?' Norton gave the doorman a boozy double blink. 'Why? What have I done?'

'You gotta have a collar on your shirt.'

'A collar on my shirt?' Les couldn't believe it. The shirt was a Preswick and Moore Susie had brought back from Melbourne for him as a present for looking after the flat and giving him the arse at the same time. It was pure Toorak Road, South Yarra, and cost $175. Even if Side Valve probably stole it. Norton looked the doorman right in the eye. 'I'll bet you're a good local boy, aren't you?' You could hear the wooden cogs inside the doorman's head go round as he grunted and nodded something at the same time. 'Yeah, and you've lived here all your life. Well, there's this new style out. Not T-shirts. Just good cotton or linen shirts with no collars. They're sometimes called grandpa shirts.'

'That's what I said, mate,' droned the doorman. 'You gotta have a collar on your shirt to get in.' He was dumb, but polite.

39

After walking all the way down the hill, Norton wasn't particularly in the mood for being dicked around for no reason. He was ready to tell the doorman to get stuffed, throw his five dollars on the counter and go in and if the doorman wanted him out he could try; and any of his mates, too. Les was about to make a move when a half dapper-looking bloke in a grey suit with a name tag walked in the door.

'Hey, mate,' said Les. 'Are you the boss here?'

'Yes, I'm the night manager.'

'Well, what's all this "I can't get in without a collar on my shirt"? Where do you think I got this? Out of the church bin across the road? Besides that, I've just spent a fortune in the restaurant upstairs with some people who are guests here. And I happen to be a doctor.'

'That's quite all right, sir. Don't worry about it.' Grey Suit made a gesture and looked tiredly at the doorman. 'Brian, next time, try and use some discretion, will you?'

'Use some what?'

Norton leant over and put his face about two inches away from the doorman's. 'What he's talking is brains, Brian. If you don't know what that means, look it up in a dictionary. You'll find it between arsehole and cunt.' Les smiled thinly, paid his five dollars and walked inside.

There was a passageway, then the gents and ladies on your left near an alcove leading to a fire exit. The dance floor was on your right, a raised area behind that, then the DJ's stand above another fire exit opposite. Pillars, stools and tables led to the bar at the rear and some steps led to another lounge area against the wall on the right. It was all black and silver with chrome railings. Soft lights, spinning laser balls and TV screens above the dance floor. House music and FUCKIN' LOUD. Norton walked straight into 'Kiss Your Lipps' by Tokyo Ghetto Pussy at warp ten and besides almost making his gums bleed, it nearly blew his head off. Christ almighty! What was that? Like a terrorist who'd just been hit by a stun grenade, Les made it to the bar where, even though it was a little quieter, he had still had to yell to get a Bacardi and orange. He got that and peered around through the cigarette haze. There were about forty or so people in there, including a handful of Asquith Annies and Roseville Rogers flopping around on the dance floor trying to look hip and bored at the same time. Perched behind a perspex barrier was the ponytailed DJ in a black vest and, of all things, a white T-shirt. He had this gaunt, crazed look on his face as if, seeing it was the last Wednesday night and there weren't many in the place, he'd drive the ones that were there either mad or out the door with this full-on, esoteric, techno-cyber-beat. He slipped into 'You Belong to Me' by JX, and Norton felt as if all the fillings in his teeth were going to fall out. Shit! I can't see myself lasting too long in here, he blinked, when once again he felt like someone was looking at him and this time it wasn't a reflection.

Les couldn't quite believe it. It was a detective he knew from Maroubra. A stocky, red-headed bloke something like himself, in a white polo shirt and jeans standing near the cigarette machine in the corner with another solid, dark-haired bloke and two blondes. He was a mate of the cop Les knew in Forensics, a bloke called Mick Les had met when he was out from

Hawaii. Actually he walked into the station when Les was getting questioned over his old ute and smoothed things over. The look on the cop's face was pretty much the same as Norton's. A half-concealed smile combined with, 'What the fuck are you doing here?' Only one way to find out, thought Les, and strolled over, quietly and casually, not shoving his hand out, just in case he might have been on a job.

'Well, Steve, what can I say?'

'I know exactly what you mean, Les, so I'll go first. What the fuck are you doing here?'

'I'm staying at Price's place for a week.' Apart from George's nephew Les told the detective pretty much what he was up to. 'And so far, apart from nearly getting my ear-drums shattered in here, it's been pretty good.'

'Yeah, I know what you mean,' agreed Steve the detective, as the DJ cranked the volume up another couple of notches.

Norton edged a little closer. 'So what's your story, Steve? What are you up to?' Steve seemed a bit hesitant. 'I know. You don't have to tell me. It's drugs, isn't it? It's always drugs. There's a cripple in a wheelchair with two dope plants in her backyard. Like that one down in Wollongong. Your mates in the TRG and you're both going round to bust her and punch the shit out of her.'

'Ohh, get fucked will you, Les.'

Norton shook his head. 'Tch-tch-tch. Isn't that terrible language to use on a member of the public? No wonder we all hate you.'

'You're a big shit-stirring cunt.' But there was

42

something in Norton's cheeky banter that got Steve. It could have been pride. It could have been being half drunk. 'As a matter of fact it's not drugs for a change, thank Christ! We're after a box of machine guns.'

'Machine guns?'

'Yeah, about half-a-dozen CAM-STAT X-911s from America. And a thousand spaghetti bullets.'

'What?'

'Teflon-coated things. They burst inside and shred up all your stomach. Like spaghetti.'

'Sounds nice.'

'Yeah, just great. We got to get them before this bikie gang does. The bloke I'm with's in the Feds. We're off to Newcastle tomorrow.'

Norton thought it might be good manners to change the subject. He'd had a bit of a dig and only proved that good cops do have a prick of a job at times. And Steve was one of the good ones. 'And is that how you met the two lovelies?'

Steve winked. 'Reckon. And in course of duty, too, I might add.'

'Of course, Steve. And half your luck, mate. They're not bad sorts.'

'Yeah. We just had dinner with them. They live at Green Point or something.'

Norton was about to say something when Steve's mate tapped him on the shoulder. They had a quick conversation with the two girls then Steve turned back to Norton.

'We got to get going, Les. I'll probably bump you back in Sydney.'

'Okay, mate. Look after yourself.' They exchanged a

quick, firm handshake. 'And Steve, just remember the old saying.'

'What's that?'

'If you're gonna pull a scam, watch the video-cam.'

'Thanks, Les, I will. You cunt.'

Steve gave a bit of a wave and they were gone, leaving Norton on his own again. He strolled absently towards the dance floor straight into 'Right Kind of Mood' by Herbie. He finished his drink as the music battered him back to the bar. He ordered another drink then turned around and got battered by 'Forever Young' by Interactive. What the fuck's going on? grimaced Norton. This is diabolical. Norton felt concussed. It was as if someone was belting him over the head with a piece of downpipe and if the music had gone any faster they would have started going back in time. It's me. It has to be me. I'm turning into an old fart, a square. But looking around it wasn't only Les. Everybody in the place looked like they'd had enough too; including a couple of Asquith Annies shuffling listlessly around on the dance floor with their bottles of mineral water. The DJ had won the night. He'd beaten them all into the ground. Or the floor.

I don't know what it is, cursed Norton, but this ain't fuckin' me. He gulped down the last of his Bacardi and fled out the door into the foyer where two teeny boppers were lying on the lounge, exhausted, in front of the same doorman. Norton walked up and put his face about two inches away from the doorman's again.

'Why didn't you kick me out earlier when I told you to, you fuckin' imbecile,' he screamed. 'Thanks heaps, you hillbilly.'

With his head still reeling and his hearing half shot,

Norton left the doorman blinking and spun out the front towards the main door. He didn't know where he was going. Anywhere into the night to try and clear his head. There were two couples waiting for taxis in front of the revolving door as well as a girl standing on her own. Les stopped suddenly, almost bumping into her, his face still a mask of shock, horror and bewilderment.

'Christ almighty, that music. Sorry.'

The girl half smiled. 'You've been in the disco.'

'Yeah, I think that's what it was. Bloody hell! The Ukrainians wouldn't have shoved the Jews in there.'

Still half numbed from the neck up, Les stepped over in front of the shops and tried to clear his head. After a few moments his brain started to settle when he noticed another reflection in a window, turned around and pointed.

'You're not the—?'

'That's right. I live next door. I saw you upstairs earlier.'

Norton nodded. 'Yeah. I'm . . . up here for a week,' he replied absently and then looked at the girl for a moment or two. 'Anyway, I'm Les.'

The girl looked at Norton for a moment or two also, then took the offer of his outstretched hand. 'Caroline.'

'Hello, Caroline. Nice to meet you.'

Caroline ponged a bit of wine, but she wasn't too bad a sort tucked tightly into a denim top, white T-shirt, jeans and gym-boots. Her face was attractive enough with a small, plump mouth and nice teeth. But she had the strangest eyes; narrow and lidded and an intense violet blue that almost seemed to radiate in the soft, surrounding lights of the hotel.

'So what brings you down here anyway, Caroline? I'm just a poor mug tourist and should have known better.'

'I was with—two friends. They're staying here. Now I'm waiting for a taxi.'

'You been waiting long?'

The violet eyes narrowed and flashed. 'Yes,' she hissed. 'And there's four bloody people in front of me.'

'Yeah, that's the way it goes.' Les looked at her half sorry, half amused. 'Well, I don't want to seem rude, Caroline, but I'm off.'

'How are you getting home?'

'I'm gonna walk.'

'Walk!?'

'Yeah. It's only about ten minutes. And I want to get the cigarette smoke off me and get some fresh air. I'd offer you a lift but I didn't bring the rickshaw.' Norton looked blankly at the blank look on the girl's face. 'Goodnight, Caroline. Hope you get home all right. I'll probably see you around.' Les smiled and turned away. He'd just reached the corner when he heard a voice behind him.

'Hey, wait a minute.'

Les stopped for a moment as Caroline caught up with him.

'Hang on. I'll walk up with you.'

'You may as well,' shrugged Norton. 'You could be there all night.'

The girl stood looking at Norton for a few seconds. 'Just promise me one thing, Les. Les? That is your name, isn't it? Les?'

Les nodded. Hello, here it comes. You're not the Boston Strangler, are you? You won't try and rape me

46

on the way home? 'Yes, that's right, Caroline. My name's Les. I'm staying next door to your place and I own the blue Holden out the front. Now what's your problem, Caroline?'

'If I fall on my arse going up that fuckin' hill, will you give me a hand?'

Norton smiled at her. 'Seeing that you're such a lady, Caroline, how could I possibly not?'

They trudged on up the hill towards where the steep grade began. Norton didn't quite know what to say or what to think. Here he was walking home with the girl next door who was reasonably attractive. Yet there was something about her that seemed a bit strange. Was it her eyes? Her attitude? There was one thing about Caroline for certain, though—she was out of condition. They hadn't got more than fifty metres before she was puffing and panting. Les was eyes ahead, marching along, glad to be getting some fresh air when he heard a voice behind him.

'Hey, hang on, will you? I can't bloody keep up.'

'Can't keep up?' Les slowed down for her. 'Christ! We haven't even started yet.'

'Ohh, shit!'

They headed off again. It was getting steep now and would get even steeper. But Norton was soldiering along, going all right, even half enjoying it, when he heard a curse hanging in the air behind him. He turned around and Caroline had stopped dead with her hands on her knees sucking in what oxygen she could. Les turned back.

'Come on, Cathy Freeman. You can do it. I know you can.'

Caroline was stuffed. Her violet eyes glared up at Les in the moonlight as if it was all his fault. 'I'm going back to get a fuckin' taxi,' she gasped. 'This . . . is fuckin' ridiculous. You're an absolute idiot.'

Les looked at her while she got her breath back, and had half a mind to leave her there. But if something happened to her or she died from a heart attack on the side of the road he'd probably get the blame for it.

'Listen. Take hold of my belt.'

'What?'

'Grab the back of my belt.'

Les turned around and got Caroline to grip his belt and the back of his jeans, then he took off. Only instead of charging straight ahead he tacked up the hill like a yacht, with Caroline hanging on the back sort of slaloming back and forth across the road. It wasn't all that hard and Caroline even seemed to like it, swinging away and getting a free ride at Norton's expense. They made it to the top okay except that by the time he reached the crossroad the strain of his belt cutting into his stomach muscles had Les busting for a leak. He told Caroline to go on ahead while he jumped behind a tree and hosed away in the dark. She was waiting for him when he caught up, still fiddling with the top of his fly.

'Enjoy yourself?'

'Yeah. There's a lot of ants over there aren't real happy though.'

They fell into step. Caroline still wasn't breaking any records, but compared to before she was belting along like a two-year-old out from the fence. She was even able to engage Les in a rambling conversation.

It turned out she was a schoolteacher and originally

came from Dundas. Her parents had sold the house so she moved up here with a girlfriend who was a nurse when she got transferred to a school at Empire Bay or something. Now she was being transferred to a school at Wyong and she was going to Sydney tomorrow and she'd be back on Friday or Saturday or something. Les told her he was an executive with an oil company in Adelaide and raced BMWs in his spare time. No, he wasn't married. His career and overseas travel jetting back and forth to America, Europe and England unfortunately prevented that. They nattered on some more and before Les knew it they were out the front of Price's. Norton thought about inviting her in for a drink, but she still seemed a little odd and it was a bit close to home and if they did happen to get into it or whatever he'd have her hanging around all the time.

'Well, goodnight, Caroline,' he said politely. 'That was a lot of fun. I'll probably catch up with you before I go back to Adelaide.'

The girl next door seemed to tilt her head for a moment and the violet eyes flashed again. 'Would you like to come in for a cup of coffee?'

'Yeah, why not.' That's you, Norton, Les told himself. Got a backbone like a saveloy. But it's not like I'm stuck with her in my place.

A pathway at the left angled down beneath the house next door to Caroline's flat; she fumbled in her pocket for the keys, opened the door and turned on the light. It was painted mainly white with touches of blue. Two bedrooms on the left ran off a hallway which led to the loungeroom and kitchen and a door to the back verandah. The bathroom was opposite the end bedroom. The furniture was comfy, if cheap, black corduroy. There were a few prints and posters on the walls, indoor plants, a coffee table, a small TV and a mini-stereo on a set of shelves with some books and a handful of CDs. About the type of place two girls would share to save money. Les had lived in worse.

'Not a bad place you've got,' he said, pretending to admire an old Jimi Hendrix poster. 'Where's your girlfriend?'

'Night shift. Take a seat in the lounge while I get out of these clothes.'

'Righto.'

Les sat down on a small sofa as Caroline turned the stereo on to some FM station blurting out the usual hits and memories leaving Norton listening to 'Ride Like the Wind' by Christopher Cross while she used the bathroom and then got changed. This oozed into ELO's 'Telephone Line' and then she was back in a pink and yellow floral dress buttoned down the front and a pair of battered black Kung Fu slippers.

'Getting ready for a bit of Tai Chi, Caroline?' joked Les.

'Something like that.'

She stepped back, hissed and threw a snap kick at Norton's face. He moved his head and automatically brought his hand up as it missed him by a whisker. It wasn't meant to be funny. It was kind of 'mess with me and this is what you'll get, you sexist bastard'. Norton wasn't very impressed. As well as being a little strange, Caroline definitely had a nasty side to her. I think it'll be one cup of coffee and out of here, he thought. This sheila's a cowboy boot short of a linedance.

'You're a regular Bruce Lee, Caroline,' he smiled mirthlessly.

'That's me all right. So how do you like your coffee?'

'2SM.'

'I gotcha.'

Caroline fiddled around in the kitchen. There was the sound of water boiling and jars being opened while 'Love Theme from St Elmo's Fire' seeped out of the stereo. Then she was back and Norton was handed a mug of coffee that wasn't sweet enough and tasted exactly like—cheap instant coffee.

'Nice,' remarked Les, forcing down a mouthful.

'Mmmhh. So's mine.' Caroline sat down on a sofa between Les and the stereo. 'And why don't you call me Carol.'

'All right, Carol.'

They nattered on about nothing in particular with Carol giving Les these strange, furtive looks every now and again as if she had something on her mind besides coffee and small talk. She seemed kind of nervous or edgy and kept turning around to change stations on the radio even though the music was all pretty much the same. This suited Les, however, because every time she reached over to the radio he'd tip some of his coffee into an already sick-looking parlour palm next to the sofa. She turned back, leaving Cat Stevens' 'Wild World' playing, to find Les with his mug tilted back draining the last drop of his coffee.

'Well, that was nice, Carol,' he said, putting his mug on the coffee table. 'I might get going.'

'Already?'

51

'Yeah. There's a few things I have to do tomorrow.' Les got to his feet and smiled. 'Anyway, thanks for the coffee.'

Carol put her mug down next to the tuner and stood in front of Les. 'I'll walk you home.'

Norton looked at her for a moment. 'That's okay. I can get a taxi. There might even be a bus along soon.'

'No. I'll walk you home.'

Norton gave an indifferent shrug. 'Okay. Please yourself.'

Carol left the lights on and they went out the front door with Les leading the way. Well, figure this out, mused Norton as she padded up the stairs behind him. I'm not quite sure what to do here. This tart's got fuck-all sense of humour and she's definitely not playing with a full deck. But she's got nice legs and a good pair of tits. It's a hard one. They hardly had time to talk before they were at Price's house; Les pulled back the flyscreen, half opened the front door and turned around.

'Well, thanks, Carol,' he said. 'I should be all right from here on, I think.'

'You think so?'

The violet eyes flashed again, and Carol pushed herself up against Les, forcing him through the front door, and slammed it behind them. Then Caroline attacked. She didn't even wait to get into the bedroom. Grabbing Norton's belt buckle, she started tearing at it, pulling his jeans down and forcing him onto the floor.

My God, thought Norton as he lay helpless on his back, it's date rape again. Carol whipped Norton's boots and jeans off and Les did his best to stop her by

52

undoing the front of her dress. She had the odd roll of fat but her generous boobs were tucked tightly into a white lace bra and a dainty pair of matching knickers just covered her ted. Norton tried desperately to save his honour, but Mister Wobbly had other ideas and was soon up and away, roaring and ready to go. Carol gave his dick a few strokes, running her fingers round the knob and Les was expecting a nice bit of a polish to start proceedings. Instead she lay back against Norton's outstretched left arm, whipped off her knickers then got up and straddled him, sliding up and down slowly but steadily. Her ted was warm and firm and a little dry at first. But it didn't take long for things to start juicing up and proceed along swimmingly. In fact it felt pretty good and Les closed his eyes for a moment as a few tiny shivers went up and down his spine.

He slipped Carol's dress over her shoulders letting it catch on her elbows and fall round her waist, then did the same with her bra straps sitting her boobs up in the bra as he licked his fingers and began stroking her nipples till they stuck out like two soft, pink jelly beans. Carol started getting a head of steam up, oohing and aahhing, as she went faster and faster. Then she started screaming, howling and crying as if she was having the time of her life, but dirty on herself for doing so at the same time. It was a strange one all right. But not to Mr Wobbly. All the noise was like music to his evil little ears. Before long he was getting ready to burst his boiler and Norton's head was banging against the floor. He held her by the love handles round her waist and started shoving up as Carol came down. Carol screamed and howled, her hands planted firmly on Norton's shoulders as the dark Melrose Place hair flew from side to side while she rocked up and down. Les gave it a few more shoves, then several good ones and finally two big ones, howling himself as Mr Wobbly exploded and Carol drained every last drop out of him. Norton rose up and shook for a moment, then Norton collapsed like a house of cards and so did Mr Wobbly. Carol lay back against his left arm again and lay there shuddering and shaking, puffing and panting in pretty much the same condition as Norton. After a little while Les got his shit back together and gave Carol's stomach a gentle rub.

'Hang on a sec,' he said. 'I'll get a towel.'

Carol stiffened and the violet eyes flashed in the soft darkness. 'No, I don't want a towel.'

Without saying another word, she got up, grabbed her knickers, did up a couple of buttons on her dress then turned and ran out the door, slamming it behind her. Norton lay on the floor wondering what was going on, his eyes following her rapid, if somewhat strange, departure.

'Well, if you don't want a fuckin' towel, I won't get you one,' he called out to no one in particular. 'Suits me. You could have at least kissed me goodnight, though.'

Well, what a fuckin' nutter, Les chuckled to himself. I knew she was off the air. But it suits me. At least I don't have to stuff around saying goodnight and making more coffee or whatever. But what a weirdo. And it's right next door. Norton shook his head and started gathering up his clothes. Anyway, I'm having a shower and hitting the sack. That wasn't quite my idea of a good root, but it was better than a kick in the nuts with a Doc Marten, I suppose.

Les drank two glasses of orange juice, then had a long, hot shower. He wasn't quite singing in there, but he was certainly chuckling to himself a bit. He cleaned his teeth and, because Mr Wobbly was a bit sore where Caroline had pounced on the poor little fellow when he wasn't quite ready, Les rubbed a bit of Savlon-D along the sides. The ointment soon relieved the chafing. In fact, it was better than that and Norton suddenly found himself feeling a bit toey again. Must be all this clean, fresh air he chuckled to himself again. Wonder if I should go and knock on the lovely Carol's door and make sure she got home safely. No, I think I'll hit the sack, thanks all the same.

Les climbed into a clean pair of jocks and a T-shirt, turned out all the lights except the bedlamp and climbed under the sheets. Well, so much for my first day's holiday up here. I wonder what tomorrow will bring? He was just about to turn out the light when there was a solid knocking on the front door. What the—?

Norton got up, walked round and opened the door. It was Carol. This time she had her hair pinned back and was wearing a baggy, knee-length T-shirt with Sylvester the cat on the front.

The violet eyes flashed in the dark. 'Where's your bedroom?'

'Right this way,' replied Norton, closing the door behind her as she barged straight in.

She followed Les into the bedroom and, without saying anything, threw herself on the bed. Les would have a liked a bit of foreplay; even a little kiss or two would have been nice. But Carol wasn't interested in any lovemaking. She'd left her knickers at home and all she wanted was a root. Oh well, mused Les, I s'pose I ain't doing nothing for the next fifteen minutes or so.

The next fifteen minutes went closer to half an hour as Norton lifted her T-shirt up over her boobs and gave it to her every which way but loose. Carol squawked and squealed, snorted and grunted, moaned and groaned and even sobbed and sniffled at times. It was weird sex and for some reason, instead of feeling any affection for Carol, Les found himself hating her and just wanting to pound her into the ground. He couldn't figure out whether she fancied herself as the ultimate super screw, or she was some kind of mixed-up, half-baked feminist or whether she was teasing him, laying it on with a trowel tonight and the next time she saw him either play hard to get or ignore him altogether. Whatever the answer, the bottom line was Carol was nuts. And I'm nuts, too, thought Les, for getting involved with her. This is getting to be a drag. Les raised Carol's ankles up over her head and like a ten-pound hammer with a five-foot swing belted out the finale as the girl next door let go one tortured scream that seemed to hang in the air for about five minutes. Though, after half an hour, Les had to admit the end result didn't feel all that bad.

Again they lay there side by side in a pile of twisted limbs and sweaty bodies as Norton's heart settled down and he got his breath back. When he was breathing normally again, Les looked over at Carol, gave her belly a rub and wondered if the magic words would work again.

'Hang on a sec. I'll go get a towel.'

The violet eyes flashed under the bedlamp. 'No, I don't want a towel.'

Caroline jumped off the bed, straightened her T-shirt, then ran down the hall and out the door again. Well, there you go, thought Les. Works every time. And that ratbag's teaching kids. Norton shook his head and swung his legs wearily over the bed. Buggered if I know.

Les had another shower and more Savlon-D, then changed back into his jocks and T-shirt. He had another glass of orange juice and while he was standing in the kitchen drinking it his eyes moved in the direction of the house next door. Mmmhh, I wonder? he thought moodily. He went through the kitchen closets till he found what he was looking for, went back to the bathroom again, then the front door, then turned off the lights and went back to bed. He was about to switch off the bedlamp for the second time when there was another knock on the door. Yes, I fuckin' thought so.

Les got up, opened the front door and there was Carol, barefoot this time, wearing a blue check, hangout shirt.

'Whereabouts is your loungeroom?' she demanded.

'Right here, sweetheart.' Les picked up the plastic bucket of water he'd placed by the door and dumped the lot right over Carol's head almost drowning her. 'Now, fuckin' piss off.'

Carol let out a hideous, startled shriek, spun around and ran off down the front pathway leaving a tiny trail of wet footprints behind her.

'Are you sure you don't want a towel?' Les yelled out before he shut the door. Shaking his head, Norton put the bucket back in the kitchen, then turned out the lights and crashed into bed for the last time; out like a light himself.

Les didn't feel too bad and was in half a good mood as he wandered into the kitchen at eight the next morning warbling a few notes of the old Neil Diamond song 'Sweet Caroline' in his shorts and yesterday's blue T-shirt. Outside it was shaping up for another nice day; sunny, with a few clouds around and a light southerly blowing. He got some sausages out of the fridge and, although he was hungry, he didn't particularly feel like cooking anything and making a mess. As he was contemplating things three old kookaburras landed on the railing around the small sundeck outside the kitchen. Les watched them watching him through the flyscreen door, then cut up one of the sausages and laid it along the railing. It took about two seconds for the kookaburras to start squawking and carrying on amongst themselves as they attacked it.

'It's all yours, boys,' said Norton, smiling at their antics. 'I'm going down the beach to get the paper, have a swim and get some breakfast down there. Have a nice day.'

Les threw a towel in his overnight bag and locked

the front door. There was no sign of Carol out the front and apart from a few magpies and a woman watering her garden just down the street, no sign of anyone. Les got in the Berlina and drove down to Terrigal, where he got a parking spot under the pine trees in almost the same place as the day before.

The morning sun was sparkling on the ocean and a few people were either walking around or having a swim when Les strolled across the park to the promenade. S'pose I may as well dump my gear in front of the shower block, he thought, climbing out of his shorts and dropping his sunglasses on top of his towel.

As he jogged across the sand, Les thought he recognised one of the men he'd seen sitting outside the surf club the day before, only now he was coming out of the water carrying a paddle in one hand and a blue racing ski on his head. The tide was half out and there were no waves; Les charged straight in and started wallowing and splashing around in the clean, clear ocean. This soon had him feeling on top of the world and after a good blast of cold water in the shower block Les was feeling even better again. Then he changed into his shorts and a pair of dry Speedos and locked his bag in the car. Now it was breakfast time.

Restaurants and coffee shops ran right along the main drag. The paper shop was straight across the road and a few doors down on the corner of a narrow, blocked-off laneway was a skinny little place called Coffee Corner. The punters seated inside looked to be mainly locals so Les got the paper and wandered down.

Small wicker chairs and tables were spread around a colourful mural of Terrigal Haven on the wall and delicious cooking smells drifted through from a cramped kitchen at the back. A bustly little bloke in a striped polo shirt and glasses was waiting on the tables while two blonde girls did the cooking. Les ordered two toasted ham, cheese, tomato and onion sandwiches and a mug of flat white. They soon arrived and were delicious—scrumptious even—and the coffee wasn't much short of sensational. He didn't have to pick James up till eleven so Les took his time flicking through the paper while he enjoyed his toasted sandwiches. He finished his coffee just as two women seated beneath the mural decided to attack a packet of cigarettes and kindly share the smoke with everybody else in the restaurant. Well, that was good timing, thought Les, as he paid the bill then walked back over to the car.

Back at the house Les had a bit of time to spare so he turned the stereo on in the lounge and stared out the window through the trees behind the house at the glimpses of ocean beyond. Les was gazing at nothing in particular when he noticed what looked like a white soccer ball bobbing around by the edge of the pool. I wonder how that got there? he mused. Probably Carol. It's either got a message on it or a bomb inside it. To kill a bit of time, Les thought he'd go down and take a look.

It was a cheap plastic thing with a design on the side. Norton scooped it out of the pool and gave it a couple of bounces when he heard voices drifting up from behind Carol's flat. That's where it's come from, nodded Les. The kids next door have kicked it over. He walked over to the fence to toss it back.

The owner next door was wrestling around a red and

blue tent with what must have been his wife and two children. He had dark hair, a moustache and glasses, and his wife was blonde. A boy about four had fair hair like his mother and the daughter about six had dark hair like Dad. They were all whooping and hollering around the tent as they tried to get it up, tried not to get in each other's way and tried not to laugh at the same time. It was quite a funny scene and Les was trying to think of something it reminded him of. He was staring away, possibly a little rudely, and it dawned on him just as the husband looked up and caught his eye.

'I've seen this movie before,' Les called out. 'It's the Griswolds.'

The bloke looked at Les for a moment, then laughed. So did his wife. 'Yeah, right,' he answered back. 'Hey, I've seen all those videos. They're great.'

'Yeah, I don't mind them myself,' said Les. 'Where are you off to? Wallyworld?'

The bloke laughed again. 'No, actually we're going up to Myall Lake on the weekend. I just got this thing last night.' He looked at the tent and shook his head. 'I'll get it together somehow.'

'You mean *we'll* get it together, don't you, dear,' said his wife.

'Didn't I just say that?'

Norton thought he'd leave the Griswolds to it. 'Hey, is this yours?' he said, holding up the ball.

'Ohh, yeah, the kids must have kicked it up there. Sorry about that.'

'That's okay.' Les tossed the ball down to the kids, who immediately started kicking it around the backyard. 'I'll see you later.'

'Yeah, righto mate.'

Norton glanced at his watch and went back inside the house. He poured himself a glass of orange juice and sipped that while he tidied up his room, then changed into a pair of jeans and a white T-shirt he bought in Montego Bay with Ire Jamaica on the front in red, green and yellow. After finishing his orange juice, he put the glass in the kitchen sink, got a tape, then climbed behind the wheel of the Berlina and headed for Kurrirong Juvenile Justice Centre.

With 'Big Man' by Redneck Mothers bopping out of the stereo, the drive through Erina was a breeze and Les was past West Gosford and the Woy Woy turn-off and heading up the mountain road towards the gaol before he knew it. He turned right at the garage like it said on the directions he was given, and then past a football field or some kind of grassed oval dotted with trees and edged with a low white railing. There were more trees and blocks of old, colonial-style houses painted cream and blue with galvanised iron roofs, a boom gate and speed humps. Then Les turned right and went about another kilometre. This brought him onto a driveway set in nice bush surrounds with a fabulous view of Brisbane Water on the right and the gaol in front and on the left. There was a perspex or glass wall about ten metres high alongside the driveway, a metal fence topped with barbed wire the same height behind that, then the concrete buildings that looked just like a modern, maximum-security gaol for young offenders. A small grass circle propping up the flag sat in front of a windowless concrete building with one large, metal gate and a smaller blue door on the left.

Les was right on time, but not quite sure what to do, so he cruised slowly up to the gate and started to read a sign bolted to the Besser bricks. He got as far as PLEASE NOTE. VISIT PROCEDURE. IDENTIFICATION MUST BE SHOWN PRIOR TO ENTRY TO THIS CENTRE when the blue door opened and a young bloke wearing jeans, gym-boots and a purple Billabong T-shirt, and carrying an overnight bag, stepped out. Les leaned across and opened the door and he climbed into the Berlina closing the door after him.

'Thanks, mate,' he said, in a soft, clear voice.

'That's all right, James,' answered Les. 'My pleasure.'

A voice crackled over an intercom. 'Would you mind not blocking the driveway. It's a turning area.'

'Yeah, righto,' said Les, even though no one could hear him with the window up.

'Ahh, blow it out your arse,' said George's nephew, adjusting his seat belt.

'Yeah, fair enough,' said Les.

They drove back up the driveway. As Les slowed down for some speed humps he decided to check James out.

'So, how's things? Okay?'

James turned to Les and started checking Norton out at the same time. 'Yeah. Not too bad, thanks.'

James was slimly built, shorter than Les and very, very goodlooking. Neat black hair wisped across two jet-black eyebrows which were set above a pair of lively brown eyes. His nose, slightly flattened though not broken, had a small bump over the bridge. A set of perfect white teeth almost sparkled from a smooth face with a suntan George Hamilton would have envied and a tiny cleft in James' chin reminded Les of his uncle back in Sydney. James could have been a little grained or worldly-wise from doing time, but if George's nephew was nineteen, Les rode a skateboard and listened to silverchair. This struck Les as a little curious. Something else the big Queenslander thought he picked up about James made Les chuckle a little to himself as well.

'Anyway, I'm Les,' he said, offering his hand. 'Can I call you Jimmy?'

'Sure. Why not.' Jimmy's handshake was brief but firm as he continued to check out Norton and accepted his open, if maybe unexpected friendliness. 'Hey, that's a choice T-shirt, Les. Where did you get it?'

'Jamaica. Montego Bay.'

'Fair dinkum? Have you been there?'

Les nodded. 'Too right. Yah I nung. Respec, mon. Jah Rastafarri.'

'Hey, good one, Les.'

They drove on, picking up a little speed. 'Yeah, I been there,' said Les. 'And I know all about the black problem, Jimmy.'

Jimmy's smile faded a little. 'Oh, really?'

Norton nodded again. 'Fuckin' oath. And I know just how to fix it.'

'Do you now? And just exactly how would you fix this "black problem", Les?'

'Well, if I was running Jamaica, the first thing I'd do is bring back slavery.'

Jimmy was incredulous. 'You'd what?'

'Bring back slavery. Shove 'em all back in chains and flog the shit out of them and work the cunts into

64

the ground. That's all they're good for, the lazy black bastards.'

Jimmy gave Les a double, triple blink. 'You're fuckin' kidding.'

Norton shook his head adamantly. 'No way, mate. And back here, the first thing I'd do is shove a bomb under ATSIC and blow it to the shithouse. Then shoot the lot of the whingeing bastards.' Norton looked evenly at the horrified look on Jimmy's face. 'Well, not really. What I'd do is get all the whites out of Australia and leave all the abos here with an AK-47 each, a thousand rounds of ammo and a few flagons of plonk. Then come back in about a month and there'd be none of the cunts left. Well, maybe a few. But fuck them—we'd just poison 'em like they did back in the good old days. Maybe gas 'em this time.'

Jimmy's eyes stuck out like two ping-pong balls as he recoiled from Norton's despicable tirade. 'I don't fuckin' believe this,' he said. 'Turn the car round and take me back to the nick. You're completely fucked.'

Norton gave Jimmy a double blink along with a look of shock and confusion. 'Jimmy,' he said. 'You're not—you're not a fuckin' abo, are you?' His eyes still bulging, Jimmy nodded almost imperceptibly. 'You're a bloody koori. Well, I'll be buggered. I honestly thought you were a white man.'

'Sorry to bloody disappoint you.'

'That's all right. I should've known, though.'

'How do you mean?'

'By the chip on your shoulder. You've all got one, just some are bigger than others. Yours'd be about average, I'd say.'

'Well up yours, too. You fuckin' boofheaded big red-neck goose.'

Norton grinned and made a gesture with one hand. 'Hey, think nothing of it. I stole your country, didn't I?'

'Ohh shit!' Jimmy looked at the floor, looked at the stupid smirk on Norton's face, then stared out the passenger window. He knew he wasn't going to get far with Les and now that he knew where Norton was coming from he felt not only relieved but had to try hard not to laugh himself. He kept his feelings to himself for the time being, however, and they were past the Gosford turn-off before he spoke.

'So just what do you know about me, Les?'

'What do I know? Jimmy, all I know is you're George's nephew. You're bunged up in the nick on a dud pot charge. There's some Elliott going down in there and they've got you out till next Wednesday while they sort it out. I happened to be up here and they asked me to keep an eye on you till then.'

'Is that what they told you?'

'That's it, mate. Do I need to know any more?'

Jimmy shook his head. 'No. That'll do for the time being. I'll fill you in on a few other things as we go along.'

'Fair enough. And did they say anything to you about me?'

'Enough.'

'Well, there you go, Jimmy. I guess enough is enough.'

'Yes, Les. I guess you're right.'

They crossed the old Punt Bridge and approached the Avoca turn-off.

'Hey, turn right here, will you, Les.'

'Okey doke,' replied Norton. The lights were green, so Les hit the blinkers and turned right at a garage and a boatyard into Avoca Drive.

The road curved its way through gently rolling hills thick with trees and past houses dotted along the side of the road mostly hidden from view by more trees. Norton got a glimpse of Brisbane Water on his right, then they went through Green Point shopping centre. A bit further on the traffic slowed up for some road-works, so Les tried for a bit of light conversation with Jimmy. But George's nephew seemed preoccupied with something else. All he would mention was his family came from around Empire Bay and he went to school at Terrigal. Didn't Les see them all waiting for him outside the gaol along with all his mates? Les left Jimmy's sarcastic remarks hanging in the air and, apart from the stereo playing softly through the speakers, they drove on in silence. The road continued on through more heavily timbered hills and valleys; the air was fresh, the sun was out and Norton was enjoying the drive. They went past the Davistown/Saratoga turn-off when Jimmy pointed ahead.

'Pull up over here, will you, Les.'

Norton stopped the car outside a flower stall built onto an old sandstone house. Buckets of flowers and pots of seedlings and indoor plants were stacked under a wooden, lattice-work front next to a sign saying KIN-CUMBER FLOWER HUT. SHOW YOUR LOVE WITH FLOWERS.

'I won't be a sec.' Jimmy jumped out of the car, then got back in a minute or two later with a bunch of flowers.

'Carnations,' said Norton, taking a couple of sniffs. 'They sure smell nice.'

'Like I said, Les,' replied Jimmy, doing up his seat belt, 'there's a lot of things you don't know about me. This is one of them.'

'Fair enough. So where to now?'

'Keep going straight ahead. I'll tell you when to turn.'

'You're the boss.'

Les slipped the Berlina into drive and they were off again. Before long there were more houses, then Les got another glimpse of water and Kincumber shopping centre was on the left and opposite was a McDonald's and a KFC. Behind them Les thought he glimpsed a hotel just back from the water. They went through another roundabout near a retirement village and Jimmy pointed again.

'Chuck a donut at the next roundabout and come back this way.'

'One donut coming up.'

Left of the roundabout the road continued on to Avoca and Terrigal; right was Empire Bay Drive. Just back from the corner Les circled right past a tiny church with a graveyard surrounded by a low, white picket fence and small trees. He drove back a short distance when Jimmy pointed again.

'Pull in here.' Les eased the Berlina off the road and cut the motor. 'You can wait here if you want,' said Jimmy, undoing his seat belt. But the way he spoke, it sounded more like an invitation to join him.

'No, I might stretch my legs.' Les undid his seat belt and got out too.

Beneath a gnarled old tree, an iron gate with a chain and hook was set into the picket fence. Jimmy opened it and Les closed it behind them. Up close the little, vine-covered sandstone church looked even smaller. Two trees almost side by side sheltered it on the right and on the other side a church bell was set in the fork of a grey, sunbleached log. The grounds and graves were all well kept and a gentle zephyr rippling the trees in the midday sun gave the tiny church and its surrounds a distinct, natural beauty tinged with peace and serenity.

Les followed Jimmy through the tombstones to where the churchyard sloped down to a corner on the right, next to the road and a house next door. He stopped in front of a granite slab set into the grass beneath an overhanging tree with branches that low they almost touched the ground. The granite tombstone was hewn roughly at the top but highly polished with neat, gold lettering across the front. Les edged forward as Jimmy bent down and placed the carnations in front of it. The gold lettering said 'Rosemarie Rosewater', when she was born and when she died and beneath that:

Farewell dear mother, thy days are past.
You did your best while life did last.
God called you home, it was his will.
But in my heart you're living still.
God shall wipe away all tears.
ISAIAH XXV

'Your mother, Jimmy?' Les asked softly. Jimmy nodded. 'She was only young, mate. What happened? If—'

'She had a heart attack.'

Les nodded. He got the picture, or as much of the picture as he needed for the time being. 'I'll see you back at the car, Jimmy.'

'Yeah, I won't be long.'

'You take all the time you want, mate.' Les turned away quietly and left Jimmy Rosewater alone with his thoughts.

Instead of waiting in the car, Les leaned against the passenger-side door and gazed back at the little church and its surrounding graveyard. He'd barely met Jimmy. But in the brief time since he had, Les tried to form a rough opinion of George Brennan's nephew. He was heartbreakingly goodlooking, but there was no mention of a girlfriend. Whether the cops had loaded him up or not, Jimmy was still a bit shifty. That's why he was in the nick? His face was too clean to be a fighter and he didn't have the attitude of a young thug. But he stood up to Les earlier, so he had spirit and definitely wasn't weak. He didn't have or seem to want many friends, so he was a bit of a loner. Nor did he have any time for his relatives. But he was obviously very close to his mother. It didn't say anything on the tombstone about her being the beloved wife of whoever, so Les guessed Jimmy was probably illegitimate; he mightn't even know his father. And going by the dates on the grave, and if Jimmy was around twenty, Rosemarie was about fifteen or sixteen when Jimmy was born and only somewhere in her early thirties when she died. It was rather sad and Les was a little sorry he'd revved him up like he did earlier, considering the poor bludger had just walked out of the nick and still probably didn't know where he was.

Still, he managed to bounce back pretty smartly. One thing was for certain about Jimmy, though—with those looks he'd be unbelievable burley to take out chasing women. They'd be hurling themselves at him like javelins. No, Jimmy was all right. But summing up what Les knew about him so far. Jimmy's favourite saying would probably be one of Norton's. Know everyone. Trust nobody. And paddle your own canoe.

Les watched him as he came through the gate and closed it behind him.

'So how are feeling now, Jimmy? All right?'

Jimmy nodded. 'Yeah, I feel good.' He gave Les a wrinkled sort of smile. 'In fact, Les, I couldn't feel better.'

'Good on you, mate.' Les stepped back and opened the door for him. 'So where to now?'

'Terrigal.'

'Terrigal it is.' Les closed the door after Jimmy, then walked round and got behind the wheel.

Les didn't bother driving back down to the round-about. There were no cars around so he tromped the Berlina and scorched straight across the double white lines. The sign said Terrigal/Avoca and they were following more winding road set amongst more hills thick with trees and John Anderson was crooning 'Hillbilly with a Heartache' through the car stereo when Jimmy finally spoke.

'I have to pick up a bag at a friend's place. It's not far from Uncle Price's.'

'You know Price's joint?'

'Yeah, I've stayed there with George a few times.'

'Ohh, right,' nodded Les absently.

'When we get there, come inside and I'll show you something.'

'Yeah?'

Jimmy nodded. 'Remember in the papers about a year ago? A bloke called Baxter went off his head with a shotgun and shot four people in a house. Three young girls and a bloke. Then he drove off and shot two other people?'

Norton nodded slowly. There'd been that many shootings and killings in the last twelve months, not counting the ones he'd been involved in, he'd lost track. 'Yeah, I think so.'

'Well, this is the place.' Jimmy's face went grim. 'I knew one of the girls, too. I used to buy chocolates where she worked. She was eighteen and pregnant. Just about to get married.'

'And he shot her with a shotgun? Sounds like a nice bloke.'

'Yeah, real nice,' said Jimmy. 'The cunt.'

They went past the Avoca Beach turn-off. The road curved up, then straightened out with the ocean on the right and farms on the left. Dams shone in the gullies, the hills were thick with trees and Les could hardly believe he was only an hour or so from Sydney. It was like being right up the North Coast. They came onto the road that took them past Price's street. Jimmy told Les to go left and he drove down the same way he walked the night before when Jimmy said to stop near the steep hill Les had dragged Carol up. Norton pulled up in the driveway of a two-storey, yellow brick house with trees out the front, a double garage below and stairs on the left that angled up to a patio and a

72

residence above. Les got out of the car and followed Jimmy up the stairs. The brown door was open and inside a young girl with dark hair wearing a black tracksuit was smoking a cigarette and watching TV. Jimmy knocked a couple of times, she looked up, smiled and walked over.

'Jimmy. How are you? We got your message.'

Jimmy nodded. 'Yeah, I got five days off for being a good bloke.'

The girl laughed. 'Yeah, that'd be right. Come in.'

'Louise, this is a friend of mine—Les.'

'Hello, Les.'

'Hello, Louise. Nice to meet you.'

The upstairs unit was spotlessly clean with light brown carpet, comfy furniture and white walls. An open archway off the lounge led to the kitchen and on the left when you walked in was a wooden cabinet with the TV and stereo. Laminated prints of Harley-Davidsons and American Indians hung on the walls and next to the kitchen was a full-length, laminated print from *Reservoir Dogs*. A two-litre swing bottle of Jim Beam sat on the TV cabinet with more motorbike and American Indian bric-a-brac. The laundry was in a corridor left of the kitchen, then the bathroom and bedrooms.

'So, where's the boys?' asked Jimmy.

The girl gestured with the cigarette. 'On the toe. The fuckin' Tarheels have got a shoot-to-kill order on them. So they pissed off till they sort it out.'

'Christ! What the fuck happened?'

'Ohh, it's just a big fuck-up. Two Tarheels got their legs broken and it wasn't even Wade and Peirce. They were in Sydney.'

Jimmy's face darkened and he shook his head. 'Jesus, they're a bunch of pricks.'

'Don't we all know it.'

'So, where are they?' Louise gave Jimmy a blank look. Jimmy nodded. 'Yeah, righto. So is my bag here?'

'Yeah. It's in the garage. I'll just find the key.'

As Louise went to the bedroom, Jimmy turned to Norton. 'Have a look at this, Les.' He took Les into the kitchen and pulled back the window curtain. Across the bottom of the glass was a crooked row of small fracture holes.

'Shotgun pellets?' said Les.

Jimmy nodded. 'Come here.' He led Norton to the corridor and pointed up to the ceiling. There were more holes. 'See this.' Jimmy pointed to one of the bedroom doors. There was a long scrape mark near the keyhole and the doorknob was all uneven as if it had been hit with a hammer. 'One of the girls tried to lock herself in here and that's where he bashed the door open with the butt of the gun.'

Norton ran his hand over the doorknob. 'Lovely.'

'Now have a look at this.' Next to the front door, faint marks were still visible running down the wall. 'He got one here. And—'

Louise returned, holding some keys. 'We'll go down through the laundry, Jimmy.'

'All right. Have a look around, Les. I'll be back in a minute.'

'Yeah, righto.'

While Jimmy and Louise were gone, Norton perused the unit. The marks were against nearly all the walls with four in one room where the gunman must have shot two people twice. Although the marks had been scrubbed and painted over, the force of the blast must have sent blood deep into the concrete because, despite several coats, it still kept seeping through. Beneath the white it looked as if someone had splattered about a dozen tomatoes against the walls and it had all run down to the carpet. It was macabre and Norton tried to picture what it must have been like in there when the killer burst in and opened up with the shotgun. Three terrified girls and one bloke all trying to hide. Almost unimaginable. Les was shaking his head and looking at some more pellet holes he'd found in the ceiling when Jimmy struggled into the loungeroom with a blue, canvas carry-all almost as big as himself.

'Christ, what have you got in there, Jimmy?' asked Les. 'A baby elephant?'

'Just a few odds and ends,' he puffed, dropping it on the floor. He turned to Louise. 'Well, I'll give you a ring or whatever. But I definitely have to see Peirce. So—'

'Don't worry, Jimmy. That'll all be sweet. But ring me when you get to the house and give me the number.'

'Okay, Lou. I'll see you then.'

Jimmy went to pick up his bag and Les took it. 'Here, let me. You'll end up with a hernia.'

'Oh, thanks, Les.'

'I'll see you again, Louise.'

'Yeah, you too, Les.'

The bag was certainly heavy. But Les managed to

get it down the stairs and onto the back seat of the car a lot easier than Jimmy would have.

'Where to now, Jimmy?' he said, closing the door. 'Home?'

'Yes. Home, James. I wouldn't mind a quick swim, then a long shower. Get the smell of that fuckin' nick off me.'

'I understand perfectly, James. It's not real good, is it?'

'You can say that again, Les.'

There were one or two things Norton would have liked to ask Jimmy, however he thought he might let it slide for the time being. Les hit the ignition and they drove the short distance to Price's house.

'Righto, Jimmy. I think you can manage now.' Les dropped Jimmy's bag near the top of the stairs. 'Where do you want to doss? I've got the room at end of the hall.'

'There's one near the pool'll do me.'

'All right. Well, there's coffee and food and all that in the kitchen if you want. Just help yourself. I'll be down the pool having a read if you want me.'

'Okay, Les. I'll sort my stuff out and see you in an hour or so.'

'Take your time, mate. There's no hurry.'

Jimmy got his bag and lugged it downstairs while Les went to his room and changed into an old pair of shorts and his thongs then got a glass of orange juice and took it into the loungeroom. Jimmy must have had the same idea as Norton when he first arrived, because by the time Les had tuned the stereo to some FM station and started staring out the window, Jimmy had left his gear and jumped straight into the pool also; except

Jimmy didn't worry about Speedos. Les watched Jimmy's not-so-white backside gliding easily through the water and thought that, as well as looking fairly fit, he didn't have a bad swimming style either. Go for your life, mate, Les smiled. You only got a week, then it's back to the puzzle. Les drifted back to his room to get his book and sunglasses. By the time he got to the pool the only sign of Jimmy was a few wet footprints and the sound of someone singing in a shower. Les settled down on a banana-lounge and started reading. He was getting into stories about the Einsatzgruppen and Babii-Yar when Jimmy strolled casually round the side. He was wearing neatly pressed, white Alberto Biani shorts with an alligator skin belt, a brown Banana Republic T-shirt and tan Mezlin loafers. With his Iridium Oakleys jammed into his eyes he looked like he'd just walked out of a spread in *GQ* magazine.

'So how are you feeling now, Jimmy? You've certainly brushed up okay.'

'Yes, well I'm not quite into the all-Australian, Shanghai-riding boots and stubbies look—which is obviously your particular go.' Jimmy gave Les a thin, pearly white smile as Norton self-consciously scrunched his toes in his old thongs. 'And as to how I feel—as a matter of fact, Les, I'm hungry. What about you?'

'Jimmy, I'm always hungry.'

'Okay, let's do lunch.'

'Do lunch? You don't fancy a barbecue or something? I got some grouse steaks in the fridge.'

'I'd love to, Les. But I left my can holder back in the nick. Along with my Fatty Vautin cookbook and my thongs.'

Les folded his book. 'Okay, lunch it is.'

'And, Les, try and wear something a little decent, will you? The place I've got in mind is sort of—respectable.'

Wear something decent, Les. The place is respectable. Norton's eyes narrowed and darkened slightly as he climbed out of his old shorts back in the bedroom. Then he caught sight of himself in the mirror and smiled. You started it, smartarse. You've got no one to blame but yourself. He changed into a pair of Levi shorts, a blue Nautica T-shirt and black, lace-up Road Mocs and gave his hair a quick comb. Jimmy was waiting in the kitchen drinking a glass of orange juice like the French Consul sipping Beaujolais. He gave Les a quick once-up-and-down, followed by a grudging nod of approval.

'So where are we doing lunch, James?'

'A place called Waves. Opposite the carpark next to Terrigal Surf Club.'

'Okay. Let's go.'

Jimmy rinsed his glass clean and they walked out to the car. After Les put on his seat belt and started the motor he turned to Jimmy.

'Just one thing, Jimmy, before we go.'

'Yes, Les.'

'If this place is so—respectable, how come they let you in there?'

Jimmy didn't blink. 'Because I generally take a moron redneck with me, get the management to rob him blind on the bill, then make sure he leaves a substantial tip.'

Norton didn't blink either. 'Fair enough.'

The restaurant was above a surf shop and an art gallery. Les found a parking spot in the carpark opposite and they walked back across the street. A blue awning with 'Waves' written across it in white sat above a short passageway leading to a set of stairs that angled up to a blue railing. Les stepped in and was almost on the front step when he heard Jimmy call out.

'Where are you going?'

Jimmy was standing on the footpath with his arms folded. 'In here,' replied Norton. 'This is it, ain't it?'

'What are you going to drink with your meal? Coca-Cola? Les, please. Some wine, surely?'

'Fair enough.' Norton rejoined Jimmy and they started walking towards the other shops. 'Hey, Jimmy, if you're going to get a flagon of cheap Moselle, shouldn't we be going to that pub over near the bridge? I doubt if that bottle shop'd have any goonis.'

'Droll, Les. Verrry droll.'

The woman was behind the counter puffing on a cigarette while she talked to a customer. Jimmy walked across to the white wines, had a quick peruse, then picked out a bottle and placed it on the counter.

'Have you got a bottle of this slightly chilled, Sheri,' he asked.

The woman looked at the bottle and put down her cigarette. 'Sure have, Jimmy.' She took the bottle and replaced it with one from a small chiller near the front wall. 'By the time you get to the restaurant that should be about perfect.'

Norton looked at the label then at Jimmy. 'Mount Mary Vineyard. Lilyvale Chardonnay. Is that any good?' Jimmy looked at the woman. The woman looked at Jimmy. Then they both looked at Les. Les looked at the price. 'Christ! It'd want to be.' Norton knew Jimmy had absolutely no intention of paying, but he was still a bit slow getting the money out of his pocket.

'Well,' said Jimmy, 'don't stand there like a stale bottle of piss, Charlie Brown. Pay the woman.'

A cosy indoor dining room faced you as you walked into Waves with a large outdoor dining area overlooking the beach on your right. A bushy-haired woman wearing jeans and a crisp, white shirt was checking something at a small counter near the door. She looked up and smiled happily as they walked in.

'Hello, Jimmy,' she said. 'How are you?'

'Pretty good, Dyane,' answered Jimmy. 'Nice to see you again.'

'You too, Jimmy. Always.'

Jimmy handed her the bottle of wine. 'Have you got a nice table on the—?'

'For you, Jimmy, always. Always.'

Dyane led them out to a bright, spacious, terracotta-tiled balcony edged with white brick and dotted with customers eating off white tables shaded by blue umbrellas. Two extensive greenboard menus sat either side of the balcony above several ceramic pots full of parlour palms and indoor plants. She settled them at a table right at the edge and Les could see all the way to Wamberal and across to the boats in the Haven. A pleasant breeze drifted over the tables and you were far enough above the traffic to watch it but miss the noise and any car fumes. Without ignoring Les, Dyane had a few more words with Jimmy then came back with his wine in an ice bucket and two menus. She poured them a little over half a glass each, smiled again, then went over to have a word with a waitress and some customers at another table.

'Well, cheers, Les,' said Jimmy.

'Yeah, same to you, mate,' replied Norton.

The chardonnay was nice. But, unfortunately, Les had to admit wine was just wine to him. He could tell good from bad, red from white, then after that it was just all plonk. Price and George were wine buffs to the point of being Nazis and spent a fortune on the stuff at times. Les would listen to them waffling away about vintages and bouquets and whatever with rich punters back at the club and it bored the tits off him. He'd tried to appreciate fine wines on several occasions but to no avail. Even French champagne gave him indigestion. Try as he might, Norton was a wine philistine and preferred a glass of cold mineral water with a meal any time; especially sitting out in the sun during the middle of the day.

'So, what do you think?' asked Jimmy, swirling his glass gently like a typical wine-nazi-cum-connoisseur.

'Yeah, not bad,' conceded Norton. 'Could be a bit colder, though.' Les got some ice, dropped it in his glass, swirled it around vigorously with his fingers, then licked them. 'Yeah, that's better.'

Jimmy shook his head in disgust. 'I don't believe anybody can be that crass. Why don't you put some cordial in with it?'

'Not a bad idea,' agreed Les. 'They got any Lime Green Kooler in here? That would complement this wonderfully.'

Dyane came back with her notepad. Jimmy ordered a dozen Oysters Natural and Pan-Fried Cajun Coral Perch Fillets with sour cream. Les thought he might have the same only with a Malaysian Prawn Laksa for an entree, plus garlic bread, a side salad for two and a large glass of mineral water. When Dyane left them, Jimmy sipped his wine, crossed his legs and sat back. Les took a couple of sips of wine, watching Jimmy as he drank. He also watched the women at the other tables. Young and old, they were all pitching furtive glances at Jimmy; two young blondes to Norton's left were almost drooling. Whether Jimmy was aware of this or not, Les couldn't tell because of the sunglasses. But he was kicked back, looking around him and no doubt revelling in the more than pleasant surroundings. Though going from a cell to a first-class restaurant in barely a few hours, there would be something wrong with you if you didn't preen a little. Norton's mineral water arrived and he took a mouthful.

'Well, Jimmy. What do you reckon? I could think of worse places to be.'

'Yeah.' Jimmy started singing with a bit of a punk British accent. 'Like down in a sewer. Or on the end of a skewer.'

'The Stranglers. "Rattus Norvegicus".'

'Hey, Les, you know your music.'

'Warren—the bloke I live with—he's got the CD.' Les took another mouthful of mineral water. 'You didn't seem to mind some of the stuff I had playing in the car.'

'Country and Western. Are you kidding?' Jimmy started to laugh. 'Rural-influenced contemporary music. In fact, I've got a surprise for you later, Les.'

'You have?'

'Yep. We're going out for a couple of hours at six o'clock.'

'We are? Where?'

'Over to Avoca. I reckon you'll love it. So don't get pissed.'

Norton shrugged and nodded to the ice bucket. 'Not on that shit, I won't.'

The entrees arrived. Jimmy's oysters were creamy, plump and fresh that day, and he ate them like a gentleman. Norton's laksa was rich, spicy, full of succulent prawns and noodles with seasoned, fried shallots on top and, despite a finger bowl, he ate it like a caveman. Then, hard as it was to believe, the cajun coral perch was as good or even better. Two fat fillets of delicious blackened fish that fell apart on a bed of shredded lettuce into the sour cream. If Norton had been a dog, he would have run out to the kitchen and started rooting the chef's leg. They slipped, slopped and slurped away, getting into the salad and garlic bread as well till there was nothing left. Les was good on the tooth. But for his size Jimmy wasn't bad either and despite a bottle of wine he didn't appear to be the slightest bit drunk.

Les raised his second glass of mineral water. 'Well, Jimmy, I've got to hand it to you.'

'My choice of restaurants?'

'That. Plus you've drunk a whole bottle of wine and haven't carried on like a drunken abo.'

'Really?'

'Yep. You haven't picked a fight with the owner. You haven't abused any of the other customers and asked them what they're looking at. And you haven't called

83

me a boofheaded white cunt and told me I stole your country.'

Jimmy sniffed indifferently. 'Why bother? You don't need me to tell you that. Besides, you're driving me around, picking up the tab—you even carry my bag for me. As far as I'm concerned, you're just a goosey big mug.' Jimmy drained the last of his wine and blinked at the look on Norton's face. 'Les, Les, I'm sorry. You're not. You're not a mug, are you? Good Lord, why didn't you tell me?'

What could Norton say? He'd been completely hoisted with his own petard. 'Jimmy, I reckon you could make carrot cake out of cow shit.'

'Too right, Les. I might be temporarily bunged up at the moment, but I sure as hell ain't climbing up mug's hill on the slippery side.'

'So what do you want to do now?'

'I wouldn't mind going for walk. Walk the meal off. Just get out in the open for a little while.'

'Good idea, Jimmy. Whereabouts?' Les nodded over the balcony. 'Terrigal.'

'Avoca. I like it down there.'

'Okay, let's go.'

As they got to their feet Jimmy pointed to the bill. 'Oh, and Les, don't forget a substantial tip.'

Norton grinned and patted his stomach. 'You don't have to worry about that, Jimmy.'

With Jimmy giving directions, Les drove past the Haven and on up the hill to the North Avoca turn-off. Jimmy explained how you couldn't drive directly to South Avoca because of the lagoon in the middle, but you could get there easy enough walking along the

84

beach, which was what they were going to do. The
road led down, then on past a cluster of shops; Les
pulled up in a small carpark next to North Avoca Surf
Club.

'We may as well leave our shoes in the car,' suggested Jimmy.

'Good thinking, 99,' said Norton, kicking his off
then locking the doors.

There was one other car in the carpark and two surfies standing on a wooden platform above some bush
checking out what the gusty sou-easter had done to the
waves. Les followed Jimmy through the bushes split
by a fenced-off pathway that led to the sand and a sign
saying NO DOGS, NO LITTERING, NO TRAIL BIKES, etc,
next to a swing-top garbage tin. Between the sign and
the garbage tin was a pile of empty chip packets,
flavoured-milk cartons and softdrink cans and several
dog turds.

Jimmy pointed over to the water's edge. 'The tide's
half out. It'll be good walking on the wet sand.'

'Yeah,' agreed Les.

As he followed Jimmy across the beach, Les had a
look around and checked things out. A small point
jutted out on the left, beneath a towering headland
thick with scrubby bush that almost hid a number of
houses nestled amongst the trees. More houses ran up
the green hills to a huge, blue water tower bulging out
against the sky. Further along the treeline Les thought
he could make out where Price's house just missed the
best part of the view. To the south, a wide curve of
beach, a little like Bondi only longer, ended at another
surf club and three towering headlands thick with

more trees and bush. All the houses and units around the beach seemed to end near the surf club and just back from the middle of the beach was a lagoon; back from the beach on the other side of the lagoon was a row of tall Norfolk Island pines. A few clouds had started to drift over and the sou-easter had stiffened, but Les was still surprised how few people were on the beach.

'We'll just walk down the south end and back,' smiled Jimmy. 'It won't take long.'

Norton shrugged. 'Whatever you reckon, Jimmy. I'm easy.'

Jimmy strolled off along the water's edge, kicking at the few small waves trickling in, waving his arms around, skipping flat stones across the water and just enjoying the bit of freedom they'd somehow managed for him. Les was happy to fall behind a little and let Jimmy do his thing and skipped a few flat stones across the water himself. He was also thinking of checking out some of the local real-estate agents' windows before he left. After Sydney, the Central Coast just seemed to get better and better. A couple of joggers went around them, and a fat woman puffed along with a cocker spaniel almost as fat as she was on a lead. Then they walked past the lagoon and the pine trees, finally stopping at a shallow rockpool in front of the surf club. It was more sheltered at the south end and a few mothers were splashing around with their children in the pool while the beach inspector sat in his four-wheel drive keeping an eye on what few swimmers there were splashing around between the flags.

'I'll tell you what, Jimmy,' said Norton looking around him, 'compared to Sydney, this place is God's own.'

'Yeah,' answered Jimmy. 'The land of the three Bs.'

'The three Bs?'

'That's right. Builders, bastards and boofheads.'

'I don't quite get you.'

'Well, every prick up here with a hammer and a bag of nails reckons he's a builder. The place is swarming with bastards—I can vouch for that. And believe me, Les, there's no shortage of boofheads.'

'Ahh, come on, Jimmy. That's just the chip on your shoulder talking. You'll find boofheads everywhere. This place is tops.'

'Yeah, righto. Come on, let's start walking back.'

They headed back the way they came, taking their time with Jimmy in front and Les following. Just past the lagoon, Jimmy spotted something washed up on the beach. It was an old piece of roofing batten a little less than a metre long, baked black and hard from the sun and the salt water. He picked it up and started twirling it around; first like a drum majorette, then across his chest and up under his arms like he had a nunchuku. Whatever Jimmy was doing it had a definite technique and Les was curious—that curious that Les wasn't watching where he was going and, of all things, he trod on a poor dead bee.

'Yeow, shit! You bastard!'

The sting went in just under his big toe and though the pain wasn't excruciating it hurt enough and was certainly annoying.

'I don't bloody believe it,' cursed Les as he flopped

on his backside and rubbed his toe with wet sand. 'It could only happen to me.'

Jimmy was still strolling along, playing around with his stick and Les was about to call out to him when he saw a movement coming down the beach to Jimmy's left. A big, ugly, burly man in a blue cap, old shorts and a sweatshirt with the sleeves hacked off came walking across the sand with a big, black Alsatian just as ugly as he was. It had no collar or lead and was just plain mean and vicious and out looking for something to bite or kill. There were no cats or dachshunds around, so as soon as it saw Jimmy it snarled, drew back its fangs and went for him. Les was about to warn Jimmy when the owner called out to him.

'Run into the water!'

Jimmy turned around, saw the dog coming at him and spun the stick into his right hand.

'Run into the water, you fuckin' goose,' yelled Blue Cap, the owner.

The Alsatian charged at Jimmy and was just about to sink its teeth into his thigh when Jimmy smashed the stick down across its snout. The dog howled with pain and crashed onto the sand front legs first, like a horse going down in a Western movie. Before it had a chance to let out another yelp Jimmy belted it across the snout again, only harder this time. That was the last thing the Alsatian was expecting. It literally dogged it. It stuck its tail between its legs and, yelping and screeching, tore off up the beach towards North Avoca and parts beyond. The owner watched his heroic killer attack dog disappearing into the distance and came charging over.

'What the fuck do you think you're doing?' he bellowed at Jimmy.

'What am I doing?' answered Jimmy. 'Stopping myself from getting my leg torn off.'

'Why didn't you run in the water like I fuckin' told you?'

Jimmy's temper started to rise. He was entitled to an apology, but instead he was getting abused. 'Fuck running in the water,' he snapped. 'You're not even supposed to have the fuckin' thing on the beach. And where's its fuckin' lead? Lucky I wasn't some poor little kid.'

'Fuck the lead. And fuck the sign,' bellowed Blue Cap. 'If I want to bring my dog down the fuckin' beach, I'll fuckin' bring it down.'

'Good. And if the rotten thing comes back and tries to bite me again I'll give it another belt in the head, you fuckin' big goose.'

'What!? Ohh fuck you, you poofy-looking little cunt.'

Blue Cap charged at Jimmy and shaped up to throw a big looping left.

Oh-oh, thought Norton, I'd better make a move here or Jimmy's face is paste. That mug's a bit big for young James. Les ignored the bee sting and started to run over. But he didn't need to.

Jimmy stood where he was and as the bloke moved in he brought the stick down across his wrist then backhanded it across his shin all in the one movement. The bloke yelled and cursed with pain, not sure whether to grab his wrist or his shin first. Before he got a chance to do anything, Jimmy bent down behind him, shoved the stick between his legs near his ankles, turned it around and jerked back tripping Blue Cap face-first into the wet sand. Norton was stoked. Hey, good one, Jimmy. Now shove the stick right up his arse. Jimmy stepped back smiling as the bloke wiped the sand from his face and lumbered to his feet.

'Why, you fuckin' little cunt!' he screamed with rage and pain.

Blue Cap glared at Jimmy then charged at him again, this time throwing a big angry right. Making it look easy, Jimmy crouched under the mug's right, letting it slide behind him, shoved the stick up under the mug's right armpit and over his shoulder, stuck his left leg in front of Blue Cap's right knee, pushed the stick and bent over at the same time. Blue Cap went sailing over Jimmy's hip, head-first into the sand again, somersaulting onto his back. Les was even more stoked than before. Hey, we got one bad-arse, mother-fuckin' nigger here. Go, Jimmy, go. He was wondering what Jimmy was going to do next when two blokes about the same size and wearing much the same clothes as Blue Cap came running across the sand. They looked at Jimmy holding the stick, then looked at Blue Cap who was now half on his knees trying to get his breath back.

'Hey, Thommo, are you all right?' said one. 'What's goin' on?'

'I was walkin' along the beach,' howled Blue Cap. 'And this little cunt in the poofy shorts hit me with a lump of wood.'

'What! Why you fuckin' little yuppie cunt.'

Blue Cap's mates started to move towards Jimmy.

Les thought it was now high time he did put his head in. Jimmy might have been okay at what he was doing. But there were two of them and they were both twice as big as Jimmy. Les ran over and stopped in front of them.

'Bad luck, boys. The yuppie's not on his own.'

'Who the fuck are you?' said the first one.

'No one,' answered Les. 'But I'm with him.'

'Well, too fuckin' bad,' said the other.

Just as he spoke, the first one threw a big right at Les. Les pulled his chin in, stepped inside it and slammed a short right under the bloke's heart. He gasped with pain and his eyes bulged as Les snapped a left hook into his jaw that mashed up the inside of his mouth, chipping and knocking half the fillings out of his teeth. His mate thought this was about the only good chance he was going to get, so he ran at Norton, throwing all sorts of punches. Les took a few around the shoulders and a couple on the top of his head, then stepped back and snap-kicked the bloke in the solar plexus. He stopped dead in his tracks just in time for Les to slam a left-right combination into his face, breaking his nose. He barely had time to close his eyes and give a tortured grunt of pain when Les grabbed him by the hair and brought his face down into Norton's knee coming up, smashing the rest of his nose across his face in a splatter of blood and snot. He hit the sand face-first and started snoring.

The other mug was still on his feet, not feeling very well, and fast realising he wasn't going to get any better. In desperation he threw a big, slow right at Les. Norton stepped outside, letting it go past his face then jammed his left forearm up under the bloke's chin, pushed his right elbow up with his right hand and kicked the bloke's legs from under him with his left foot. The bloke landed heavily on his left side and Les banged two withering short rights into his jaw, breaking it and smashing up a few more teeth. There was really no need, but Norton thought he might stomp on the bloke's groin a few times, 'Jake the Muss' style, just for fun. So he did.

Blue Cap saw all this and started to panic. 'I'll get the police,' he howled. 'I've got a mate's a cop in Gosford.'

'Have you now?' said Norton, walking towards him. He turned to Jimmy. 'Eric,' he said, slowly and distinctly, 'give me that stick.'

'Sure . . . Vernon.'

Les took the piece of roofing batten and jammed one end into Blue Cap's mouth, straight through his teeth, over his tongue and halfway down his throat. Blue Cap moaned a painful gurgle through the blood and smashed teeth and clutched at his face. Les looked at him for a moment then gave him a couple of quick whacks over the ear just for being a mug.

'When you can talk again, shit-for-brains, say hello to your copper mate for me. Come on, Eric, let's go back to the hotel.'

'Good idea, Vernon. I don't think I like it down here.'

They walked off, leaving the three heroes bleeding and moaning on the wet sand. No one appeared to have seen anything, but Les threw the piece of roofing batten way out into the sea all the same.

'Just in case that big sook does call the cops, we don't want anybody noticing us.' Les grinned. 'We're just a couple of tourists walking along the beach, Eric.'

'That's us, Vernon,' winked Jimmy. 'Two yuppie tourists.'

'I'll tell you what, Jimmy, you're not bad with the bloody thing. Where'd you learn that?'

'Kukishin ryu. Off a Japanese bloke I know in Sydney. I can't fight to save my life, Les, and I'm not interested. But give me a weapon of some description and I'm pretty sweet. Anything from a can opener to a biro to a gun—I'm there.'

'I can see that, James.'

'Hey, don't worry about me. You're not bad yourself. Not fuckin' bad at all.'

Norton shrugged. 'I get by.'

'But what was I saying about boofheads, Les?'

'Yeah, but you can't judge everybody by those three dills.'

'Mmmhh. It's a good thing I did find that bit of stick though. I'd have a big piece missing out my leg now and he wouldn't have given a fuck. "Run into the water." The fuckin' imbecile.'

Les shook his head and started to laugh. 'You know it's funny, Jimmy. Every time I come up here, I finish up in a fight on the beach and crazy women jump my bones.'

'What do you mean?'

'I'll tell you about it later.'

They got to the sign saying no dogs were allowed on the beach and Jimmy stopped. 'Hey, Les.'

'Yeah?'

'What do you call a boomerang that doesn't come back?'

'Fucked if I know. What?'

'A stick. Jesus, you are a mug, Les, aren't you?'

Norton shook his head. 'Not really. It's just that I wouldn't shock your sensitivities by mentioning a racist joke like that. But it's droll, Jimmy, all the same. Verrry droll.'

Back at the house, Jimmy said he wanted to make some phone calls, sort a couple of things out and put his head down for an hour; he'd see Les back in the kitchen at six, then they'd head over to Avoca. Les poured two large glasses of orange juice and Jimmy took his downstairs with him, leaving Norton in the kitchen figuring out what to do with himself. It was still a fairly nice day outside and a bit of exercise wouldn't go astray, like a run or a good solid walk up and down the hills around Terrigal to check out the neighbourhood. That'd be an idea. Instead, Les decided to glide up and down the pool for a while in the clean country air. After leaving a message on Price's answering machine to say the eagle had landed and mission accomplished so far, he got his goggles and a towel and did just that.

It was delightful down by the cabana with the afternoon sun still streaming down while the birds sang to each other in the surrounding trees. As Les was breast-stroking a few laps he found himself smiling and thinking about George's nephew. You couldn't help but like him. He had a ton of style, didn't mind a joke and if you wanted to get clever with him he gave as good as he got; plus, for his size he was pretty willing. The little prick was up to something, there was no two ways about that. But if Jimmy was trying to hustle up a few dollars while he was out good luck to him; and if there wasn't too much heavy shit involved he might even give him a hand. All the things Les wanted to ask him he'd leave till the weekend was over and they were sitting around the house with nothing to do. And there was plenty he wanted to know. George's nephew was an intriguing little bloke. It's funny though, thought Les, as he pushed himself off the end of the pool and started backstroking for a while. If I had a nephew as sharp as him I'd bring him down to Sydney, kick a few dollars in and start him up in some kind of business. Still, maybe he just likes it up here on the Central Coast. Norton spurted a mouthful of water up towards the clouds, the sky and the trees. Can't say I blame him.

Les finished his swim, then sat around and read his book till the sun started to go down and the first of the mosquitoes arrived. He had a shower and a shave, changed into his blue tracksuit pants and a plain grey sweatshirt, then walked into the kitchen and got a glass of water. Jimmy walked in about five minutes later wearing a triple-tone green Sergio Tranchetti tracksuit and white Fila trainers.

'So how are you feeling now, Sticks?' asked Norton.

'Pretty good, big Les.' Jimmy opened the fridge and poured himself a glass of milk. 'What about you?'

'Good.' Les gave Jimmy a quizzical smile over his glass of water. 'So, where is it you're taking me, James?'

Jimmy smiled back over his glass of milk. 'You reckon you like country music. We're going linedancing.'

95

'Linedancing?'

'Yeah. You ever been?'

Norton shook his head. 'No, can't say I have.'

'Well, now's your big chance, cowboy.'

'Shouldn't we be wearing R. M. Williams boots and ten-gallon hats? We look more like we're going to do a Claudia Schiffer workout.'

'These are only lessons. And I want to catch up with a few old friends.'

Old friends, mused Norton? I thought he said he didn't have any? 'Okay, fair enough.'

Jimmy finished his glass of milk. 'Well, come on, Gina Jeffreys. Let's get cracking.'

'Righto. Bootscootin' it is.'

They rinsed their glasses in the sink and walked out to the car.

The drive didn't take long. Brooks and Dunn belting out 'Momma Don't Get Dressed Up For Nothing' had barely faded into Long John Hunter doing 'Evil Ways' when Jimmy told Les to turn left at the Avoca Beach roundabout. A few hundred metres or so on the right they cruised past a long, low building with gardens out the front round a flagpole and a sign above saying AVOCA BEACH MEMORIAL CLUB. A row of windows faced the roadway and in the light behind Les could see people playing the pokies or sitting around while they sucked on their middies, schooners or whatever. Jimmy told Les to turn right at a street running along the side of the club where he found an empty spot amongst a row of cars angle-parked to the kerb. After Les zapped the car doors they walked down to a pathway leading to the main entrance and straight in through a pair of double glass doors. A corridor on the right angled off to the bar and main lounge. There was an office on the left and ahead was a large room with a dark-haired woman about forty wearing jeans and a loose white shirt seated at a table by the entrance collecting the money. As soon as she saw Jimmy, a big, happy smile spread over her face.

'Hello, Jimmy,' she beamed. 'How are you, love? Haven't seen you for a while.'

'Yeah, I've been on holidays. How are you, Edna?'

'Good.' Edna's voice dropped an octave or two. 'Especially when I see you, Jimmy.'

Jimmy blew her a kiss. Les paid her and followed Jimmy through the door.

Inside, about fifty or so people, mainly women, were seated at chairs and tables round the walls hung with honour rolls, a portrait of the Queen and other RSL bric-a-brac. In a corner at the far end was a closed-up bar and at the opposite end near the door was a stage with the toilets in the corner next to it. Most of the women ranged from forty to sixty with a few younger ones and a handful of blokes in their late thirties or early forties and a few teenagers, but not many. Nearly everyone wore jeans and T-shirts and elastic-sided boots, with the odd vest and a few hangout shirts. Les and Jimmy were definitely the only ones wearing tracksuits. A lot of the women reminded Les of 'The Golden Girls' on TV and the way they were all sitting around nattering happily he figured that as well as getting in a bit of bootscooting, they caught up with the local gossip over a few drinks with their friends and neighbours. Whatever and whoever they were, it seemed to be a friendly little scene and they all smiled and waved when Jimmy walked in.

'Well, what do you reckon?' said Jimmy, as they sat down at an empty table not far from the corner near the gents.

'I don't know,' shrugged Les. 'It looks all right so far. Wish I'd worn a pair of jeans, though.'

Just as Norton said that the instructor got up on stage and took hold of a microphone with a long lead behind him. He was tall with thick, dark hair wearing black jeans, R. M. Williams boots and a black Lee Kernaghan T-shirt.

'Righto,' said the instructor, 's'pose we may as well get started.'

He'd no sooner spoken when there was a stampede onto the dance floor and everybody, including Jimmy, formed up lines and picked out their favourite spots on the floor. Les found himself in a line four back from the stage, between two golden girls wearing jeans and white T-shirts with 'Memorial Club Bootscooters' on the back.

'All right,' said the instructor, untangling himself from the lead, 'we'll start off with the Honky Tonk Stomp, which is two right fans, two right heels forward and two right toes behind.'

Les watched the bloke as best he could from where he was and watched the people around him while they went through it a couple of times to the sounds of people stomping and shuffling their feet on the floor. The instructor went on with something about frieze left, right, left with a 180-degree turn left and hitch right to more shuffling and stomping. Then something about hitch left, frieze right, two right stomps or whatever and they started again.

'Okay, youse all got that?' said the instructor.

There was an avid chorus of 'yes' before Norton had a chance to say no and the instructor said, 'Righto, let's try it to some music.' He flicked to a track on the CD player—'Honky Tonk Man' by Dwight Yoakam burst out of some overhead speakers and away they all went.

There was only one word to describe Norton's first attempt at linedancing. Horrible. No matter what he did, or how hard he concentrated, Les just couldn't get it together. There were only about two dozen steps to the song, then stomp your foot and start again. But Les couldn't figure out when. It was like there were a hundred steps to remember and he was trying to divide it by four left feet; and to make matters worse, the golden girls around him with their blue rinse hairstyles and sensible boots glided around the floor like they were the queens of Memphis. Jimmy was there, too. Les stole a quick glance over at him and Jimmy was bootin' and scootin' around the floor with his thumbs hooked in the front of his tracksuit pants as if he'd grown up in Texas. He even bent his knees and dipped his shoulders and did it with attitude. Naturally there were a few on the floor that weren't too crash hot, but no one was down at Norton's level. The track finished, the instructor pressed the repeat button and before Les had a chance to work out which way he was facing they were all off for the second round. The only saving grace for Les was that nobody gave a shit how good or bad you were. Everyone was having too much serious fun enjoying themselves and the music to worry.

'Righto,' said the instructor, when the track finished for the second time. 'Youse've got that together. Now let's do the Bartender Stomp. And that starts with a frieze right and scuff your left foot. Then frieze left and tap your right foot next to your left. You got that?'

'Yeaaahhh,' chorused everybody on the floor.

Everybody except Norton. His mind screamed, 'No!' But it made no difference. They went through the steps twice, then the instructor hit the CD player and 'Baby Likes to Rock It' by The Tractors started pumping out of the speakers and away they all went again.

'Jeez, youse are getting good,' said the instructor when they finished. 'You must be practising somewhere else.'

Yeah, bloody terrific, thought Les. Now to add to his woe he could feel rivulets of sweat running down his face, around his neck, then down his chest and back.

'Okay,' came the voice on stage. 'Now let's do the Chattahoochie. And that starts with a swivel heels left, centre, left, centre. Step right back forty-five degrees, left together and clap.'

Christ! This bloke's kidding, thought Les, after they went through the routine twice. There must be two hundred steps. Who does he think I am? James fuckin' Brown? Les was still trying to work out how he was going to jump out and jump his right foot in front of his left then swivel on the balls of his feet when the instructor hit the CD button and 'Chattahoochie' by Alan Jackson started twanging out from the speakers. Les bloomphed, clumsied and perspired around till mercifully the instructor called a halt.

'Righto, let's have a drink of water or whatever.'

Les went back to their table, sat down and wiped the sweat from his eyes, leaving Jimmy on the dance floor chatting to some women before he came over.

'So, how's it going, Gina?'

Les smiled up at him through sweat-filled eyes. 'I think I'm getting it. I'm not buggered or nothing. But Christ! Talk about sweat—it must be trying to concentrate on all those steps.'

'I can dig that, Les. Concentrating wouldn't be your go at the best of times.' Jimmy gave Les a slap on the shoulder. 'But don't sweat it, baby. If anyone asks, just tell 'em Diamond Les was in town.'

'What do you mean?'

Jimmy pointed to the dance floor. Where Les had been standing in the line was a trail of sweat drops in the rough shape of a diamond. 'Ohh shit!'

'Like I said, Les, don't sweat it.' Jimmy took a glance at the Hermes Captain Nemo on his wrist. 'I'm going to talk to some friends, then we'll give it another hour and split, okay?'

'You're the boss, James.'

Jimmy walked over, sat down and started talking to a table full of women as some other women drew chairs up around him. Les went into the gents, had a long drink of water and wiped as much sweat off as he could with paper towels. He came out just in time to get his backside down then straight up again for another stampede onto the floor to find his place in line.

'Righto,' said the instructor. 'Youse are all looking pretty good from up here. This time we'll do the Linda Lu.'

The instructor ran everyone through the steps twice and away they went again. Les flopped around the dance floor leaving another diamond-shaped trail of sweat in his wake plus a couple of right-angled triangles too. A few people dropped out. But Les persevered and despite sweating like a pig and clumping around like a dinosaur with a club foot was actually starting to get the hang of it by the end of the second session; at least he could tell the difference between two buttermilks, a slap right behind and a forty-five twist step. The instructor called time off for a drink. Les gulped down some more water, wiped away more sweat and sat down again just as Jimmy came over.

'I was watching you during the last one, dude. You're almost getting the knack of it.'

'That's me, baby,' replied Norton. 'I'm a regular redneck daddy.'

'Yep. You've got your wheels spinnin' and the pussy grinnin'. Anyway, it's time to go.'

'Suits me. Back to the house first?'

'Yep.'

'Then where?'

'I'll tell you when we get there.'

'Okay, let's vanish.'

Les stood up and headed for the door, Jimmy waved goodbye and blew kisses to the golden girls like Liberace walking off stage at The Sands in Las Vegas, then they walked out to the car. As he opened the doors, Les noticed the lights alongside the club had picked up a few wisps of steam coming from his arms and neck whereas Jimmy hadn't even raised a sweat. So he thought it might be an idea if he kept his big mouth shut or Jimmy would bury him. Except for the stereo in the car they drove back to Price's house pretty much in silence. When they got there, Les headed straight for the kitchen and the fresh chilled orange juice. So did Jimmy. Les poured two tall glasses, handed one to Jimmy, then gulped down half of his.

'Well, here's to bootscootin', Jimmy. That was fun.'

'I thought you'd like it once you got the idea.'

'In fact, I might even back up again next week.'

'Good on you, Gina. Who was it said white men can't dance? Or is it jump?'

Les looked at Jimmy for a moment then put his orange juice on the sink. 'Hey, before I forget—I got something for you.' Norton went to his room and came back with a wad of notes which he handed to Jimmy. 'Price gave me a stack of money to look after you with before I left. I can't see me spending it all, so there's five hundred there—more if you want it.'

Jimmy looked at the money and slipped it in his pocket. 'Thanks, Les.' Then he looked at Norton for a moment also. 'And I just might have something for you too.' He went downstairs and came back with a vest on a coathanger.

It was the most unusual and original vest Norton had ever seen. Beautiful, soft brown leather cut in a 'V' pattern down the front and sides, the rest was all cut from faded blue jeans. But whoever made it had cut the pockets from the fronts of the jeans to form pockets in the front of the vest and the back pockets of the jeans with the monograms on them to somehow form the back of the vest. Four shiny brass studs ran down the front, the lining was blue silk with more pockets inside. Les had never seen anything like it in Sydney and if he had it would have cost an arm and a leg.

'Shit! Where did you get that, Jimmy?'

'Off a bloke up here who makes them.'

'Christ! He must be a genius.'

Jimmy started to laugh. 'Actually they call him Crazy. I got it off him for another bloke. But the bloke copped a faceful of SG pellets, so he won't be needing it.'

'Was he a bikie?'

Jimmy nodded. 'So if you want it, it's yours.'

'If I want it! Are you fair dinkum? Fuckin' oath.'

Jimmy shrugged. 'Okay, it's yours.'

Les took it off the hanger and tried it on. It fitted perfectly. 'Jesus, Jimmy,' said Norton, patting the pockets. 'This is the grouse. Thanks heaps. I don't know what to bloody say.'

'Don't worry about it. And I might have another surprise for you. You hungry?'

'Funny you should say that, Jimmy, but I am. Must be this country air. And all that bootscootin'.'

'Good, 'cause I'm going to take you to the grouse.'

'What? Even better than that last place?'

'Maybe. We'll see. And you can get on the piss if you want to. I've got us a lift.'

Norton's eyes flashed to the fridge and the Bacardi. 'Fair dinkum. I don't have to drive?'

'Nope.'

Norton shook his head in disbelief. 'Jimmy. You're my God Heart. You are my fuckin' Elvis.'

'A bop-bop-a-lula. A lo-bam-boom. I'll see you back here in an hour.' Jimmy headed for the stairs, then stopped. 'Hey, why don't you wear that vest tonight?'

A sheepish grin formed on Norton's face. 'Funny you should say that, Jimmy.'

Back in his bedroom Les couldn't believe his luck. He looked at himself in the mirror and patted the front of the vest. Well I'll be buggered. What a good bloke that Jimmy is. And the fuckin' thing fits like a glove. He turned around a couple of times to have a look at the back, then took it off and hung it in front of the wardrobe ready to wear that night. Anyway, time for a tub. He got out of his sweat-soaked clothes and climbed under the shower. Yep, nothing wrong with young James, he thought, as he soaped away all the sweat and BO. Funny, though, how he always refers to Uncle George as plain George and Price as Uncle Price. Still, he's probably known him since he was a kid and it's just a sign of respect. Better than calling him Mr Galese all the time. And I call nearly all my uncles by their first name. He turned off the hot water tap and stood under the cold. Call me what you like, just don't call me late for dinner.

After he dried off, Les changed into a pair of jeans, a blue denim shirt and his Road Mocs, then slipped a tape into the stereo, not too loud, and attacked the Bacardi, vodka and OJ. Before long, each one started to taste better than the first and each track started to sound better as well. Psycho Zydeco were rattling into 'Feet Don't Fail Now' and Les was in the kitchen about to make another drink when Jimmy walked in wearing a pair of Collezione Di Carlo jeans, a plain, white Polo Ralph Lauren T-shirt that made his skin look like it was glowing, the same trainers and the same tracksuit top with a mobile phone in the pocket.

'So how are you feeling now? You look like you're having a good time.'

Les tinkled the little bit of ice left in his glass. 'Unreal. You want one?'

Jimmy shook his head. 'I doubt if we'll have time. My man should be here any minute now.' Just as Jimmy spoke there was polite knock at the door. He looked at his watch. 'Right on time. You ready?'

Les put his glass in the sink. 'I'll just get this grouse vest I got in my room.'

Norton went to his room then turned off the lights and the stereo and they walked to the front door. Standing under the front light was a dark-haired man with a warm smile wearing a black suit and tie.

'Mr Rosewater?' he asked.

'That's me,' said Jimmy.

'This way, sir.'

Parked out the front was a huge, black stretch limousine with lights running along the side and across the back. It looked like the *Achille Lauro* without the funnels. The driver opened the back door and they piled in.

'Nice one, Jimmy,' said Les, sinking his backside into the plush upholstery and spreading his legs around.

'Doesn't everybody take a limo when they dine out?' replied Jimmy.

Les stared at Jimmy for a moment. Shit! You're starting to remind me of someone, he thought. He was just about to say something when the driver started the engine.

'Peeches was it, Mr Rosewater?'

'That's right, but I want to call into the bottle shop at Terrigal first.'

'No problem at all, sir.' The driver slipped the limo into Drive and they cruised up to the crossroad.

'Seeing as you chose the restaurant, Jimmy, would you like me to choose the wine?'

'Sure, Les, and make sure they serve it in two polystyrene cups.'

They took the scenic route paste The Haven followed by a lap of the block then the driver double-parked outside the bottle shop and opened the back door. Jimmy ran into the shop and was back about five minutes later with a bottle in a paper bag and the woman from the bottle shop after him.

'Listen, mate,' she yelled. 'You wouldn't know red wine from Red China, you little shit.'

'Possibly,' replied Jimmy. 'I know one thing, though. If you were a wine, you'd be a Russian Moselle. Full bodied, but with very little taste. Goodnight, madam.'

'You know what you can bloody well do.'

Jimmy climbed in the back, the driver closed the door and they drove off with the woman still yelling abuse from the footpath.

'What was that all about?' asked Les.

'Nothing. Just a joke.'

'You got a funny sense of humour. She looked like she wanted to kill you.'

'Bullshit. She loves me.'

'Yeah,' conceded Les. 'I think they all do, don't they?' He looked in the paper bag. 'So what are we drinking? Rosemount Estate. Balmoral Syrah. Is that any good?'

Jimmy looked at Les and shook his head without saying anything.

They did another victory lap of the block, cruised up the hill out of Terrigal, turned right on the roundabout at the bottom, then stopped just on the other side of the bridge outside a small, white-painted restaurant with a sign on the awning above saying PEECHES. A full glass window faced the street from behind a phone box and apart from a motel across the road, it was tucked happily away on its own and secluded from everything else.

'I'll give you a call when we want to leave,' Jimmy said to the driver as they got out.

'Whenever you're ready, Mr Rosewater.'

They entered through a sliding glass door where a young blonde girl greeted them and took Jimmy's wine, then sat them down at the right-hand wall next to some mirror tiles. The restaurant was quite compact with a pleasant, personal kind of ambience. White chairs and tables with crisp white tablecloths were set evenly around grey carpet and olive green walls. Above them, down lights in the brown ceiling reflected through the spinning fans and melded into the light flickering from a number of candles set in chunky wine glasses on each table. The walls were hung with lots of comically unusual framed prints. Rows of babies' bums, pigs' bums, rustic-looking old blokes in hats and glasses, bums on seats and other things, all of which seemed to suggest the owner had a pretty good sense of humour. The waitress returned with Jimmy's wine and a bottle of chilled water just as a portly man with grey hair and a happy face framed in a pair of glasses and wearing a chef's outfit stuck his head out of an alcove at the rear of the restaurant.

'Hello, Jimmy,' he called out. 'How are you, mate?'

'Pretty good, Bernie,' answered Jimmy. 'How's yourself?'

'All right, mate. I'll come and see you soon as I get a chance.'

'Righto, Bernie.'

'You know 'em all don't you, Jimmy,' smiled Norton.

'That's me, Les. Know all of them. Trust none of them—'

'And paddle your own canoe,' cut in Norton.

'Hey, right on, white boy. 'You know, I think I like you, Les. You're a man after my own heart.'

Norton was going to say something, but decided to order from the fairly extensive greenboard menu at the opposite end of the restaurant.

Whatever some of the diners at the other tables were eating, it looked good and smelled even better; Les was tempted to ask a couple what they had. Instead, he went for the Brains sautéed in bacon and herb butter and served in a basil and tomato sauce for an entree and Veal Fillet Medallions sautéed in tarragon butter and served in a mushroom velouté. Jimmy went for a Caesar salad and pork medallions seared in garlic butter in a Dijon mustard sauce. Jimmy sipped his Balmoral Syrah and Les sipped water while they nattered away about nothing in particular. Then the food arrived, along with the fresh bread rolls.

Norton's brains arrived in a bowl of creamy, rich sauce full of finely chopped herbs and diced tomato.

He took one mouthful and nearly fainted at the table it was that good. Jimmy's Caesar was huge, crisp as early morning and full of herb croutons, anchovies and bacon pieces in a thinner sauce than usual, but twenty times tastier. They bowled that over pretty smartly and next up was the veal and pork. Norton's veal was not only a taste sensation in a beautiful, brown sauce, it was that tender he could hardly tell the pieces of veal from the slices of mushroom. He had a taste of Jimmy's and it was just as tender, only the sauce slightly more tart with the perfect amount of spices; and all accompanied by fresh, steamed vegetables with a thin, cheese sauce. Les would like to have said something but he was too busy eating. Then it was all gone.

'Well, what do you reckon, Les?' asked Jimmy.

'What do I reckon? Jimmy, that was absolutely sensational. I don't think I've ever tasted anything like it.'

'I told you it was something special. Listen, I'm just going to duck out and see Bernie and shout him a glass of wine. I'll be back in a few minutes. You want sweets or coffee?'

Norton shook his head. 'No. I couldn't fit any sweets in and coffee'd only take away the taste of all that grouse food.'

'Fair enough.'

Jimmy left Norton with nothing much to do except pay the bill, leave a substantial tip and study the greenboard menu with the idea of coming back and eating everything on it twice, maybe three times. Jimmy returned, patting his stomach.

'So where to now?' asked Les.

'Down Terrigal Pines for a while.'

'Whoa. Hang on a sec there, Jimmy baby,' protested Norton. 'I'm not going in that fuckin' disco. I was in there for ten minutes last night and that music made me burst out in boils. And all these running sores spread over my back and arms full of pus and gangrene. Thanks a lot, but no fuckin' thanks.'

Jimmy made a defensive gesture. 'Don't worry, Les. I know exactly what you mean. No, we'll just go up the Baron Riley Bar. There's a girl sings in there tonight and she's pretty good.'

Les could taste a nice cool one already. 'I'll certainly be in that.'

Jimmy pointed to a row of lights out in the street. 'Anyway, the pumpkin coach is here. Let's hit the toe.'

The girl smiled and opened the front door for them, the driver smiled and closed the limo door for them and they headed for the hotel.

Compared to the previous night, Terrigal Pines Resort had come to life. The beer garden was full of people of all shapes and sizes, though mainly very young; some were queued up on the steps getting checked for ID, others were queued up waiting to get in the disco, more were either milling about or walking around out the front. The limo pulled up in the driveway and the driver got out and opened the door.

'I'll let you know when we're ready to leave,' said Jimmy.

'No problem at all, Mr Rosewater,' replied the driver, giving them both a polite smile.

There were a few people out the front waiting for taxis or just hanging about and as the limo pulled away

111

they gave Les and Jimmy a quick glance in case they might have been someone special. Les was about to walk inside when he stopped dead. Two bouncers were standing outside the revolving door half-arguing with some man or something. He was fairly well built with thick black hair and wearing a black Phantom T-shirt tucked into scruffy, blue jeans with a full-length, green velvet cape over his shoulders. On one hand was an old gardening glove with the fingers cut out, in the palm of the other glinted a large green talisman. The man had a strong jaw-line and wild, demented eyes going everywhere, but Les couldn't make out the rest of his face because it was painted green.

'Listen, Crazy,' said one of the doormen, 'for the last fuckin' time, you can't come in. Now will you piss off.'

The bloke screwed up his green face in anguish and waved his hands round in front of it in tiny gestures. 'But my friend, my friend, I am the Shamash. The Shamash must get in. It is important. It is written in the stars and across the moon. Grrhgnngh nkhmmh marrggh glizznkjh.' The cape screwed his face up even more and went into this ramble of indecipherable gibberish, still making gestures with his hands that reminded Norton of some weird Arab trader haggling in a bazaar.

'I don't care if it's written on the wall in the shithouse, Crazy,' said the other bouncer. 'You're still not fuckin' getting in. Now piss off.'

'Aaarrghh rhnhtt grshlirp oorghiij,' begged the man in the cape.

'What in the fuck's that?' said Les.

'Christ! I just hope he doesn't see me,' answered Jimmy.

At the sound of their voices the man spun around in a flourish of glinting, green talisman and swirling cape. As soon as he spotted Jimmy his eyes lit up and spun round wilder than ever.

'James, James, my friend. It is you. It is ordained. It is written in the stars. It is truly the prophecy. The great one has . . . grrnhhh arrghnnh sckrorghhn nyennnhh.' The man went into another hail of complete gibberish, then knelt at Jimmy's feet and kissed the back of his hand.

'So what's up, Crazy? They won't let you in?'

'Aarrrghjkt.'

'And you've got no money.'

'Zzzjghrrngh.'

'Well I can't fuckin' help you.'

'Aaarrrghnjrghnjjkkngh,' howled the thing in the cape.

'Ohh, for Christ's sake. Here.' Jimmy pulled out twenty dollars and gave it to the cape who immediately went into even greater raptures, bowing in front of Jimmy and kissing his fingers.

'Oh, blessed one. Oh, pearl of the lotus flower. Light from ten thousand suns. Jewel of the cosmos. I will make you a jacket. I will make you a vest. I will . . . aarrgghhhjjkkgh ghrzzjvviijkll.' Then he noticed Les. He stood up, walked across and started pawing at Norton's vest. Les wasn't quite sure what was going on, whether he was trying to pick his pocket or what, and was half thinking of putting one up his ribcage. 'This vest. This vest. I know it. You wear a creation of the

113

Shamash. Aarrghjklnmghj.' He looked up at Norton. 'You are blessed. Greatness is upon you. You walk the shining path. The universe . . . nnggrrhllkjhgh.'

Norton shook his head then for some strange reason pulled a twenty out of his pocket also and handed it to the cape. 'Will you please go away.'

'Aaarrggghnjggrhtzzklnmmh.' The cape went into even bigger raptures again. 'I am leaving. I am leaving. Oh, efendi. Oh, chosen one. This worthless pile of rags is leaving.'

'Good. That's the best news I've heard all night.'

'But before I go,' the cape held up the talisman in the palm of his right hand, 'what do you see here, my friend?'

'A lump of green glass on a piece of tin can.'

The cape shook his head adamantly. 'No. It is the sacred stone of the Pharisee.'

'Go on.'

'And do you know what the sacred stone does?'

'I wouldn't have a fuckin' clue,' said Norton.

'Turns me into Michael Jackson.'

The cape turned side on, pointed the hand with the gardening glove on it up in the air and struck a pose like John Travolta in *Saturday Night Fever*, then moon-walked down the driveway, through the people and off into the night. Norton looked at him in bewilderment for a moment, then he and Jimmy walked past the doormen and through the revolving door.

'What the fuck was that all about?' Les asked Jimmy.

'That's Crazy—the Shamash. He likes a drop of Jack Daniels.'

114

'Crazy?' Norton shook his head. 'Stark raving mad'd be more like it. The cunt should be wearing a fuckin' straitjacket. Not a cape.'

'He's also the bloke that made your vest.'

'What!?' Norton stopped dead. 'That gibbering, drunken idiot made this? Why didn't you tell me? I'd've slung him another twenty bucks and got him to measure me up for another one. Where do I find him?'

'Don't worry, Les. From now on, he'll find you.'

They climbed the stairs to the Baron Riley Bar.

It was nowhere near packed, but there was quite a good crowd. All the tables were taken with couples or small groups of friends, as were the stools round the bar, and between the serving area and the dance floor stood a group of men with name tags drinking mainly beer on some company account. Instead of the piano player an attractive, dark-haired girl in a black leather vest and matching skirt was seated on a stool strumming a guitar in front of a sequencer. As they walked in she was warbling 'All I Want to Do is Have Some Fun' and doing a pretty good job; two couples were on the dance floor and most of the tables were singing along as well. She was that good Norton started to join in himself as they crossed to the bar.

'What do you want, Jimmy? I'll get them.'

Jimmy thought for a moment. 'Get me a Bacardi and orange with a dash of strawberry liqueur.'

'Sounds all right. I might even have one of those myself.'

This time Les got a tall barman with a Canadian accent, along with another pleasant smile, and soon had the two drinks.

'Why don't we stand over there.' Jimmy took his drink and pointed to an archway near the corner of the bar closest to the pool area.

'Yeah, righto.' Les followed Jimmy over and had a sip. 'Hey, not bad, James.'

'Yeah, I noticed what you were drinking earlier. It's not quite the same. But it's still a nice way to go.'

'Gee, I drank some nice rum when I was in Jamaica.'

'Yeah?'

Les related to Jimmy an anecdote or two about Jamaican rum and margaritas in Florida. Jimmy said he picked up a taste for good wine after working in a winery for a while and doing a course in it. Now it was a bit of a hobby. Beer always bloated him and if he went out he liked cocktails or light rum. They nattered about this and that while they checked out the punters and talked about the singer, who did an Oasis song, then an old Van Morrison, and took a break. Jimmy got the next two drinks and they stayed near the archway listening to a tape playing through the speakers. A couple round the end got up to go and left two empty stools. Les was about to point this out to Jimmy when he noticed a woman seated near the corner, leaning around gesturing to him. She was barely sitting a few metres away, so Norton started to check her out. She looked around forty with corporate-style, brown hair and a very pretty, very foxy face. A denim skirt with a long split up the side and a maroon, knitted top displayed enough flat, hard boobs and tanned arms and legs to show she was madly into aerobics. Next to her, a girl about thirty with pale blue eyes and short black hair tucked behind her ears got up

116

to get something from her pocket. She was wearing a short-sleeved white shirt tucked into faded blue jeans and was a bit more solid than the older one with much bigger boobs. The older one gestured again. What the hell? thought Les, starting to walk over. I wonder if she's seen *Taxi Driver*?

'Are you talkin' to me? Are you talkin' to me? You talkin' to me? Me? Are you talkin' to me?'

'Listen, come here,' said Maroon Top. She took Norton by the elbow. 'Are you and your friend gay?'

'What!?'

'I want to know, are you and your friend gay?'

Les gave her a blank look. What she said was hardly worth an answer, let alone any witty kind of verbal repartee. 'What a stupid bloody question. What would you have said if I'd have come over and asked you if you and that scrubber with you were dykes?'

'Oh, well you know what I mean.'

'No, I don't know what you mean.'

'All right then. You're not poofs.'

'Thank you. And if you ever say that to me again, I'll hit you with my handbag.'

'Listen, why don't you and your friend come and join us. There's two empty stools there.'

'Hang on.' Les went back to Jimmy.

'What's going on?' he asked.

'Do you want to come over and have a talk to these two potatoes. I don't know them, but there's a couple of stools there and it's better than standing up.'

Jimmy took a look over Norton's shoulder. 'Yeah, why not. I'd just as soon sit down. And if they get too punishing we can ignore them.'

'What'll we tell them?'

'I don't know. You think of something. I'm just a poor dumb abo.'

They walked over and shuffled the stools around; Les finished up next to the older one and noticed she was drunk, but not as drunk as her girlfriend.

'Anyway, I'm Les and this is James.'

'Megan,' said the older one.

'And I'm Paula,' said the other one, already drooling over Jimmy and wondering how he'd managed to fall into her lap.

'So, are you two up here on holidays?' asked Megan.

'No,' said Les. 'We own a string of fashion boutiques on the North Shore and we're up here buying some clothes off a local designer.'

'Who?' asked Megan.

'The Shamash. The Chosen One.'

'Never heard of him.'

'You've never heard of the Shamash?' said Jimmy. 'El Crazino.'

'No.'

'Me neither,' said Paula.

'Then you have surely not trodden the golden path. Nor been blessed by the Messiah of the sacred delicious. Grrnhhgjkknllgh.'

Megan and Paula looked at each other then back at Jimmy. 'What?'

'Don't worry about it,' said Les. 'Your day of atonement will come. Zzzjkkgrnjllknh. So what do you two girls do?'

They both worked for the same bank, different branches, and tomorrow was an RDO so they were

118

both out on the drink and having a bit of a knees-up. Megan had two kids and was divorced and, like Norton guessed, was an aerobics princess and sometimes taught classes. Paula was single, had never been married, played netball and was a lifesaver at some beach and rowed in the boat crew. They lived together at Copacabana, had got a lift over with Paula's brother and were catching a taxi home. Megan was into Jack Daniels and Paula was hitting up on Bundy and Coke.

Les ordered four of what he and Jimmy were drinking and handed them round. The girls thought the drinks were delightful and it helped break the ice. Not that the ice needed much breaking. Paula was Jimmy's for the taking and Megan was all Norton's way. Normally Les didn't get off on older women. It wasn't a hangup about age or anything. It was just that he'd had a couple of liaisons with divorcees when he first arrived at Bondi and it was okay. Except that when you'd see them down the beach with their children the next day you knew what the kids were thinking and it didn't exactly make you feel like beating your chest. Then if the ex-husband happened to come ambling by you didn't quite feel like striking up a bright and breezy conversation with him either. Besides, there were that many younger, single women running around Sydney, why bother? But Megan was one horny aunty. Fit as a fiddle with sexy eyes and a film star face. And this was up here, not home. If Megan wanted to come back to the house later on for more cool ones and a bit of the other, ripper. It was truly the prophecy. Grrrnghjkklng.

The night proceeded swimmingly. The girl in the

black vest got up and did more songs and more drinks went down including four Chocolate Surprises. Then the singer cut into Bob Marley's 'Is This Love?'

'Ooh, this is one of my favourite songs,' said Megan. 'Come on, Les. How about a dance?'

'Yeah, righto.' Les got up, leaving Paula boozing on next to Jimmy.

There was plenty of room on the dance floor and Megan started flouncing and posing around doing more of a Jane Fonda workout to show everybody how fit and healthy she was, as much as dancing. Les looked at her for a moment and thought, oh well, here goes nothing, and started linedancing. Somehow he managed to get away with it. A frieze here, a couple of buttermilks there. Do-si-do and away we go. Megan was taken aback and surprisingly impressed by Norton's amazing versatility. She even tried to join in herself, but couldn't quite hack it. Norton was just too cool. The singer slipped into 'Blue Suede Shoes' and Norton started bootscootin' again. After the last Chocolate Surprise he even threw in a bit of attitude. When that finished Megan didn't fancy being upstaged and said she wanted to sit down, which suited Les; even though he was doing it easy this time around, the denim and leather vest didn't quite cool him down. When they returned to their stools Paula said she wanted to go to the ladies. She was breaking her neck to go sooner but, like a good Aussie girl, there was no way in the world she was going to the can on her own and leave her very best girlfriend.

'You'll be here when I get back, won't you, Les?' said Megan, picking her handbag up off the bar.

'With every single beat of my heart. Oh, pearl of the lotus flower.'

'I think I'm beginning to like you, Les.'

'There's worse blokes out there than me, Megan.'

Norton took a swallow of his drink and as soon as they were out of earshot turned to Jimmy.

'Well, what do you want to do with these two scozza's, Jimmy? That aunty's a bit of a horn. I wouldn't mind dragging her back to the gaff and seeing if she wants to play hide the sausage. How do you feel about the clubbie?'

'Paula? Paula's got a jam melon for a head and about as much style as a pig with mad cow's disease.'

'Yeah, but she hasn't got a bad set of tits.'

Jimmy reflected into his glass for a second. 'Yeah, fuck it. Why not? At least she's better than what I've been looking at lately.'

'Righto. Well, here's what I reckon we ought to do . . .'

The girls came back and sat down looking both relieved and like they'd had a good tete-a-tete in the ladies. Jimmy waited till they sat down and picked up their drinks.

'Listen, it's all right in here, but we're getting sick of it. You want to come back to our place? There's a pool, music, plenty of booze. If we get our fingers out, I got us a lift.'

'Who with?' said Megan.

'My aunty's going to pick us up.'

'Your aunty?' said Paula. Jimmy nodded. Paula looked at Megan for an answer she didn't need. 'Sure—why not.'

'Okay. Let's go,' said Megan.

121

They finished their drinks, the girls picked up their things and they walked downstairs to the foyer.

'This aunty of yours,' said Megan, sounding a trifle suspicious, 'she must be a sweet old thing to come out and get you in the middle of the night?'

'She is, and I love her dearly,' replied Jimmy as they got to the revolving door. 'And here she is now, God bless her, right on time.'

They came out the other side just as the limo rocked to a halt and the driver got out to open the door.

'Where to now, Mr Rosewater?' he smiled.

'Straight home, thanks.'

'Certainly, sir.'

'Some aunty,' blustered Megan, as they bundled in the back. 'You bastard, Jimmy.'

'Yeah, but I'm a nice bastard.'

'Is he ever!' said Paula, placing her hand on his knee.

The ride home was fairly uneventful. By the time Paula almost had her seat belt on they were out the front. Jimmy told the driver he'd call him when they were ready, Les opened the door and they all swarmed inside.

'Ooh, what a beautiful house,' said Megan. 'Who owns it?'

'I do,' answered Jimmy.

'It's beautiful. I love your furnishings.'

'Where's the toilet?' asked Paula.

Norton motioned with this thumb. 'That way.' Paula walked down the hall and Les turned to the others. 'I might hustle up a cool one.'

'Good thinking, 99,' said Jimmy, ushering Megan into the kitchen.

By the time Paula got back Norton had four large Bacardis together and they all trooped into the lounge-room and sat down. Les rummaged through his tapes, picked out one he'd been playing earlier and slipped it into the stereo.

'What are we listening to?' asked Megan.

'Some rural-influenced contemporary music,' replied Les.

'Some what?'

Norton adjusted the volume, a woman's quick giggle came through the speakers and Gina Jeffreys started hoofing into 'Girls Night Out'. 'Nothing wrong with this,' said Norton.

'Hey, I've seen this clip on Channel Two,' said Paula. 'She's great.'

'Reckon,' winked Les.

'Come on, Les,' said Megan, tapping her foot. 'Give us a linedance.' Norton smiled and shook his head. 'Come on, you big wooz.'

'All right. You want linedancing? Come on, Jimmy, you and me.' Jimmy shook his head also. 'Come on.'

'Oh, all right.' Jimmy stood up and looked at the blank expression on Norton's face. 'Remember The Honky Tonk Stomp, Les?'

Les nodded slowly. 'You lead, Jimmy.'

There was plenty of room in Price's lounge; Les fell in behind Jimmy and went for it. They bootscooted around the floor with Les just about getting there, though it wasn't hard to see who was the better of the two. The song finished and they sat down to drunken applause from Megan and Paula.

One track slipped into the next, Jimmy got another

round of drinks, they all got a little closer to each other and it wasn't long before Paula was all over Jimmy. Not that Les and Megan weren't getting along famously, even if Les did see her giving Jimmy the odd glance at times. Les was blowing in her ear about nothing much in particular when he noticed a movement on the other side of the room and Paula was dragging Jimmy downstairs. Megan saw them leave also.

'Gee, I hope Paula will be all right,' quipped Les.

'Surely you're not worried about Paula, are you?'

Norton looked at Megan for a second. 'It was . . . I say it was a joke, gal.' He put his arm around Megan's waist and drew her towards him. She stiffened and put her arm on Norton's elbow. Les drew his arm away.

'I don't normally do this, you know.'

Norton shook his head adamantly. 'I'm bloody sure you don't. And may I say neither do I.'

'You don't?'

'Of course not. Normally I run a self-support group for single mothers at Manly.'

'Yes, I'll just bet you do.'

Les went to give her a quick peck on the lips. Megan let go of Norton's arm, put a front half-nelson on him and shoved her hot, sweet tongue halfway down his throat. Hello, thought Norton, trying to suck in some air, I don't think Aunty Megan's acting quite normal tonight.

They licked, kissed, wrestled and groped all over the lounge till Norton decided to come up for air. He just about had Megan's maroon top off and she almost had his fly undone.

'Why don't we brush this and go into my bedroom? It's nice and comfy with a great view of the street.'

'Show me the way.'

Norton took Megan's hand and led her along to the bedroom and switched the light on next to the bed. She took her dress off while Norton wrestled his way out of his jeans and shoes. When he turned around Megan was standing at the end of the antique wooden bed in a pair of skimpy, purple knickers, shaking the hand-crafted cedar slats. Shit, don't wreck the bloody thing, thought Norton.

'Hey, Les,' she breathed, her eyes seeming to glow in the soft light from the bedlamp.

'Hey, yes.'

'How about tying me up?'

'How about what?'

'Tie my hands to the end of the bed.' Megan lay back on the mattress and spread her arms out behind her. 'Come on, tie me to the bedstead.'

Norton stared at her with a blank expression on his face looking for the right words. Like, what with? 'Yeah, righto,' he nodded dumbly.

Megan writhed on the bed. 'Oooh, good.'

Christ! What's all this about? pondered Les. And what am I going to use? Rope? Electrical cord? I only got one belt. Hang on. He rummaged around in his bag of training gear and found two sweat bands he'd cut from an old white T-shirt.

'Ooh, yes,' squealed Megan. 'Perfect.'

'Good. I brought them along specially for the occasion.'

Megan let her arms out comfortably behind her and Les tied her wrists to the wooden slats in a bow. Tight, but not that tight so she couldn't get out of them if she

125

wanted to. He finished tying the last bow and was still wondering if this was all a big joke. Some sort of . . .?

'Now gag me.'

Exactly what I was thinking. 'Sure, just hang on a sec. I got an old football sock here somewhere.'

'What did you say?'

Les went to the drawer, got a clean hankie, folded it and tied it round Megan's mouth. 'There. You happy now?'

Megan nodded enthusiastically. 'Mmmrrrmmpphh.'

Norton stood back from the bed for a look at what he'd done. In one sense Megan looked sensational; all trussed up, her whippy body straining against the ties and writhing about on the bed in just her knickers. It was definitely some sort of weird turn-on. On the other hand, her eyes peering up at him from between the corporate hair-do and the hankie in her mouth, Les thought she looked absolutely ridiculous. And what if Norton had been some sort of a nutter. The stupid bag either trusted him or took things for granted. Then Norton started laughing. Hey, wait a minute. I *am* a fuckin' nutter.

Megan strained against her bonds. 'Mmmrrrmmph. Mmrmphh.' It sounded like 'What are you laughing at?'

'Don't go away,' said Les. 'I'll be back in a second.'

'Mmmmrrrmmphh.' It sounded like 'What are you doing?'

'I'm just going to get a red-hot coathanger and a chainsaw.'

'Mmmmmrrrmmmppphhhh.'

Norton went out to the kitchen and started rummaging through the cupboards. Now where did I put that fuckin' thing? I know I bought one. Ahh yes, here it is. He went back to the room where Megan was still trussed up on the bed and held up one of those little, plastic honey bears and flipped back the tiny, yellow nozzle.

Les smiled down at her. 'I always . . . I say I always like a little honey on my crumpets, Megan.'

He slipped Megan's knickers off, gave her nice, neatly shaved, aerobic-princess ted a wipe with a towel then started squeezing honey all over it. Megan snorted and cooed through her gag and writhed around on the bed. Les squirted honey in her navel and across her flat, firm boobs then squirted some more in her puss before putting the cap back on the honey bear and placing it under the bed.

'Okay, Megan baby,' he said, starting to sing as he took off his jocks. 'Say you will when you won't, but uh-uh, honey don't.'

Norton started licking the honey off Megan's boobs before slowly working his way down to her navel. He'd squirted on a bit more honey than he first thought and it took a while to get off but Megan didn't seem to mind so far. She wiggled her toes and moaned into the gag like it was some slow torture. Finally, he ran his tongue down a trail of honey to her ted, shoved his face in and went for it. Megan's eyes flickered and spun round and the corporate hair swished from side to side as Norton sucked honey from every nook and crevice he could find it. She kicked her legs up, thrashed round on the mattress and strained at her bonds almost ripping the antique wooden slats from the end of the bed. Norton couldn't make out what she was saying under the gag, but it sounded like she was having a good time. In fact it was a good thing Megan did have the gag in her mouth or she would have started letting the ships at sea know what a good time she was having. Not that Norton wasn't enjoying himself. Megan's antics were turning him on that much he was laughing with glee. And somewhere in the middle Mr Wobbly was banging his head around dying for a piece of the action, too.

The honey was starting to run out so Norton got his hands under Megan's backside, lifted it up and buried his tongue and face as far into her ted as he could get it. His tongue was coming to the last of the honey when Megan clamped her legs around Norton's head in some kind of sexual Indian death-lock and tried her best to rip it off his shoulders. Les licked up the last drop then screwed up his face and closed his mouth as Megan let him have it. Les rattled his head from side to side for a last few seconds then came up before he either suffocated or drowned. Megan lay back with her head to one side, chest heaving and her legs apart. It looked unbelievably inviting and by now Mr Wobbly was a complete basket-case.

Les picked up the towel from the end of the bed. 'Righto, Megan,' he said, giving her and his face a wipe, 'now it's my turn.'

Les slipped Mr Wobbly in, wanting to give her heaps. The only trouble was, Norton's balls felt like they were on fire and ready to burst, testosterone was almost pumping out of his ears by the gallon and Megan's ted was that warm, sweet, moist and tight the whole thing was just about over before Les even had a chance to get started. He gave a few good shoves, a few more, then arched his back, moaned with pure delight and emptied out in about a minute flat.

He left Mr Wobbly in for a moment before pulling him out, then whether Les was a bit stuffed or not watching what he was doing, he miscued and fell off the bed, hitting his head on the floor. But even though it hurt, instead of going crook, Norton starting laughing. He climbed back up on the bed and lay down next to Megan gurgling and gubbling away fit to bust. He was lying there, tears rolling down his cheeks, when he felt a knee bang into his ribs, then another one.

'Huh? Oh shit! Sorry, Megan. I almost forgot.' Les undid Megan's wrists and removed the gag, then lay back on the bed still chortling away.

Megan glared at him and rubbed her wrists. 'And just what are you laughing at?' she demanded.

'What am I laughing at? What do you think I'm laughing at? Oh, I don't know. Probably because I'm happy. Because I feel good. Shit! You have to admit it was fun.' Megan didn't appear to think so. 'Well, I had a good time anyway.'

'You're laughing at me, aren't you?'

'Well . . . probably. Yeah, but it's just the whole silly scene.' Megan still wasn't laughing. 'All right then. If my laughing offends you, I'm sorry. I promise I won't laugh again.' Norton had another look at the expression on Megan's face then burst out laughing again, harder than ever.

'Very bloody funny.' Megan got up from the bed and found her clothes. 'Where's the toilet from here?'

Norton pointed a feeble finger. 'Straight through there.'

'Thank you. I'll see you outside.'

'Yeah, righto . . . honey pie.'

Norton heard the bathroom door slam and fell back against the pillows almost getting tangled up in one of his sweat rags. After a while he settled down. Christ! What did I do wrong? Isn't sex supposed to be enjoyable and to relieve tension or something? Les shook his head. Buggered if I know. You just can't seem to win these days. It must be those stupid magazines they read. He got into a pair of shorts and a T-shirt and went out to the kitchen to get a cold glass of orange juice, where he was surprised to find Jimmy sitting on his own in the loungeroom sipping a Bacardi and watching TV. Les poured himself a drink then went down and joined him.

'So what's happening? Where's the beautiful Paula?'

Jimmy gave Les a derisive look. 'The clubbie? I threw her in a taxi and pissed her off.'

'No limo?'

'Limo! I should have made the cunt walk.'

'Shit! What happened?'

'I get downstairs with her. Get her on the bed and she drops those big boobs out in front of me, so I'm keen. Then she says she wants to go to the loo. Fair enough. So I'm waiting here with a horn that hard you couldn't push a thumbtack into it. And I hear crash, bang, thump. The drunken fuckin' moll's fell arse over head in the laundry, broke the iron and the ironing board, then pissed herself.'

'What?'

'She's come back in and there's a big wet patch right across her jeans. I just about told her to get fucked.'

'So you threw her in a cab?'

'Wouldn't you?'

'Yeah, I s'pose so,' agreed Les.

Jimmy shook his head in disgust and took a sip of Bacardi. 'So what happened with you and the aunty? At least she had a bit of style.'

Just as Jimmy spoke the bathroom door opened then closed. 'I'll tell you about it later.'

Megan came into the loungeroom all tidy and cleaned up, looking like butter wouldn't melt in her mouth. She sat down away from Norton and close to Jimmy.

'Hello, Jimmy,' she said pleasantly. 'Where's Paula?'

'She went home. She wasn't feeling very well.'

'She'd had a fair bit to drink.'

'Yes, so I'd noticed.'

'Can I get you a drink or something, Megan?' asked Les.

Megan gave Les an icy stare. 'No, thank you.'

'Okay, I think I've had enough myself. I'm just about knackered.'

'Then why don't you go to bed?'

Les gave Megan a double blink. 'What about . . .?'

'I'd like to sit here and watch TV with Jimmy for a while.' Megan turned her back on Norton. 'You don't mind do you, Jimmy?'

Jimmy gave her a syrupy smile. 'No, not at all.'

'What are you watching?'

'Some old Jack Nicholson movie. It's not bad.'

'Sounds good to me.' Megan got up and sat down on the lounge next to Jimmy. 'Mind if I have a sip of your drink?'

'Help yourself. I'll get you one if you like.'

'That would be lovely, Jimmy.'

Norton watched them for a second, then stood up. 'Okay, I'll see you in the morning, Jimmy.'

'Righto, mate. See you then.'

'Goodnight, Megan.'

Yeah, all right. Les went to the bathroom, cleaned honey, sweat and pubic hair from his teeth, then climbed into bed somewhere between the sweet patches, the sweat patches and the wet patches and switched off the light. Well, how was that for a nice brush-off? he thought as he stared up at the ceiling for a few moments. And all I did was have a good time. I just hope she doesn't take her rotten mood out on poor young Jimmy. Norton started to laugh again. I've got a feeling she won't, somehow. The filthy old thing. Les chuckled away in the darkness and before he knew it he'd laughed himself to sleep.

Whether it was the country air, all the good food or what, Norton wasn't sure, but the next morning he was feeling pretty good when be bowled into the kitchen wearing a pair of old shorts and a T-shirt around nine. He was even singing what sounded like 'Sugar. Ooh honey, honey.' A note on the kitchen table put a temporary stop to his warbling.

'Les. I got to bed a bit late. Could you wake me by one? Thanks. Jimmy.'

Norton looked at the note again, then tossed it in the kitchen-tidy. Yeah, I'll bet you got to bed late, you rotten little shit. After you stole my girl off me. Bastard. Les shook his head. Shit, I'd better not laugh. I'll only get into more strife. He poured a glass of orange juice, had a look out the window and figured out what to do. It wasn't too bad a day; sunny, with a few clouds around, a bit of a southerly ruffling the tops of the trees. However, it wasn't a matter of what to do. It was what *had* to be done. His sheets. If they dried out he'd

133

have to break them up with a piece of four-by-two to get them in the washing machine. I'll do that, then have breakfast down the beach again. Stuff cooking anything. Les finished his orange juice, then bundled up any dirty T-shirts as well and trotted downstairs to the laundry.

Jimmy was right about the iron; it was completely stuffed. Luckily there was a spare one in the kitchen. And the ironing board was only bent. Les straightened it out then dumped his washing into the machine. Instead of detergent, he thought as he tipped in the Radiant, I should throw in a few carrots and onions and a cup of barley. Make some soup. Consommé of crumpet. Avec honey. I wonder what sort of wine young James would choose to complement that. Being a connoisseur he should know. Hope the noise doesn't wake the poor bludger up.

Les turned the dial and quietly closed the door; there was very little noise at all. While his washing was going round, Les tuned into some local FM station on the stereo and, with OMC's 'How Bizarre' playing softly in the background, stuffed around tidying up his room and the few glasses in the kitchen from last night. Then he went down to the pool and did some exercises, some swimming and thought there could be worse ways to start the day. While Jimmy snored on peacefully, Les hung his washing out, had another swim around, then climbed into a pair of Levi shorts and a green Rainbow Warrior T-shirt, ready for some breakfast. By now Norton felt more like brunch than coffee and sandwiches. Some fish and chips from that place he saw when he drove into Terrigal. He locked the front door, took the long way down to the beach and got a parking spot outside the resort across from the pine trees. The south end of the beach was well sheltered from the wind and there were a few people swimming, lying on the sand or walking about. Les locked the car and strolled up past the shops to the Flathead Spot.

The fish shop was doing quite a nice little trade when Les walked in. He ordered two pieces of hake and a medium chips and looked at the fresh seafood on display and the posters on the walls while some big bloke with black hair and sidelevers that reminded him of Elvis Presley said if he wanted some extra grouse prawns he'd just got in some super fresh ones from Myall Lakes. They did look good and Les thought he might come back later and grab a kilo. The fish didn't take long to cook. Les got a bottle of lemonade from the fridge, paid the woman, then walked back down to the south end, found a seat under the pine trees and ripped in. Norton was right about the Flathead Spot. The food was sensational. I don't know, Les thought as he squeezed more lemon on the fish and stuffed more crisp, golden chips into his mouth, the bloody nosh up here just seems to get better and better. I'll end up eating myself to death. He finished his food and drink, threw a few scraps to the seagulls, then dropped his rubbish in a bin right at the very end of the pine trees near an open air shower. Parked next to it and well past the No Parking sign was a big, white four-by-four with an equally big, white boat behind it on a trailer. It was a twin-hulled, space-age looking thing with twin outboard motors on the back, aerials, depth sounders and other gizmos all over the place. Les was patting his stomach and absently looking at the boat, wondering which buttons you pushed to work what, when he heard a familiar voice behind him.

'Righto, knackers, get your eyes off the boat. Or you might get a toe right up the blurter.'

Norton turned around. It was J.D. Gloves, wearing his familiar fishing jacket and cap over a pair of jeans and trainers.

'Gloves,' said Les. 'What's doing, mate? How's things?'

'Good, Les. What are you doing up here?'

'Didn't Price tell you? We're blowing up the local swimming pool.'

Gloves looked over Norton's shoulder to the one below them. 'You won't fuckin' need what you used last time.'

They each had a good laugh over their private joke for a minute or so as a woman walked past pushing a stroller. Les told Gloves how he was staying at Price's house for a week and enjoying it, although he didn't mention Jimmy for the moment. Gloves said he was up here testing the boat Les was looking at for close-to-shore fishing. He'd just driven up with the reps, who'd walked over to the resort to pick up two Canadian fishing writers that were staying there. He was just keeping an eye on things and watching out for parking cops while they all got their shit together. Norton agreed there were worse ways of making a quid and wished Gloves luck.

'I'll tell you what,' said Les, 'it's not bad up here, Gloves. You come up here much?'

'The Central Coast? Christ, Les, I've been coming up here for over twenty years.'

'Yeah? Shit! What was it like then?'

'A bit different.' Gloves pointed to the resort. 'That used to be the old Florida Hotel. There was a fruit shop on the corner. Down the back where all those boutiques and restaurants are was all old wooden boarding houses and a church.' Gloves started to laugh. 'I used to come up here with fuckin' George.'

'Brennan?'

'Yeah, when we were sort of young blokes. He had this nutty aunty had a farm over at Empire Bay and we used to stay there. She was stark raving mad. Completely crackers.'

'George never mentioned this to me,' said Les.

'We used to come up here all the time to get away from our wives when we first got married. We'd either drive up in George's white Ford convertible or my red Holden, towing an old aluminium fishing boat. It used to take six months to get here then.'

'And you and George used to come up here fishing?'

'Yeah, fishing.' Gloves gave Les a wink. 'And a bit of porking as well. Young George didn't mind kicking his heels up back then. He was a real good dancer and all the little sheilas loved him with his flash car. We had some funny times together up here, me and George.'

Norton shook his head. 'You and fat George cutting into the young spunks. I'd like to see that.'

'And young's the word, too,' said Gloves. 'There was a high school not far from aunty's farm and we didn't mind driving past in George's convertible with the music blaring when the girls were walking home in their school uniforms.'

137

'Nice pair of louts,' said Les.

'Yeah,' agreed Gloves. 'Hey, don't say nothing about this to George. I don't think he wants anyone to know about his mad aunty. She poisoned her husband and someone else and they ended up shoving her in the rathouse. So don't say I mentioned it, will you.'

'No, that's sweet,' said Les. 'I still can't picture George Brennan as a cool swinger, though.'

'Ohh, mate, that fat heap used to look like Kirk Douglas once. Right down to the hair and the dimple on his fat chin.'

'I can just imagine. What about you, Gloves? Who did you used to look like?'

'Paul Newman. Only with more iridescent eyes.'

'You mean bloodshot, don't you?'

Gloves was trying to think of something to say, when four men came across from the resort wearing red and blue coveralls and caps covered in badges or cotton windcheaters and carrying camera gear and bags. Les said goodbye. Gloves said he'd see him in Sydney, then they piled into the four-by-four and drove off towards the boat ramp in the Haven.

Les watched them disappear over the hill then turned around and stared out over the ocean. So George, you fat cunt. You're always bagging me about the clickers up where I come from and my nutty family. And all the time there's a full-on loony-tune in yours. That'd be about bloody right. But as for a lazy, fat heap of shit like you ever being even half a good sort, let alone a good dancer and a pants man—that'll be the bloody day. Norton watched a few small swells wash over the sand towards the rocks then glanced at his watch. It was nearly time to wake the boarder. He drove home and was surprised to find him in the kitchen looking very together in a clean T-shirt and shorts, finishing off a nicely prepared meal of steak and eggs.

'Jimmy, what are you doing up? I was just about to cook you breakfast and bring a tray round to your room.'

'You couldn't cook it as good as this, white boy. I don't mind you carrying my bags and driving me around, Les, but don't bother about getting me my meals.'

Norton looked and took a sniff at what Jimmy had left. 'I don't blame you. Any coffee left?'

Jimmy nodded towards the stove. 'So where have you been?'

'Down the beach. I did some washing, then went down and had a feed of fish and chips under those pine trees. It was tops.'

'Yeah. It's nice down there in a light southerly.'

Les got some coffee and sat down. 'So how are you feeling, James?'

'Terrific. Can't complain one bit.'

'Good. And so you should after stealing my girl off me, you rotten little cunt.'

Jimmy shrugged indifferently. 'Well, you know how it is with us well-hung blacks.'

'Listen, Jimmy, the only time a black's well hung is when you can't get your finger between the rope and his neck. That was an awful, low thing you did to me last night, especially after I just gave you five hundred bloody bucks.'

'Well, what did you expect me to do, you goose? The poor woman was frothing at the mouth, especially after what happened with you.'

'Oh, yeah, and just what did Megan the Merciless say happened with me?'

'As soon as you got your jeans off you shot your bolt. You were hopeless.'

Les stared evenly at Jimmy for a moment. Why spoil his fun. 'Yeah. It must have been all the cream in those Chocolate Surprises. But shit, she was a horny bloody thing.'

'Tell me about it. She went off like a Hezbolah suicide bomber. You should have seen us linedancing in the nude with the sun coming up. It was sensational.'

'I can imagine. No wonder you're having steak for breakfast.'

Jimmy smiled at the look on Norton's face and nibbled on a piece of toast. 'So what have you got planned today, Les? Anything?' Norton shook his head. 'I have to be down Terrigal in about an hour. Is that okay?'

'Sure. What's the story?'

'I've just got to see a bloke for a few minutes. That's all.'

'Righto. Just let me know when you want to leave.'

'Thanks, Les.'

They sat around talking for a while, both of them agreeing that, apart from Paula breaking the iron in the laundry, it was a funny old night and at least she didn't get a chance to break the phone in Jimmy's room. Les was even prepared to forgive Jimmy for stealing his girl. Les had another half a cup of coffee then Jimmy washed up and went downstairs. While he waited for

Jimmy, Les sat in the loungeroom and took it easy. He had no plans. Whatever suited Jimmy suited him; especially at night. Just take him out, stand him there and the girls start waving. Les didn't mind running second. He was in the kitchen checking out the booze supply when Jimmy walked in carrying his overnight bag. Sticking out one end was a leather handle.

'What have you got there in the bag, Jimmy?' asked Norton.

'A whip.'

'A whip?'

'Yeah. You know anything about whips, Les?' Jimmy unzipped his overnight bag and handed it to Les.

'Jimmy, you're talking to an old Queensland country boy.' Les held the coiled whip in his hand for a moment. 'But this is a ripper.'

'Open it up.'

'Ohh, mate.' Les took the whip into the loungeroom and carefully uncoiled it across the carpet. It was about five metres long, counting the handle and the lash, beautifully crafted and bound in heavily oiled red and black leather. The way the thin strips of leather were bound and plaited tightly into each other made it more a work of art than just a stockwhip. 'Jesus, Jimmy, where did you get this?'

'Off a whip maker up in Charters Towers. The cove's made from tanned Argentinian cow hide, moulded round a belly of one and a half millimetre lead pickle shot.'

'Yeah,' said Les, gently turning the handle. 'Give it a finer balance and slow the action.'

141

'Right on, Les baby. Give it that extra craaccckkkk.'

'Reckon,' said Les, carefully rippling the whip across the carpet.

'The belly's wrapped in solid kangaroo hide and plaited over with another four plaits of kangaroo hide then wrapped in split pigskin. The final overlay is one piece of A-grade kangaroo hide so it's got a double layer keeper.'

'What a fuckin' pisser.'

'Check the tapered, lawyer-cane handle, Les. It's plaited over in one piece of kangaroo hide, split into thirty-two strands with a double thickness keeper.'

Les shook his head in admiration. 'This is the best whip I've ever seen, Jimmy. Bar none. What are you doing with it?'

'I got it for a bloke.'

'Not the same bloke you got the vest for?'

Jimmy shook his head. 'This bloke's still around.'

'Is that who you're going to see now?'

'No, I don't have to meet him till the weekend. So I was just going down to see if the thing still works.'

'Whereabouts?'

A strange smile appeared on Jimmy's face. 'I was thinking of on the promenade at Terrigal.'

An even stranger grin spread across Norton's. 'Sounds fuckin' good to me, Jimmy. Let's go.'

Les carefully coiled the whip up, Jimmy put it back in his bag and they walked out to the car. Jimmy hardly said a word on the way down. But he had this enigmatic look on his face and Norton surmised that George's nephew was up to something. Les found a parking spot outside the resort opposite the butcher shop; he zapped the car doors and they walked across to the park. People were either walking about or sitting around eating their lunch and sipping drinks.

It seemed to be mid-tide. But as there wasn't much beach left, what swimmers or sunbathers there were, were sitting in a fairly tight group on the short strip of sand in front of the surf club. The happy-faced bloke wearing glasses that Les had seen on the microphone the day before was still working at the canteen serving a woman and two kids with ice-creams and drinks. About half-a-dozen tanned, fit-looking men in Speedos, and going a bit thin on top, were sitting in front of the first-aid room. One man with a moustache had a cigar, a sponge, a bottle of iodine and a packet of Band-aids. Another bloke with dark hair going a bit in the front was sitting in front of him with his arm out. Les recognised him as the bloke he saw walking up from the water with the surf ski. As he watched, the bloke with the cigar stubbed it on the other man's arm, let it sizzle for a moment, then wiped it with the sponge, tipped some iodine onto the burn before covering it with a Band-aid. The other bloke never flinched. He just sat there talking with the others while they all listened to the songs playing on the radio in the first-aid room.

'What the fuck's he doing?' asked Les.

'Burning off melanomas,' answered Jimmy.

'Skin cancers? Why doesn't the cunt go to a doctor?'

'The bloke with the cigar is a doctor. You're not back with your arty-farty friends in Bondi now, Les. Anyway, hang on, I got to go and see a mate of mine.'

Jimmy walked over to the man in glasses who had just finished serving the mother and her two kids. He looked surprised when he saw Jimmy and made a quick, almost nervous gesture with his hands.

'Jimmy? What are you doing here? You don't have to come round till Monday, Tuesday. Whenever.'

'I just couldn't wait till then, Reg.'

'Oh, Christ!'

'So, how's the zurfglub going, Reg?'

'The zurfglub's going great, Jimmy. It's all sweet. Don't worry about it.'

'What about the gandeen?'

'The gandeen's going great guns, too. Everything's . . . cool, Jimmy.'

'No, it's not. It's going bad. You know what you need, Reg?'

'Not you, Jimmy. Go away.'

'Advertising.'

Before the man in glasses had a chance to do or say anything, Jimmy had darted behind the counter, got hold of the microphone and was back out the front uncoiling the whip.

'Righto, you lazy bastards down there on the beach, listen up and pay attention.' Jimmy's soft voice boomed out of the speakers and across the sand. The group of people on the beach stopped whatever they were doing and turned towards the promenade. Even the people swimming and in the park looked around. 'You've been bludging off us lifesavers for too long and you give us nothing in return. Not even bloody thanks. We ought to let you all drown, you ungrateful pricks. Anyway, the surf club needs your help. So on behalf of myself and Reg at the gandeen, Terrigal Surf Club is now having . . . a whip round.'

'Jimmy, please. No.' The man in glasses was too late.

Jimmy put the microphone down, ran the whip out in front of him then started twirling it anti-clockwise above his head. He spun it round three times then brought it down hard in front of him. Instead of a craaacckkk, like Jimmy said earlier, there was more like a BANG! As if someone had fired a gun. Except the sound was more beautiful, crisp and clear. It had the desired effect. The people on the beach nearly jumped a foot in the air and the ones in the park almost dropped whatever they were eating or drinking. Even the bloke getting the skin cancers burnt off looked up when the doctor dropped his cigar. Jimmy started twirling the whip once more, then cracked it again. And again, and again; each one sounding louder than the first. Jimmy wasn't all that big, but he knew what he was doing and the whip was so beautifully weighted and balanced he couldn't go wrong. He cracked it another couple of times then picked up the microphone.

'Okay, you bastards. Reg from the gandeen will now be passing the hat round. So dig deep. And talking about hats . . .'

Sitting wide-eyed at the foot of the steps was a small group of Asquith Annies and Roseville Rogers—all staying at their parents' weekender and having like a really, incredible, totally, just-so-good day at the beach, like you know, wow. One dork in a pair of John Lennon sunglasses and a pair of monstrously baggy shorts had a multi-coloured, peaked cap on his head with a tiny propeller on it. Jimmy moved across to the top step, whirled the whip round his head twice then bent slightly and cracked it sideways over the dork's cap with a neat, sharp bang! The propeller flicked slightly up in the air then spiralled slowly down onto the sand in front of him like a dying moth. Jimmy ran the whip out in front of him then turned to the man in glasses.

'Righto, Reg, what are you waiting for? Unless you want me to try for a cigarette in your mouth.'

Reg shook his head. 'You're right, Jimmy. What am I waiting for?' The man in glasses slapped a red and yellow beanie on his head, grabbed a plastic bucket and headed towards the stunned people on the beach who were now digging frantically in their pockets.

'If I'm not here on Monday, Jimmy, just stick a note under the door. Anything you like, mate.'

'See you later, Reg.' Jimmy put the stockwhip back in his overnight bag, gave Les the nod and they started walking back across the park. 'I've always wanted to do that,' he smiled at Norton.

'Well, you certainly got your wish,' replied Les. 'Who's the bloke in the glasses?'

'That's Reg. He's a retired magistrate and the surf club's social secretary. He's a top bloke. If anyone's on weekend detention, he gives them jobs. Like cleaning up the surf club or painting the church or whatever. I'm supposed to report to him while I'm out. Me and Reg are good mates.'

'Yeah, I could see that. The poor bludger was terrified of you.'

'Get out, you cunt. He loves me. They all love me.'

'Hey, Jimmy,' said Les, 'fair crack of the whip, mate.'

146

'That's precisely what I gave him, Les.'

Norton could see this line of conversation was going nowhere. 'All right, so what do you want to do now?'

'Nothing. I wouldn't mind just hanging at home round the pool. Have a few cool ones, listen to some music I got. Maybe have a read.'

'Sounds good to me. You like prawns?'

'Yeah.'

'Well, I might get some at that place where I got the fish and chips. You want to grab a bottle of plonk? Or do you want to drink what I got at home?'

Jimmy thought for a moment. 'I might get a nice white. Then have a few Bacardis later. You got any money on you?'

'Yeah, and while you're there, get a bag of crushed ice.'

Les gave Jimmy a hundred dollars and said he'd see him back at the car. By the time Les got two kilograms of Myall Lakes prawns off 'Big Elvis' at the Flathead Spot, Jimmy had the bag of ice plus two bottles of Lindeman's Hunter River Porphyry and they drove home.

Les had noticed an esky in the garage earlier. After changing into an old pair of shorts and organising a towel, sunblock and his book, he packed the esky with ice, booze, orange juice and prawns. Then he strolled down to the pool and made himself comfortable on a banana-lounge. Jimmy came out of the house not long after with a book also, plus a small bag of CDs, an extension lead and a fairly hefty ghetto-blaster.

'You didn't have that in your bag, too, did you? said Les. Jimmy nodded. 'Christ. What haven't you got in there?'

'You'd be surprised, Les,' Jimmy said, looking evenly at Norton. He opened a bottle of wine and poured himself a glass, then plugged the ghetto-blaster into the nearest power point and sat it down next to the cabana so the noise would bounce off the wall and the tiles round the pool. Les watched and wondered just what Jimmy had in store for him as he got a CD from his bag, slipped it into the ghetto-blaster, adjusted the graphic equaliser and pressed the button.

'All right, Les,' he said, settling back on another banana-lounge with his glass of wine. 'Tell me if you like this. And if you don't, too fuckin' bad.'

The ghetto-blaster had a great sound; especially positioned where Jimmy had put it. Les sipped his Bacardi, OJ and strawberry vodka as the sounds of a calypso, mardi-gras band, whistles blowing, maracas rattling, came bouncing out of the speakers. The music quickly faded away then this cool, soft American voice said, 'Hey, Jimmy, do you know somebody in Miami that can get me a passport real quick?'

'Oh no.' Norton threw back his head nearly spilling his drink. 'Don't tell me, Jimmy, you're a fuckin parrot-head.'

'Hey, right on, baby.' Jimmy was ecstatic. 'I don't believe it, Les. You're into Jimmy Buffett, too?'

'Yeah, sort of. Warren's got some of his CDs, so I get a bit of it at home.' Les gave Jimmy a half-smile. 'Whether I like him or not, it looks like I'm going to get it all afternoon anyway.'

'That,' replied Jimmy, 'and I might have something else snookered away in there, too.'

Les raised his glass as 'Everybody's Got a Cousin in

Miami' cruised easily out of the speakers. 'Whatever suits you suits me, Jimmy. There's heaps worse things I could be doing than sitting round a pool drinking piss, eating prawns, and being a parrot-head for the afternoon.'

'Fruit Cakes' went into 'Barometer Soup'. Norton read his book, peeled prawns, got a pleasant glow sipping Bacardi and every now and again fell in the pool to cool off and freshen up. Jimmy sipped wine and did much the same. Like Norton said, there could be worse ways to put in a day. Some Jimmy Buffett CD cut out. Jimmy put it back in his bag and took out something else.

'Righto, Les,' he said, settling back with another glass of wine, 'tell me if you like this.'

'What have we got now?'

'Pale Riders.'

'Never heard of them.'

'There's a lot of good Aussie music around you don't get to hear on radio,' said Jimmy.

'That's true,' nodded Les.

'They live in Sydney but they come from a place in Tasmania called Penguin and they're starting to get a big cult following. They're good.'

'If you say so, Jimmy.' Norton sipped another Bacardi and listened. The music was a mixture of blue grass, country, folk-rock and boogie. Crystal clear harmonies, great guitar licks and heaps of energy. Les gave Jimmy the thumbs-up and made a mental note to buy the CD when he got back to Sydney. Jimmy was in a good mood from the wine and Norton enjoying his music was making his mood even better. He put Pale Riders away and pulled out another CD.

'You reckon you like rock 'n' roll, Les?'

'Sure do, James.'

'Okay. Try this. The Headhunters' "Outlaw Boogie". This belongs to Wade and Peirce. They don't know I got it. If they did they'd bloody kill me.'

The next CD was full tilt, kick-down-the-door rock with some great ballads. Some red hot covers of 'Cadillac Walk', 'Roadhouse Blues' and others and on one track the singer sounded just like Bob Seger of old. Norton made another Bacardi and another mental note. If Jimmy stole this off Wade and Peirce—whoever they were—then they certainly wouldn't know if he stole it off Jimmy. Don't leave that CD lying around before you go back inside, young master James, Les smiled to himself. 'Outlaw Boogie' boogied out. Jimmy slipped in some more parrot-head music, then said he was going inside to have a leak and make a couple of phone calls. As Jimmy walked off, Les placed his book down and thought he might strain the potatoes too. Running alongside the fence were some oleander trees and a couple of flowering frangipannis. Les started hosing away near an oleander when he heard some commotion. It was the elderly bloke with the beard abusing someone or something.

'Piss off, Golden Tonsils, you bastard of a thing,' he yelled out. 'Get away from those bloody tomatoes.'

Norton peered over the fence to see what was going on. It was a big, black brush turkey. Long neck with a yellow frill and horrible eyes set in a scruffy, half-bald, red and black head that looked like a cheap hair transplant gone wrong. It was as ugly as sin and had its eyes on a patch of choice, ripe tomatoes. Concentrating on the tomatoes, it didn't see the man with the beard come charging down the backyard, vigorously pumping a large, yellow super-soaker. The bloke gave the super-soaker another pump then from about two metres away blasted the bush turkey in the head. For good measure he also gave it a long burst up the backside. The bush turkey gave a bit of a squawk then half ran, half shuffled and half flew back into the nature reserve surrounding the houses.

'Bastard,' yelled the bloke, still firing the super-soaker into the bushes.

'Mr Radio trying to get at the tomatoes again, is he?' Les heard the man's wife call out from above.

'The rotten bludger,' answered the man. 'I'll give him golden tonsils. I'll get a longer extension on the hose and drown the bastard next time.'

The wife said something, the man checked his tomatoes, then went back up to the house.

Les shook his head, shook Mr Wobbly, then walked back to his banana-lounge. As he went to sit down he noticed Jimmy's book and picked it up to see what he was reading. *A Short History Of The World* by H.G. Wells. Les idly flicked through it and found various paragraphs in different chapters marked with pink fluoro highlighter. King Asoka. Priests and Prophets in Judea. Primitive Neolithic Civilisations. The First True Men. The last paragraph in The First True Men was outlined, so Les thought he might see what it said.

It is interesting to note that less than a century ago there still survived in a remote part of the world, in Tasmania, a race of human beings at a lower

151

level of physical and intellectual development than any of these earliest races of mankind, who have left traces in Europe. These Tasmanian people had long ago been cut off by geographical changes from the rest of the species, and from stimulation and improvement. They seem to have degenerated rather than developed. At the time of their discovery by European explorers, they lived a base life subsisting upon shellfish and small game. They had no habitations but only squatting places. They were real men of our species, but they had neither the manual dexterity nor the artistic powers of the first true men.

Very interesting, mused Norton, putting the book down as he'd found it. I wonder if that was any of Jimmy's rellies down there in good old Tasmania? I'd better not ask him though or he might think I've been snooping. Les settled back down with his book and the music. A few minutes later Jimmy came back out, picked up his book and sat down again too.

'Everything okay?' Les asked politely without being nosy.

'Yeah, sweet as a nut.'

'That's good.' Les nodded to the paperback in Jimmy's hands. 'What's the book you're reading?' Jimmy held it up. Les scanned the cover. 'Any good?'

Jimmy nodded. 'Yeah. I like to read about history.' He nodded to Norton's book. 'What's that like?'

Les held up *The Hand that Signed the Paper*. 'I haven't finished reading it yet, but so far it's pretty good. Easy enough to read.'

'Of course,' replied Jimmy. 'You hate abos. It's only natural that you're anti-semitic and you hate Jews, too.'

'Don't forget poofs and Asians. I hate them, too, you know.'

'Sorry, Les, I forgot. It must be the wine.'

'That's all right, Jimmy. What can I expect, talking to some abo half-pissed on cheap plonk.'

'Lindeman's Hunter River Porphyry—cheap plonk? You're fuckin' kiddin'.'

'Anyway, Jimmy, I don't think the book's anti-semitic. It just tells things from the other side. The Ukrainians were getting a hard time from the Russians, the Jews, and everybody else. And when the Germans arrived they were no worse off. Better if anything. So they threw in with them and gave the Russians and the Jews a hard time.'

'Like gassing and shooting them.'

'And starving them, too. Same as they did to them.'

'That's right,' said Jimmy. 'Ten million Ukrainians starved to death under Stalin. I remember reading it.'

'But you know how it is these days,' shrugged Les, 'say anything at all about the Jews and immediately you're anti-semitic.'

'Yo! Mah man. We dig that shit in the hood, brother.'

'I don't particularly wish to cop one up the blurter and I think Julian Clary's about as funny as a drunk with a shotgun, so that makes me homophobic. Make even the slightest comment about aborigines, like those few minor points I wished to discuss with you in the car when I first met you, and straightaway you're a racist. You know what I mean?'

Jimmy nodded. 'You're right, Les, it's . . . it's absolutely appalling.'

'The thing is though, Jimmy. I didn't just buy this book to read episode nine hundred and seventy-eight thousand six hundred of the bloody Holocaust. I wanted to find out what the fuss was all about and how this sheila won all those literary awards. I'll admit I got caught up in all the hype and bullshit and they managed to con me out of $13.95. But it's still not a bad read. There's even a bit of porking in there.'

'Fair dinkum? The rotten hussy.'

Les nodded. 'In a way I feel sorry for the sheila that wrote it. All the fuckin' shit she's going through. I mean, all the poor bastard did was write a book and half put one over those turnip heads running the literary scene. Now they want to burn her at the stake. She's got to get round like that Salmon Rushdon, or whatever his name is. Not game to show her head anywhere.'

'Yeah, I've seen all that rattle on TV and in the papers. It's disgusting. She's a blonde too, poor bludger.'

'There you go, Jimmy—persecution of blondes. Blondism.'

'Exactly, Les, the literati in Australia are nothing but a bunch of fascists and cunts.' Jimmy seemed to think for a moment. 'I'll tell you what, Les, you know what I'd do if I was her?'

'What, Jimmy? And I respect your opinion, because you're one smart dude.'

'Instead of running away from these pricks, I'd just hang low for a while then come back bigger and better

154

than ever. I'd get a real dark suntan, or cover myself with instant-tan. Dye my hair black and comb it up in an afro. Buy some overalls and a pair of crutches. Then come back again as a crippled, aboriginal lesbian, and say I was writing a book about my gay, HIV-positive, muslim cousin, and how he came to terms with his sexuality before he died of AIDS during the Gulf War. All those academic woozes out there trying to get a warm inner glow wouldn't be game to knock you back with a spiel like that. You'd clean up again.'

'Genius. I'm talking to a genius.' Norton shook his head in admiration. 'Jimmy, how much do you reckon you could tug in with a scam like that?'

'How much?' Jimmy peered into his wine glass for a second. 'Say fifty from the Arts Council. The Miles Franklin and the Vogel—another forty. You'd have to take out the Nita B. Kibble. Another twelve. Book sales? Over a hundred K. Not counting overseas. Shit! I reckon you'd be looking at around quarter of a million.'

'Quarter of a million bucks? Have you got a typewriter in that bag, Jimmy? We'll knock the fuckin' thing out before you go back in the nick.'

'Why don't we go one better again, Les? Do another version where girl meets boy. Girl loses boy. Girl gets boy back again. Boy undoes girl's bra-strap in the last three pages and we'll flog it to Mills and Boon.'

'Did I say genius?' Norton threw back his hands. 'There's a biro in my bag. You fill out the application form for the Arts Council. I'll find a list of gay bars in Baghdad and start the research.'

'Why don't we have a swim first, Les, and cool off?'

'I think that might be a good idea, Jimmy.'

They splashed around in the pool, drank more booze, ate more prawns and listened to more Jimmy Buffett. By then the afternoon was just about shot. Les made another Bacardi and thought he'd better see what Jimmy had planned for the evening.

'So what's on tonight, James? It's obvious by now you're the brains of the outfit.'

'Well, naturally we'll be having a nice dinner, Les.'

'I tipped that. Where are we going?'

'I'm taking you to a non-smoking restaurant, Les. The Mail Drop. It used to be the old Terrigal post office.'

'Sounds good to me. How does a non-smoker go up here, Jimmy? Those two windbag, know-alls on radio reckon if they make restaurants non-smoking it'll be the end of civilisation, big brother taking over and the restaurants'll all go broke.'

Jimmy gave Les a peeved look. 'You don't take too much notice of them, do you? Does McDonald's look like they're going bad? I had to ring up before I got out of the nick to get us a table.'

'Good one, mate. And what do you fancy doing afterwards?'

'Not much. I had a late one last night and I got a nice day lined up for us tomorrow. Another surprise for you.'

'There's an over-thirties disco on down the road. You want to have a look? You could pass for thirty with a bit of luck.'

'Club Algiers? Yeah, I saw the sign outside the hotel.' Jimmy gave a chuckle. 'So you want to try and hit on some more feral aunties, do you, Les?'

156

'Yeah. See if I can find Aunty Megan and rekindle the spark of love between us.'

'After Jimmy Superstud's been there? You're kidding, aren't you, Les. She wouldn't piss on you if you were on fire. Unless she was pissing kerosene.'

'I still wouldn't mind having a look, though.'

'Okay. But I'm not having a late one. If you want to kick on, go for your life.'

'No. I'll stick with you. Is your man coming to get us?'

Jimmy nodded. 'Of course. Would you like a lift? Or would you prefer to follow us down in the Berlina.'

'No, I'll come with you. I'll even sit down the back with you. I just thought I'd slip that one in, Jimmy. Between mates.'

Jimmy drained the last of his wine. 'Droll, Les. Verrry droll.'

They cleaned up round the pool and got rid of the prawn shells. Les took his washing in, then they watched the news over a cup of coffee and started getting their shit together. The idea of not having a late one now appealed to Les. He wasn't dog tired, but sitting in the sun all afternoon drinking cool ones had taken the edge off him just a little. And who knows what Jimmy had lined up for him tomorrow? After a relaxing shower and shave, Les changed into a pair of jeans, a crisp, white long-sleeved shirt and his spiffing new vest. No, he thought, standing in front of the mirror after daubing himself with Jamaican Island Lyme, I won't grab anything down there tonight. I'll just let them know what they missed out on. If Les looked good, Jimmy looked ten times better when Les found him listening to the stereo and gazing out the window in the loungeroom. He was wearing a black T-shirt with a brown boomerang motif across the front, tucked into a pair of black, silk Dolce and Gabbana trousers with a crocodile-skin belt and matching crocodile-skin loafers. Sitting snugly over this was a soft, black leather James Dean jacket with brown snake skins sewn into the front, shoulders and back and piped round the sleeves.

'Don't tell me the rat made that,' said Les.

Jimmy nodded. 'Hard to believe, isn't it?'

Norton was going to say something when there was a polite knock on the door.

The Mail Drop was in a side street that ran towards the ocean just behind the resort. Jimmy told the limo driver he'd ring when they were ready and they walked up the front steps to the foyer. Apart from a lick of paint here and there, the owners hadn't tried to hide that the restaurant was an old government building and the red bricks, high columns and metal railing out the front only seemed to enhance the building's charm from yesteryear. Les pushed the glass door open and they went inside. Hanging lights shone down from the high ceiling. The kitchen, wine racks and counter were on your right as you entered, and the place was full. The walls were painted in earthy browns and lime-washed white; green carpet ran beneath the cedar chairs and tables with matching cedar venetian blinds. In one corner sat a fireplace with a mirror above and a clock and other bric-a-brac on the mantelpiece. The old, government-style building and the earthy colours gave the restaurant a natural warmth and charm, but not having to peer round the tables through a haze of blue cigarette smoke gave it something else—a brightness and freshness you could almost feel.

Two waiters in black trousers and black Mail Drop T-shirts hovered round the tables, then an attractive girl with neat dark hair, wearing black slacks and a brown top, appeared behind the counter.

'Good evening,' she said with a pleasant smile.

'Hello,' replied Jimmy. 'I made a booking for two. Rosewater.'

The girl checked the reservation list. 'Right on time, Mr Rosewater. This way please.'

She ushered them to a table in the corner, sat them down and left them with the wine list. Les ordered a bottle of Grolsch. Jimmy thought he'd try the Diamond Valley Pinot Noir. Both arrived promptly.

'Well, here's looking up your old address, Mr Rosewater,' said Les, taking it all in. 'And you've done it again. I'm impressed.'

'To tell you the truth,' said Jimmy, 'it's the first time I've been here, but I thought you might like it, Mr Norton.'

There were enough scrumptious-sounding things on the menu to choose from. But seeing as Les ate most of the prawns earlier he wasn't all that screaming hungry, so he just went for Oysters Natural with lime, cracked pepper and flat bread for starters. Then Grilled Barramundi with lemon, thyme butter and potato fennel wedges. Jimmy was a bit keener on the tooth. He went for the Deep Fried Tiger Prawns with Red Curry Sauce on Asian Greens and Muscovy Duck in Cointreau Orange Sauce with a Compote of Autumn

Mustard Fruits. Coffee and sweets were even a distinct possibility.

If Norton liked the restaurant, he liked the food even better. His oysters were plump and fresh, the fish delish and everything that came with it delightful. Jimmy's was the same. He wouldn't release any prawns, but Les got a taste of the duck and half wished he'd ordered that as well. Washed down with one more beer then 'sparkling eau de maison' another top meal. They were sitting back, sipping flat whites while the waiter cleared the dishes and Les looked directly at George's nephew.

'Jimmy, how come all the restaurants in Terrigal are so good? The last time I was here I had an absolute prick of a time. Now I'm in hog heaven. I'll end up looking like one the way I'm going.'

Jimmy shrugged. 'Everything's fresh and there's plenty of competition. But just do me one favour, Les.'

'Sure. What's that?'

'Don't tell anyone in Sydney about the place. I don't particularly like having to dine with revhead westies, northside trendoids and all your arty, farty, would-be film-star friends from the eastern suburbs.'

Norton was about to say, 'How about I bring Uncle George back up?', but decided not to mention what Gloves had told him. 'All right if I come back now and again?'

'Sure,' replied Jimmy, rubbing his stomach. 'Come back any time you like.'

'Thanks, Jimmy. You want to pay the bill?'

Jimmy shook his head. 'No, you may as well. You're better at it than me.'

Les paid the bill, got a nice smile and a big thanks from the girl in the brown top and they started walking the short distance to the resort. On the way Les suggested they have one at the Baron Riley before they hit the disco.

'Before we go in,' said Jimmy, 'I have to tell you, Les, I'm not real keen.'

'Mate, if you don't want to go—sweet. Ring the limo, I can get home all right.'

'No. I'll have a couple with you. But . . .' Jimmy seemed to let it go at that.

'Just tell me when you want to leave,' said Les.

There were a few people standing around the driveway, waiting for taxis or whatever. Les was just about to head for the revolving door when a white, stretch limousine pulled up that looked about twice as long as the one they'd been in. The driver got out and opened the back door. Two skinny blondes in red and blue micro-minis and low-cut tops got out followed by a big, beefy bloke with a happy, craggy face wearing a white suit and a panama hat, which he removed to bow in front of the girls revealing an almost bald pate. Next thing a three-piece mariachi band climbed out and immediately started serenading the bloke in the white suit. They looked just like 'The Three Amigos' in their black sombreros, velvet suits and fluffy shirts as they wailed away in Spanish, playing licks on a big fat guitar, a smaller one and a trumpet. The two blondes cuddled up to the bloke in the white suit who was absolutely loving it, when he spotted Jimmy.

'James, my friend,' he boomed, 'what's happening, old son?'

'Not much, Captain,' replied Jimmy. 'What's doing with you?'

'Ahh, just taking the ladies back to my suite for cool ones,' he replied, grabbing the blonde in the red mini on the backside. 'Show them exactly what a swivelised kind of guy I am.'

'That's you, Captain.'

'I will see you, James my young friend,' he said, 'unless you wish to join us.'

Jimmy shook his head. 'Maybe some other time. You have a good one, Joe.'

'Adios, amigo.' He waved to the band. 'This way, muchachos.'

The blondes, the bloke in the white suit and the mariachi band swept through the revolving door into the foyer, then into one of the lifts. Les and Jimmy followed, then headed for the stairs.

'Who the fuck was that?' said Les. 'Don't tell me he makes clothes, too.'

'No. That's the Captain. Joe Mahoney. He's a brick-layer. Every now and again he has these massive wins at the punt. So he rents a suite in here, gets a couple of hookers and gives himself a giant spoil.'

'Does he what? I like the mariachi band. Now that is style, as my old mate Charles Bukowski would say.'

'That's what you should have had waiting for me when I got out of the nick.'

'If I'd have known what a swivelised kind of guy you were, Jimmy, I would have. Sorry, mate.'

The Baron Riley Bar was a bit quiet. A few people were seated around the bar, mainly couples, with a few foursomes or whatever sitting at various tables. The entertainment this time was a pianist with a beard and a hat crooning out ballads very much like Harry Connick Jnr. Les got the same drinks as last time and they propped up the corner of the bar closest to the dance floor. While he was checking out the punters Les realised why Jimmy seemed a little reluctant to go out. Every sheila in the place was onto him. Even three girls on the dance floor would stop in mid-step and peer around their boyfriends or whatever to ogle him. Which was nice enough. The trouble was, all their boyfriends were doing the same, only they were looking at Jimmy as if they wanted to choke him. He made an ideal running partner all right, but Norton also realised Jimmy would get a lot of shit put on him by mugs for nothing more than being drop-dead good-looking with a ton of style. And being ten lengths in front of the average goose with a comeback, plenty of heroes would want to fight him as well.

'Well, there's not much happening here,' said Jimmy. 'You want to have a look in Club Algiers? Get it out of the road.'

'Yeah, righto. Let's split.'

The piano player finished the song he was singing, they finished their drinks and left the way they came.

There was a small knot of people outside the disco, including three bouncers in black suits and white shirts and a lean, sandy-haired bloke behind them in a white tuxedo. Through the window Les could see another plumper, dark-haired bloke in a tuxedo standing under a poster of Humphrey Bogart next to four women paying admission at the counter. Les stepped back and let Jimmy go first.

'Sorry, mate,' grunted some tall bouncer with a black ponytail. 'You can't get in with a T-shirt.'

Ohh no, winced Norton. Not this again. What's the matter with these fuckin' hillbillies?

'No, he's all right,' said the bloke in the tuxedo. 'Let him in.'

The bouncer stepped back to let Jimmy in, giving him a dirty look at the same time. Jimmy gave the bouncer a dirty look in return. The bloke in the tuxedo gave Les and Jimmy a smile. Les gave the bouncer a look as if he'd like to have buried his forehead right across the bridge of his nose, then stepped inside, paid the admission and got a stamp across his wrist.

Inside it was packed. How many, Les couldn't tell— hundreds. The music wasn't quite as loud as last time but, even though the air-conditioner was working double overtime, it was hot and smoky. The dance floor was jammed and across the bobbing heads and bodies Les could see another DJ; a beefier one with thinner black hair swept back in a tight ponytail spinning old sixties and seventies pop favourites. At the moment he was belting out 'Old Time Rock 'n' Roll' by Bob Seger.

Norton pointed to the far end of the bar. 'Why don't we try and get a drink in that corner, then prop in front of the DJ?'

'Yeah, righto,' said Jimmy, sounding a little reluctant. 'I'll follow you.'

Somehow Les managed to weave his way through the seething throng, elbow his way to the bar and get four Jack Daniels and soda. Jimmy took two and they wound their way to the alcove next to the fire exit under the DJ. There was a small, empty table amongst the people seated on stools or standing beneath the chrome railing. They put their extra drinks down and Les checked out the punters.

They were mostly between thirty and forty-five with a scattering of younger ones. The women were done up mainly in skirts or dresses with low-cut fronts or lacy see-through tops and no shortage of dark stockings. Most of them were in good shape with a few wind-jammers waddling around and here and there a complete dog the average bloke wouldn't leave a burning house to get at. The blokes were wearing mainly slacks, some jeans, and long- or short-sleeved shirts of all colours and styles. Most of them were also in reasonable shape and could have been clubbies, surfies or ex-footballers. Others had guts on them like seals and were starting to part their hair in a circle. There was also the odd drunken wombat shuffling around who wouldn't find a root in a warehouse full of ginseng. Keeping an eye on everyone were another half dozen or so bouncers in the same black suits and white shirts. But everyone seemed to be enjoying themselves, dancing, talking or singing along with the old pop songs while they had a few drinks. As far as Les was concerned, it looked like a pretty good night, and at least you didn't have to put up with punishing house music and eighteen year olds pissed off their heads on two bourbons and Coke.

They'd cleared part of the section above the dance floor and two girls in short floral dresses were dancing a routine to 'Bar Room Blitz' by The Pulse for the mob's entertainment. Les and Jimmy settled back with their drinks next to a group of fit-looking women who, along with being gay divorcees, were probably aerobics junkies. One had blonde hair cut in a fringe, others had blonde or dark hair combed up, another had her hair cropped to a point on her forehead like a Romulan on 'Star Trek'. They gave Norton a few once-up-and-downs. But they were looking at Jimmy like they were all hyenas and he was a baby wildebeest lost from his mother. As usual the blokes were giving him daggers.

'Well, what do you reckon, Jimmy?' said Les. 'This is all right.'

'Yeah, terrific,' replied Jimmy. 'I've always wanted to visit the elephants' graveyard.'

'There's a few jumbo-sized arses on those stools behind us,' said Norton. 'I will admit that.'

The two girls got off the stage, the DJ threw on 'How Bizarre' by OMC and the place erupted into one giant stampede for the dance floor. Norton couldn't help himself. He caught the Romulan's eye, she nodded a big yes, Les put his drink down and they headed for the dance floor. You could forget trying to dance. Everybody just stood there and hoped for the best in time to the music. Les simply jigged up and down and turned round and round in tiny circles till he felt like he was disappearing down a sink. The Romulan's style was much the same, only she kept pumping her legs and bending her knees like she was riding an invisible exercise bike. It was good fun, though, and with a quick hit of 'Jackies' surging through him Les was starting to enjoy himself. 'How Bizarre' finished and the DJ jumped on the microphone.

'And now, ladies and gentlemen, boys and girls, it's

time for our Club Algiers dirty dancing competition. First prize—two bottles of champagne and a Club Algiers T-shirt.'

The Romulan looked hopefully at Les. Norton didn't quite feel like playing Patrick Swayze at the time. He thanked her for the dance; and she rejoined her girlfriends, while Les went back to Jimmy.

'I was watching you out there, killer,' said Jimmy. 'You've done this before. You're a full-on disco duck.'

Norton took a sip of Jack Daniels. 'I could have knocked that dirty dancing thing off if I'd wanted to,' he replied, 'but it'd be like bashing up drunks.'

Jimmy finished his first Jack Daniels. 'Quack quack.'

The DJ slipped on the song from the movie and the dance floor filled with dirty dancers, getting down and dirty trying to win first prize. The plump bloke in the white tuxedo was now standing near the DJ watching things and the thinner one was leaning against the chrome railing above the dance floor with a roving microphone. Swanning around next to him was a solid brunette, about thirty, with big boobs and a backside to match, wearing a black bikie jacket. She'd crushed herself into a pair of jeans and a low-cut top that flashed her ample cleavage to the mob below and looked like some sort of local celebrity, spotlight junkie.

'Who's the sheila in the Brando jacket with the big tits?' enquired Les.

'Blaze Montez,' replied Jimmy indifferently. 'She runs a modelling agency up here. She's a pain in the arse.'

'She's got plenty to go round,' said Norton.

The song finished and the thin bloke in the white tuxedo looked around the dance floor, then turned to the woman with the big boobs in the leather jacket. 'Well, Blaze, I can't pick it. Who do you think tonight's winner is?' he said.

There was silence in the disco as all the punters waited to see who won the dirty dancing competition, when Jimmy cupped his hands round his mouth and yelled out at the top of his voice, 'Blaze Montez sucks dogs' cocks!'

You could have heard it in Newcastle. Norton couldn't believe it, as nearly everyone in the disco looked at Jimmy.

The Romulan turned around and nodded over her drink. 'I wouldn't be surprised,' she giggled.

A hoo-ha and hub-hub ran through the place. Next thing, some bloke dressed in denim, with long blond hair, came charging down the stairs. He didn't look like a bouncer and Les tipped he was big tits' boyfriend.

'Who fuckin' said that?' he howled, then glared at Jimmy. 'You did, didn't you?'

'All right, mate,' said Les, getting between the infuriated boyfriend and Jimmy. 'He's sorry. He's drunk. He's leaving anyway.'

'I'm not talking to you,' howled the bloke. 'I'm fuckin' talking to him.'

'Fair enough,' said Les. He couldn't really blame the boyfriend for having the shits, even if the local star did momentarily stop posing and her jaw dropped about two metres. 'We're both leaving. Come on . . . Eric.'

'What?' said Jimmy. 'Tell him to get fucked. I'm not leaving. This is the grouse.'

Ohh no, thought Les.

The boyfriend made a lunge at Jimmy. Les pushed him

in the solar plexus and he went back into the Romulan and her girlfriends. A couple of the girls gave a startled scream as their drinks were spilled. The next thing they were surrounded by bouncers of all shapes and sizes; half keen for a bit of action seeing there was about eight of them and only one and a half of Les and Jimmy.

Even though they were in a completely no-win situation, Les felt like snotting a couple of bouncers just because of the way they were carrying on. But Jimmy was a little out of order and the end result would have been Les getting his nice new vest torn off his back. The tubby bloke in the white tuxedo next to the DJ looked imperiously down on the whole scene for a moment like Emperor Nero at the Colosseum, then briefly nodded his head once towards the door and gave them the equivalent of the thumbs down. Out.

Norton held his hands up in front of him. 'Okay, okay. We're leaving.'

Les put his head down and turned towards the door, not wanting to cause any more trouble. This, however, didn't stop the bouncers from applying a range of arm bars, choker holds and wrist locks so they could make a bit of a scene and toss them out a-la-carte.

'All right, you hillbilly pricks,' cursed Norton, as they were speared across the dance floor to the jeers and heckles of the dirty dancers and just about everybody else in the place. 'I'm bloody well going. You don't have to make a song and dance about it.'

Les snatched a quick glimpse of the people around him laughing and felt like a complete and utter dill. Alongside him Jimmy's feet were off the ground as they shunted him out backwards. From Norton's point of view it looked as if he were moonwalking. Oh well. So much for Friday night at Terrigal Pines Resort, thought Les, as they went past the toilets. I can't see myself getting in here again. They were just at the foyer when Les felt two hard, quick punches up under his right ribs; he wasn't expecting it and it bloody hurt. He managed to twist his head around and saw it was the bouncer he abused on Wednesday night. Les was about to abuse him again when he felt another punch crunch into his left ear, slamming it against the side of his head. He wasn't expecting this one either and it hurt worse than the other two.

Why, you rotten cunts, he fumed. Before Les knew it they were bundled unceremoniously past the people in the foyer and literally booted out the front door. Jimmy managed to land on his feet okay. Les tripped over someone's foot just outside the entrance, half spun around, then went sprawling on his backside. He managed to break his fall and got up glaring at the bouncers, his face almost crimson with both embarrassment and rage. People in the foyer and outside were looking and laughing at him, the bouncers were grouped in front of the door and there wasn't a great deal Norton could do; not unless he wanted to cop a lot more punches than he had so far and get his good vest ripped to pieces. But this didn't stop Jimmy. He got behind Les as if Norton was stopping him.

'Don't hold me back,' he said, throwing punches around Norton's shoulders. 'I'll kill the cunts. Let me at them.'

'Suits me,' said the bouncer in the black coat who'd punched Les in the head. 'Come on, you little cunt.'

Les turned around and grabbed Jimmy by the scruff of the neck. 'Come on, Mike Tyson. Let's get out of here.'

'Yeah. Piss off.'

'Go on, fuck off.'

'Yeah. Get back to Sydney you pair of poofters.'

Norton let Jimmy go and, with the crowd still laughing and the bouncers jeering, started walking towards the corner. He straightened himself up and, still filthy about getting punched for nothing, rubbed his ribs and his ear. They both hurt and you could bet he'd have bruises there in the morning.

'Well, what can I say, Jimmy?' he growled. 'We weren't even in there long enough to finish two drinks. Nice one, mate.'

'Ahh, fuck the joint,' said Jimmy. 'Anyway, it was worth it to see the look on that fat frump's face. I've always wanted to do that.'

'Yeah, well you sure got your fuckin' wish again, didn't you?' Les put his head down and started trudging up the hill.

Jimmy stopped and put his hands in his pockets. 'So, where are you going?'

Norton pointed up the mini-mountain. 'Home. Where the fuck do you think I'm going?'

'What's wrong with the limo?'

Norton gave a slow, double blink as Jimmy casually pulled his mobile phone out of his jacket. In all the fracas you'd think that would be the first thing to be lost or broken. But no. In fact, as Norton rubbed his ear and had another look, Jimmy didn't have a crease in his clothes or a hair out of place. Les could hardly believe it. Shaking his head, he turned away and noticed the church across the street. Yeah, somebody's blessed around here, he mused, that's for sure. But it sure as hell ain't me. Norton gazed absently at the church and noticed the big clothing bin out the front for the poor and needy. It appeared to be overflowing and placed round the front of it were more plastic bags of clothes and things. Then the little light bulb above Norton's head suddenly switched itself on. He turned back to George's nephew standing with the phone to his ear.

'Hey, Jimmy, how long before that limo'll be here?'

'About five, maybe ten minutes.'

Les took his vest off and started undoing his shirt. 'Here, hold these and wait here for me.' He stripped down to his T-shirt and jeans and jogged across to the clothing bin.

The plastic bags contained mostly old clothes with a few plastic toys, books, or kitchen things and whatever. Les rummaged through them looking for something that would fit. He ended up with a red and black check pyjama top, an old, grey felt hat with no band inside, a red chiffon scarf with a silver thread and a pair of white, plastic sunglasses with one lens missing. He tucked the pyjama top into his jeans, knotted the scarf round his neck, jammed the old hat on his head, then knocked the one lens out of the sunglasses and slid the frame over his nose. Not sure how he was going to work this and feeling like a complete nerd, he straightened the brim of the hat again, then strolled casually back down to the disco.

By the time he got there, all the hoo-ha had settled down and there was another knot of people out the front waiting to get in. Les gave a little smile when he saw the bouncer who hit him in the ribs standing on the right side of the door and the dark-haired one that punched him in the head standing on the left. The thin bloke in the white tuxedo was next to them and the rest of the bouncers were in the foyer getting ready to go back inside. Les got in the queue and shuffled up to the entrance, waiting for the bouncer to tell him to piss off. Instead, neither bouncer gave him a second look. Les couldn't believe it and it threw him a little. He stopped in his tracks and stared at the bouncer on his right. The bouncer stared right back.

'What's up, mate?' he grunted.

Norton absently pointed to the foyer. 'I can go in?'

'Yeah, go on, mate. You're right.'

Les gave the bouncer a wide, happy smile. 'Thanks, mate.'

The bouncer still had a look of annoyed indifference on his face when Norton dipped slightly to his left and with plenty of shoulder in it, king-hit him flush on the jaw. His back teeth shook loose; his jaw swung round the other side of his face, then swung back as Norton hit him with a right uppercut on the chin, smashing it like a china cup. He followed it with another quick left over the top that put a split round the bloke's eye about the same size as half an egg-ring. With blood bubbling out of his mouth and running down the side of his face, the first bouncer fell to his knees, then pitched face forward onto the deck; lights out. It took Les about one and a half seconds to throw the three punches and by now he surmised the other bouncer would come to life. Les was right. He turned around as the bouncer ambled towards him only to walk face-first into Norton's murderous short right coming straight at him and timed perfectly. It

173

pulverised his nose across his cheekbones, sending a spray of blood over the two closest punters. The bouncer gave a moan of pain and dropped his hands as Norton slammed a knee into his groin, doubling him up with an even louder moan of pain. As he bent forward, Les grabbed him by the back collar of his jacket and speared him head-first into the wall. He hit the deck alongside the other bouncer, lights out also.

Well, that'll do me for the time being, thought Les. I'm not that big a nark. Women were screaming, there was blood everywhere, and through the windows he could see the other bouncers coming back out to see what was going on. He was about to turn round and run towards where he'd left Jimmy when he felt someone jump on his back. What the fuck!? Les tucked his chin in and got a glimpse of a white tuxedoed arm round his face. Shit, cursed Les. I forgot to expect the unexpected. He sucked in a deep breath, gripped the two arms around his shoulders by the sleeves, bent forward sharply dipping his knees and flipped the bloke in the white tuxedo over his head. He catapulted into the bouncers stampeding through the door and they all fell in a great sprawling heap of arms and legs in the doorway. Les had a quick look then spun around ready to bolt, only to find his path blocked by yet another bouncer. It was a blonde-haired woman in a white shirt and black slacks standing in front of him in a kind of unarmed combat stance. Norton moved towards her expecting her to get out of the way, but she stood her ground and started to circle Les. She was game. She was also thinking Les might think twice before belting a woman and if she could delay him long enough the other bouncers would be on their feet and

174

able to grab him. Les turned his head quickly to see they'd just about got their act together and had blood in their eye—Norton's. Shit! Then he noticed the two parlour palms in heavy ceramic pots next to the door.

'Here, blondie, have this.' Les picked up one of the parlour palms and flung it at the woman bouncer.

The soil-filled pot thumped into her chest and the parlour palm smacked her in the mouth and she went down backwards like she'd been crash-tackled, still holding the ceramic pot with a faceful of wet dirt. By this time the bouncers were all on their feet and what should have been a quick sprint to the limo was now an attempt at the world record for the hundred-metre dash with the enraged bouncers about two metres behind him.

Les bolted down the steps in two bounds then across the road to the corner and was going all right—except there was no sign of Jimmy. Shit! Where is he? Les had a bit of a start, so he turned around for a quick look and whether it was his imagination in the dark, he wasn't sure, but the bouncers seemed to be catching up. They were yelling out to each other and those with coats on were ripping them off; they weren't giving up and they were going to have Norton's arse by hook or by crook. If I can just get a bit further up the hill, puffed Les, they might spread out a bit and maybe I can turn round and snipe a couple. If not, this hill's steep, I'm full of food, half-full of drink and in deep, deep shit. Les was about to rip the hat and pyjama top off when a row of lights pulled up alongside him and a door opened.

'Sorry, I can't give you a lift, mate. There's no room, not even down the back.'

'Like fuckin' hell there ain't.'

Les dived straight onto the floor of the limo, Jimmy slammed the door and, with the bouncers banging at the windows, they cruised off up the hill leaving the group cursing in their wake. Norton sucked in some air while he thanked his lucky stars he got away safely. Then he got up and sat down next to Jimmy. Folded neatly on the seat in front of him was his vest and denim shirt.

'Enjoy yourself, Freddy Krueger?' asked Jimmy.

'Yeah,' replied Les, 'as a matter of fact, I did. About the same as you did in the disco. Where the fuck did you get to anyway?'

'I walked back down to have a look. I saw the whole silly fuckin' thing.'

'Did you?' Les grinned and bunched his fists. 'What did you think?'

'What did I think?' Jimmy shook his head. 'I just thought what a fuckin' idiot you were.'

'Thanks a fuckin' lot.'

'No. All jokes aside, I do have to admit one thing about you, Les.'

'What's that?'

'You certainly know how to dress. That outfit suits you to a tee.'

Les looked evenly at Jimmy. 'Bullshit! You're only saying that just because I look like an abo.'

Jimmy shook his head. 'No, Les, you don't look like an abo. You look like a Queenslander.'

'That's it, Jimmy. Get fucked.'

'Droll, Les. Verrry droll. And quick too.'

The limo dropped them home and they went inside. Les got out of the old clothes and threw them in the Otto-bin saying he was going to have a shower. Freddy

Krueger probably owned the hat and the pyjamas could have belonged to someone who'd died from the bubonic plague. Jimmy said he might have one drink and watch TV for a while.

Under the shower, Les was happy to find the bruises round his ribs and on his ear weren't that bad after all and the hot water and soap got rid of all the sweat and anything else hanging around. It made Les feel good, but for some reason all he wanted to do was get into bed. He climbed into a clean T-shirt and shorts, got a glass of orange juice and joined Jimmy in the lounge-room. Jimmy was almost asleep in front of the TV, watching David Letterman. They would both have liked to have discussed the night's events, but by the time they got to see Robby Robinson and The Band and Letterman do his top ten reasons, that was about it. Jimmy said he'd see Les in the morning. Would he get him up by nine if he slept in? Okay. See you in the morning, James.

Norton switched off the TV and the lights and climbed into bed. That was when he realised why he was so keen to get in there. The fresh, clean sheets. Ahh, yes, how good's this? Les scrunched up into the pillow and wondered what Jimmy had lined up for tomorrow. Whatever it is, I imagine there'll be some-body there for him to insult. How's the little prick's form, telling me I look like a Queenslander. You can bet he got that off his fuckin' fat uncle. Despite the indignity of it all, a smile flickered round the corners of the big Queenslander's mouth. Before Norton knew it he was snoring peacefully again.

Les was up around seven-thirty the following morning, again feeling pretty good. A bit too good actually, thought Les as he sipped a cup of coffee in the kitchen and stared out the window. In fact, if he felt any better it would start to show. Hitting the gourmet trail with Jimmy was lots of fun, but what Norton needed was a bit of a hit-out to burn off a few calories. Outside was another nice day; sunny with just a light sou-easter. He got into his old training gear, including one of Megan's bonds to tie round his head for a sweat rag, threw his towel and a few more things into his overnight bag, then walked out to the car and took the scenic route down to Terrigal. He had no trouble finding a parking spot outside the resort across from the beach. But Les thought he'd be cool, so he did a U-turn across the double lines and parked beneath the pine trees facing towards the Haven.

For such a pleasant day the beach was fairly empty with just a few early risers swimming, having a jog or walking around. There was enough firm sand to run on at the water's edge; Les zapped the car, walked over and did a few stretches. As he was touching his toes Les noticed an unusual-looking pebble lying on the sand. It was dark brown, a bit bigger than an egg, with a red and white swirl through it and reminded Les of a big liquorice all-sort. Les picked it up and thought he might toss it from one hand to the other as he was running along for something to do; also if there were any more nutty dogs around that felt like biting him they could have it between the eyes. Twenty minutes up and twenty minutes back would do for a run, then from the rockpool to the surf club and back would do for a swim, Les adjusted his sweatband and sunglasses and trotted off.

The run along the beach in the sun tossing the pebble from one hand to the other while the odd wave washed in over his ankles was pure delight and Les wasn't thinking about much, except how sweet it all was. But somehow Norton's thoughts kept slipping back to Jimmy. He was a cheeky little bastard all right, yet Les couldn't help liking him; enjoying life one minute then shit-stirring things the next. He was up to something, Les was certain of that and whatever that something was, Les felt it was something to do with bikies. That was no big deal and Les doubted very much if it had anything to do with drugs. There was something else about Jimmy, however. He was probably making up for time lost while he was in the nick— that was fair enough—but it was as if he didn't give a stuff much about the future or anything for that matter. Les had been there to save his neck on a couple of occasions, but things could have gone the other way— especially last night—and Jimmy could have wound up getting his good-looking face plastered round the other side of his head. And the way he'd say, 'I always wanted to do that'. It just struck Les as a bit odd. He shook his head. Oh well, he thought, I imagine I'll find out what's going on by next Wednesday. I'd still like to know what makes Jimmy tick, though.

Les had a good head of steam up when he got back to the south end of the beach. He threw his sweaty gear in the car, put his goggles on and plunged into the sea. After the run, the swim felt even better. The water was clear and refreshing and he seemed to plough his way up to the surf club and back in no time at all. He got out and had a cold shower. Then, after drying off and changing into his shorts and his clean Rainbow Warrior T-shirt, Les felt like he was sparking on all six and ready to take on the world. Sitting on a bench beneath the pine trees, he decided to keep the funny-looking stone as a souvenir and was turning it round in his hand absently while he figured out what he should do. Or more in particular; where he should have some breakfast. Home would be best. Get the paper, then stuff round in the kitchen and sort things out from there till it was time to wake the star boarder. Les was miles away and didn't notice the figure sit down next to him. The sudden and unexpected voice gave Les a bit of a start.

'My friend, my friend. I knew it was you. It is ordained. It is truly the prophecy. Argghnszzknkgh.'

Norton spun around. 'You! What the fuck are you doing here?'

It was the Shamash, wearing a filthy, brown trench-coat belted in the middle, a battered, grey felt hat, a black Phantom T-shirt and a cheap pair of sunglasses with one lens missing. He was covered in dirt and filth from heat to foot; he stunk; his unshaven face was a mess of cuts and bruises and a black eye squinted mournfully from behind the missing lens. He reminded Les of Sam Spade after he'd just fallen under a stampede of yaks, then been mugged by grave robbers.

'Don't tell me,' said Norton. 'Let me guess. You were fulfilling the prophecy, the green talisman was stolen from you by the evil one in the castle of doom, then your flying saucer clipped a meteorite and you crash-landed through a time warp quantum.'

The Shamash shook his head adamantly. 'No, no my friend,' he croaked. 'It was nothing like that at all. I merely went for cool ones and those I thought were my friends turned upon me.'

'They what?'

The Shamash made these pitiful gestures with his hands as if he was having trouble getting the words out. 'It was late. Club Algiers was still open and knowing there are always friends of the Shamash there, I thought I would go in—and perhaps have a delicious. I walk up wearing my finest Humphrey Bogart outfit and immediately I hear the people calling. It is him. It is him. He is back. Yes, yes, I say. It is me—the Shamash. I have returned among you. I am back. I open my arms to greet my new-found friends, and walk straight into a giant king-hit. Then some crazy woman hit me across the head with a flower pot. Stop, stop, I say, it is me—the Shamash. Why do you do this? But to no avail, my friend. They beat me and kicked me, then threw things at me. Somehow I was

181

able to drag my wretched body to a dumpmaster behind the hotel where I crawled inside and went to sleep.' The Shamash screwed his face up into a mask of anguish, pain and bewilderment. 'Why would they do this to me, my friend? I am the Shamash. I do nothing but greet them with my blessings as I always do. Why? Aeeiiighrnnngh.'

Norton shook his head. 'Buggered if I know, mate. I always thought you were the chosen one, too. Do you think it might have been your shoes?'

'Shoes, my friend? What's wrong with my shoes?'

'You're not wearing any.'

'Aiieegghhnrngh.'

I don't believe it, thought Les. The poor bastard's gone up to the disco dressed like that and those boofheads on the door must have thought it was Freddy Krueger come back again. So they've belted the shit out of him. It was probably a good enough excuse, anyway. He's crawled into a dirt bin and crashed, now he's crawled out and found me. Lucky bloody Les. But there was something in either the Shamash's body language or his body odour that said he was desperate for something else besides grief counselling and male bonding. He'd also done business with Jimmy.

'My friend, do you—'

'Say no more, oh chosen one. I understand.' Les held up the pebble he found on the beach. 'You see this?' The Shamash nodded. 'Do you know what this is?' The Shamash shook his head. 'This—is the secret stone of the great charcoal filter in Lynchburg, Tennessee. Do you know what this sacred stone can do?'

The Shamash looked at the pebble as if it was hypnotising him. 'My friend, I think I am beginning to understand.'

'The sacred stone—can produce the delicious.'

'Delicious. Delicious. Yes, yes. Aarrgghhnnghnrr.'

Norton pressed the pebble into the Shamash's hand. 'Take the sacred stone and wait here till I get back. Swear you won't move from this spot.'

'My friend, I swear. The Shamash awaits your return.'

Les half jogged, half walked down to the newsagent's and got the paper. The bottle shop wasn't open, but the tall bloke was helping unload cases of wine from a van double-parked out the front. Les had the cash. Okay? Les walked out with a bottle of Jack Daniels, Coke, ice and a paper cup in a plastic carry bag. He walked back down to the Shamash who was still sitting staring at the pebble and showed him what he had. The Shamash went into raptures. It was more than the prophecy. It was a whole bottle.

'Yes, yes. Delicious. Aieegghhngrnn.' The Shamash began to kneel at Norton's feet. 'The Shamash is your servant. I am your slave, oh jewel of the cosmos.'

'Yeah, terrific. Now watch this.' Les took the pebble off the Shamash, walked over to the car and locked it in the boot along with the bag of delicious, then walked back and held the keys up. 'You see these? These are the keys to the secret cavern of the Berlina where lies the delicious. Do you want the keys?'

'Yes, yes master. Delicious. The keys. Yes. Aiieegghngngh.'

'Okay. Then I want some information.'

'My friend.' The Shamash licked his swollen lips and squinted up at Les through his black eye. 'Tell me what it is you wish to know.'

Norton sat down next to the Shamash and slowly folded his arms. 'Where do you know Jimmy Rosewater from?'

The Shamash seemed to think for a moment, then swallowed slowly. 'Jimmy is my friend. The Shamash is everybody's friend. But Jimmy is—my friend.'

'How old is he?'

'Jimmy is not young. Jimmy is not old. Jimmy is the timeless one.'

'Where does he live? Where's he come from?'

'He comes. He goes. Jimmy is a free spirit.'

'Okay. What's he do for a living? Where's he get his money from?'

'Jimmy is an arranger. If it can be done, Jimmy can arrange it.'

'Yeah, righto.' Les couldn't figure out whether the Shamash was being evasive, whether he was just a rambling drunk or whether that was just the way he saw things. Whatever the answer, he wasn't getting far, and the Shamash wasn't getting any closer to the boot of the Berlina. Les thought he'd persevere. 'All right. What happened to Jimmy's mother?'

This appeared to ring a bell. The Shamash stared down at the footpath for a moment and what little expression there was on his battered face seemed to temporarily evaporate. 'Rose was my friend. It was a bad thing. A bad thing.'

'A bad thing? Like what?'

'The men with fire in their feet. They did it. It was a

terrible thing. Nothing could be done. Poor Jimmy. Bad, bad. Aieegheegh.'

'The men with fire in their feet killed her?' Les asked slowly.

'Yes, no. They didn't kill her, but they did. Bad men.'

Christ, thought Les. I need a PhD in gibberish. This is fuckin' ridiculous. I'll try one more question and that's it. 'Who's Jimmy's father?'

The Shamash drew back and held his hands up as if Norton was going to hit him. 'I know not. The Shamash knows nothing. Don't ask me. Please I beg. Aieeegghh.'

Aha, I've hit a nerve, thought Les. 'Yes, you do. Speak, you miserable dog. Who is he?'

'I don't know. Nobody knows. Aieegghhggh.'

'The truth, dog. Speak.' Les jangled the car keys in front of the Shamash's face. 'Or lose the key to the sacred cavern . . . forever. Now tell me, what's Jimmy's story?'

'No, no. They will kill me. I will be tortured. They will gouge out my eyes with toothpicks. They will cut out my tongue. It will be the end of the Shamash. Aiieeggghhheeee.'

'It's either that,' Les jangled the keys again, 'or the end of the delicious.'

'Delicious, delicious. Aieeeggh.' The Shamash licked his swollen lips and looked as if he was going to sweat blood. 'All right,' he blurted. 'Jimmy is in the Mafia.'

'The Mafia? Ohh don't give me the shits, you fuckin' idiot. Your hat's on too tight.'

'It's true, my friend. It's true.' There was desperation

185

in the Shamash's voice. 'Bad men in Sydney. Gangsters, murderers. Assassins. They bury people. They look after Jimmy. I can say no more. I know no more. Believe me, effendi.' The Shamash seemed to roll up into a ball of fear and misery, which to Norton looked like a severe case of overacting.

Les looked at him for a moment. 'Yeah, righto, I believe you. I haven't got a fuckin' clue what you're talking about. But I believe you. Here.' Les unlocked the boot of the car, folded up his paper, then handed the plastic bag to the Shamash. 'Try not to drink it all at once.'

The Shamash grasped the plastic bag like it were the crown jewels. 'My friend, I am your servant.'

'Yeah, terrific. See you later.'

The Shamash was about to leave when he stopped and held his hand up in front of Norton. 'My friend, do you think . . .'

'Oh, Christ!' Les had about seven dollars worth of change in his pocket. He dropped it in the Shamash's hand. 'There, that's it. Now fuck off.'

'My friend, my friend, I am leaving.' The Shamash bowed a couple of times, then disappeared somewhere in the direction of the Haven.

So that was worth a bottle of Jack Daniels was it? Norton shook his head in disgust. Not counting the ice, the Coke and all my change. The men with fire in their feet killed his mother and Jimmy's in the fuckin' Mafia. And that's about it. Plus he's got a fat heap of shit for an uncle who used to look like Kirk Douglas. Norton shook his head again and stared at the ocean. You know, in the grand scheme of things, who really gives a stuff? I'm going home for breakfast. Les slapped the newspaper against his leg and walked back to the car.

When he got home, Jimmy was sitting in the kitchen wearing a pair of shorts and a T-shirt, sipping orange juice and writing something in a notepad. He finished what he was writing just as Norton walked in, closed the notepad and looked up.

'G'day, Les. What's doing? I suppose you've been down the beach again stuffing yourself with fish and chips,' he said.

'No, as a matter of fact I went for a run,' replied Norton. 'Got a bit of exercise.'

'Not a bad idea,' nodded Jimmy. 'I was watching you out the back of the limo last night and you were flat out getting up the hill, you big cheeseburger.'

Les placed his paper on the table, got some orange juice and looked out the window. 'And it looked like being such a nice day, too.'

'Come on, don't get the shits, disco daddy. I've got something nice lined up for you. Are you hungry?'

'Fuckin' starving.'

'Good. Because I'm taking you to Berowra Waters for lunch. And seeing as you don't like drinking piss with your food this'll suit you, because you're driving.'

'I'm driving to Berowra Waters?'

'No. Gosford. Then we pick up a seaplane.'

'A seaplane? Hang on a minute. How big's this fuckin' seaplane?'

'It's—not very big, Les.'

'Great.'

'Don't shit yourself. You'll love it. Then we pick

187

something up at the restaurant and bring it back with us.'

Les looked at Jimmy for a second, then shrugged. 'Okay. So what's the story? Where are we going, what do I wear?'

'We're leaving in about half an hour. The place is called Peat's Eate. It's casual. But it's also the absolute grouse. So try to look—' Jimmy seemed to think for a moment as he picked up his notepad and his glass of orange juice—'not like a Queenslander.'

I wonder what would be worse, thought Les, as he went into the bedroom to get changed, doing twenty years in a Turkish prison or spending two weeks up here with both Jimmy and Warren? It'd be a toss-up. Les left the same T-shirt on and changed into a clean pair of Levi's, his Road Mocs and a denim jacket he bought in Hawaii with Wylie Coyote on the back. He tossed a couple of things into his overnight bag and went into the kitchen. Jimmy was leaning against the sink wearing his Sergio Tranchetti tracksuit and his Fila trainers.

'What's in the bag?' he asked.

'I thought I'd bring my camera,' said Les, 'plus a towel and another T-shirt in case we ditch.'

Jimmy gave a bit of a chuckle. 'I might put my mobile in there.'

'Go for your life,' said Les, 'but if it gets wet, don't blame me.'

Jimmy did that, then looked at his watch. 'Come on, Chuck Yager. Let's get going.'

There was a bit of traffic around Erina Fair, but the drive into Gosford listening to James Blundell twanging through 'Fast Train' on one of Norton's tapes was easy enough. As they started heading along The Entrance Road Les told Jimmy about bumping into the Shamash earlier. He didn't say anything about questioning him, just how he got punched up outside the disco and had put the snip on Les for his loose change. Jimmy couldn't quite believe it at first, so Les had to repeat himself, then Jimmy started laughing fit to bust. Watching him rolling around behind his seat belt Les could see once again why women were attracted to Jimmy. All aborigines, with their brown skin and perfect teeth, have got beautiful smiles. But Jimmy's was even more of an exception. It was highly infectious and almost lit up the front seat of the car.

'You haven't got a bad smile, Jimmy,' Les told him. 'You and your abo mates should try laughing more often. It'd do you the world of good.'

'God, you're not wrong,' replied Jimmy, shaking his head. 'But that is a complete crack-up. I can just see the cunt. Yes, my friends, it is me. I have returned. Bang! Crash!'

Jimmy was still chortling away when he told Les to pull up next to a park just up from the Central Coast Leagues Club that faced Brisbane Water. Across the wide calm bay Les could see a range of low hills running towards Woy Woy and the Peninsula in the distance and on the right an electric train rattling out of Gosford Station towards Point Clare and Tascott. Les zapped the car doors and they crossed the road. A restaurant sat over the water on the left, on the right was an old Sydney Harbour ferry that had been converted into another restaurant, boats and yachts bobbed gently around on their moorings and, in between, a skinny, sandstone jetty with more boats tied up ran out about two hundred metres or so. There were a few cars parked around and several people fishing from the jetty; Les followed Jimmy out to a small wooden landing area at the end. It was a delightful day, with one or two clouds drifting across the blue sky and a light wind barely rippling the water. There was no sign of a plane, so Les stood easy taking it all in.

'Bandits at eleven o'clock and closing,' said Jimmy after a few moments.

Norton looked up to his left. A black dot in the sky slowly drew nearer then started to bank. It was a blue and white single-engine job with two pontoons and steps fixed to the fuselage and windows running along the side. It landed easily, spreading a small arc in its wake, then gradually taxied around to the jetty as the pilot cut the motor. A bloke with a moustache and sunglasses, wearing blue trousers and a white shirt with epaulettes on the shoulders, got out and tied up. He gave Jimmy a big smile and a hello, and Les too. Jimmy said something to him, then they climbed on board. There was another pilot with a moustache sitting on the right up front, then a nicely dressed young couple, sitting behind them; Les and Jimmy piled in down the back. With six people inside counting the two pilots it was a bit of a squeeze and Les was glad Jimmy wasn't any bigger. The co-pilot explained about the safety procedures if they did have to ditch and how they'd be dropping the young couple off somewhere else first before they flew on to Peat's Eate. Most of this went over Norton's head. What Les mostly noticed was that he was right up against the door, his knee almost jammed against the door handle that didn't look any different to one on a car, and if the door should open and his seat belt come undone, it would be a long, long way down. Never having been on a plane this small before, Les was naturally a little apprehensive. He didn't feel any better when the pilot turned round as they started to taxi off and said, 'We're going to have to do a cross-wind take-off. So it might get a bit bumpy and the plane might dip a little. But don't let it worry you.'

'Have you ever done a cross-wind take-off before?' the co-pilot asked him.

'Only a couple. I'm not real good at them.'

'I done one once. You want me to do it?'

'No, it should be all right.' The pilot put his hand up to his face. 'My glass eye's playing up today, though.'

'Is it?'

'Yeah, I think I got a bit of grit in it.'

The co-pilot pointed to his face. 'Do you want to borrow mine?'

'No, it should be okay.'

The others seemed to nod something. There was just a numbed silence from Les. When they got out into the open the pilot hit the throttle and away they went.

It seemed to take a while then slowly but surely the little plane lifted up and Les watched queasily as the water began falling away below them. Seconds later Les could see Lion Island, Barrenjoey Point and all the way to Sydney before they banked right over Pearl Beach and Patonga. The noise inside the cabin was almost deafening and although it seemed a little hairy at first, once Norton figured out the door wasn't going to suddenly spring open and the two pilots didn't want to ditch any more than he did, it was one unforgettable buzz. The seaplane soared on into the blue. Underneath them the Hawkesbury River looked absolutely spectacular as it encompassed Berowra Waters and flowed into Pittwater like a long, wide, emerald-green ribbon, sparkling against the lush, warm jade of the surrounding bush.

It looked that good, Norton got his camera out of his bag and clicked off a few shots out the window; then took a couple in the cabin as well.

The pilot began to bring the plane down, then banked left and Les thought the wing was going to hit the water. When the plane straightened, the pilot executed a perfect, two-pontoon landing and they began to taxi along a wide tributary, past some holiday homes set against the low cliffs that were accessible only by boat or seaplane. A couple of boats went past and waved, then from somewhere a small police launch went past and *didn't* wave. Beneath the noise in the cabin Les thought he heard one pilot mutter to the other that he wondered what they were doing here. The plane turned right, then pulled up against a pier beneath a restaurant that was all glass windows facing the water. The young couple in the front got out as a waiter came down to greet them, and a few words were exchanged with the co-pilot. Then he got back in, the pilot started the engine and they began taxiing off again.

'What do you reckon so far?' said Jimmy.

'Unreal,' replied Norton enthusiastically. 'We'll have to do it again.'

'Any time at all, Les. Any time at all.'

Norton turned back to watch the water going past. He couldn't see all that much from the window, but as they went further he noticed the police had pulled the two boats over. Next thing the pilot hit the throttle and they were soon airborne again.

This time they barely seemed to skim the trees as the pilot followed the river past cliffs thick with trees or dotted here and there with tiny, pristine golden beaches. Les clicked off some more photos and could hardly believe he was only a few minutes flying time from a huge city like Sydney. The pilot banked left to a mumbled 'oh shit' from Les, then straightened and they swished gently down on an absolutely secluded bay about the same size as Sydney Harbour. The plane taxied up to a small jetty with a few runabouts and a couple of motor launches moored alongside, and the co-pilot got out and tied up while Les and Jimmy climbed down the steps to be greeted by a young blonde girl in a white T-shirt and brown jeans and of all people, the grey-bearded pianist from the Baron Riley Bar. It was all smiles and hellos, then the girl led them across a neat, landscaped lawn dotted with palm trees. The restaurant was set beneath a shelter in a semi-circle of long wooden tables and wooden benches which faced a paved courtyard with a pergola in the middle for the piano player and his music mixer. A low cliff full of trees and shrubs sat behind the restaurant. There was a house just visible on the right, some small cabins and a pool on the left; then that was it. Absolutely nothing for miles but a huge beautiful bay surrounded by low, rolling hills thick with trees.

'What do you reckon now?' said Jimmy.

'What do I reckon?' Norton shook his head in wonder. 'I never even knew this place existed. It's unbelievable.'

'And Sydney's just down there.'

Les shook his head again. 'Unbelievable.'

There were about thirty or so casually dressed people seated around the tables sipping drinks, ducks bobbed around by the jetty, birds called to each other in the trees, and lying or roaming around the grass were three dogs, including a black and brown Doberman. The smiling girl in the brown jeans sat them down at a table near the end closest to the water and said she'd be with them in a minute. A tall, grey-haired man with a moustache came across and said something to the pilot and they walked down to the plane. They had a few more words, then the co-pilot left him and walked back up to Jimmy.

'Mr Rosewater,' he said politely. 'We might be running a little late this afternoon.'

'We're not in any mad hurry,' answered Jimmy. 'What's up anyway?'

'We're going to have to do a few trips to Pittwater and bring some police in.'

'Police?' said Jimmy.

'Yeah. Apparently some nutters have stolen two boats and shot a couple of fisheries inspectors. Then they shot up a police launch. So the police are stopping and searching all boats in the area. And we have to give a hand. But it shouldn't affect us that much. Maybe twenty minutes or so. We'll do our best, though.'

'Yeah . . . righto,' replied Jimmy.

'So have a good day,' smiled the co-pilot, 'and we'll see you this afternoon.'

'Roger over and out,' said Norton.

The co-pilot walked off and Les turned to Jimmy, who looked like he was thinking furiously. He stared at Les, then this noise suddenly came from Norton's overnight bag. Jimmy heard it and started to move. Les held up his hand.

'No, I'll get it, Jimmy. I mean, I'm your driver. I may as well operate the switchboard as well.' Les unzipped the overnight bag and handed Jimmy his mobile phone.

Jimmy snatched it and pulled out the aerial. 'Yeah. Yeah, I just fuckin' heard. Can you fuckin' believe it? Yeah. Okay. Yeah.' Jimmy looked at Les for a second. 'No, that's no problem. Yeah. Yeah. Okay, see you then.'

Jimmy pushed the aerial back in, Norton took the phone off him, put it back in the bag, then took out his camera. He aimed it at Jimmy and took a photo. 'I don't know how that'll turn out, James. You weren't smiling very much.'

Jimmy stared evenly at Norton for a moment or two. 'What are you doing tonight, Les?'

'What am I doing tonight? Hah!' Les turned round and took a couple of photos of the seaplane taxiing off. 'What do you think I'm doing? Carting you around somewhere, I suppose.'

'You fancy a quick trip up to a place called Avondale and back? It's just this side of Newcastle.'

'Sure,' shrugged Les. 'Why not? That's what I'm here for, aren't I?'

'We should be back in Terrigal by ten o'clock.'

'Terrific. Just in time for a drink at the resort and before the disco gets too crowded.'

Jimmy detected the sarcasm in Norton's voice. 'You don't mind, do you, Les?'

Les looked evenly at George's nephew. 'Jimmy, I couldn't give a shit. And I don't give a fuck what you're up to either. But if the cops arrive and start asking questions, and they find out you're a dirty, scrumbo abo who should be in the nick,' Norton smiled and shook his head, 'Jimmy, you're on your own, soul brother.'

Jimmy returned Norton's smile. 'Thanks, Les. I always knew I could count on you.'

Norton was about to say something when the girl came back and asked if they wanted any drinks.

'Yes. I'll have a Bloody Mary, please,' said Les. 'And the bloody hotter, the bloody better.' He gave the girl a wink then looked at Jimmy. 'Even if I'm driving, I can still have one.'

Jimmy looked at Les for a second, then smiled up at the girl. 'Bloody good idea. I might have one, too. But I think I'll be having more than one.'

While he waited for the drinks to arrive, Les strolled down to the water's edge and took some more photos. Another seaplane arrived with four people on board, a cruiser pulled up, a couple of boats went past towing some kids on surfboards and in the distance Les was sure he could make out the markings of another police launch. So, Jimmy, he mused, the wallopers have stuffed things up a bit at this end. Bad luck. But I knew he was up to something. Should I ask him? No, I think I'll just act the dumb heavy for the time being. If he wants to tell me, I imagine he will. Not that I really give a stuff to be quite honest. Les looked around the hills in the distance and the magnificent green bay shimmering in the sunshine. I'm having too much fun playing lifestyles of the rich and useless. He took a photo of the ducks, then strolled back to their table.

The Bloody Marys arrived, complete with a big, crunchy stick of celery, and there weren't enough Ps in perfect to describe them. Les took a healthy sip and his eyes watered, his throat burned and his taste buds started doing a Maori Haka on his tongue. Les was hungry when he got on the plane. Another sip of his Bloody Mary and he was ready to grab a wooden stool and start bashing away at the nearest rock with any oysters growing on it. There was no need. The girl arrived with the day's menu and said not to worry about ordering any entrees, she'd bring the lot over on a plate. Just order the mains. Les went for the Rack of Lamb with celeriac puree and sweet potato chips. Jimmy opted for the Quail Stuffed with Grapes, served on a bed of couscous with a citrus sauce. Minutes later the entrees arrived. A platter of king prawns caught the day before and a plate of oysters picked and washed that morning. Marinated calamari, croute emmantaloise, salad of smoked chicken fillet and roasted red pepper in a seeded mustard mayonnaise, smoked salmon fettuccine with creamy vermouth and dill sauce and Thai fish cakes. Norton thought he was going to die from overenjoyment.

While they were ripping into the entrees, the pianist walked over to the pergola, followed by the Doberman, and started plunking out 'How Much is That Doggie in the Window' and the stupid bloody dog started singing along with him. He did another song and the dog joined in again, even dropping its howl a key. It was a complete hoot.

'Thank you very much, ladies and gentleman,' said the pianist. 'Could we have a round of applause for the dog.'

Everybody clapped wildly, then the pianist slipped into all the songs he did at the resort only without the dirty ditties. Before long the mains arrived along with a bowl of perfectly cooked vegetables. They were absolutely delicious. Les washed his down with mineral water and for some reason Jimmy stayed on Bloody Marys though he didn't appear to be getting drunk. The pianist played more songs, the dog did another bracket, then a blonde-haired woman who was the owner's wife got up and belted out a few tunes in a good, strong voice and wowed them. After that, everybody got into the singing and dancing, boozing away and having a wonderful time. It was more like a big, old party among friends than an afternoon in a restaurant. Les and Jimmy got to meet some nice people and danced with a couple of blokes' wives. One couple even invited them onto their cruiser for a look and it was more like a luxury, floating home unit than a boat. After that it was back for sweets and coffee; Mississippi mud cake with tamarillo coulis and cream, and sticky date pudding with butterscotch sauce.

As an afternoon it was as good or better than any Norton had spent anywhere in the world. The only thing missing was a nice girl, because with the sun going down over the still, green waters of the bay, it wasn't only beautiful, it was truly romantic.

Les looked at George's nephew over his coffee. 'I'll

tell you what, Jimmy,' he said sincerely, 'this place is sensational. I only wish you were a sheila.'

Jimmy gave Norton a quick once-up-and-down. 'Christ, I'm glad you're not.'

Sadly, before Les knew it, it was time to go. The plane taxied in to collect them. Les settled the bill and then the owner, the pianist, the staff and just about everybody else in the place saw them off. It was like saying goodbye to old friends. Before they climbed on board, Les stopped.

'Jimmy,' he said, 'I'm stone, cold sober, but that's one of the best days I've ever had. Thanks, mate.'

Jimmy flashed his infectious smile. 'Like I keep telling you, Les—any time at all, mate. Any time at all.'

They were the only ones on the plane this time and the pilots had obviously been flat out all day, so they didn't go on with a great deal of banter this time. But the flight back into the setting sun was a breeze and the view as they left the Hawkesbury and flew into Brisbane Water was truly magnificent. Les popped off another couple of photos, the co-pilot took his camera and popped one of Jimmy and Les sitting in the back, and by the time Les finished the roll they were swishing gracefully onto Brisbane Water. As they taxied back to the jetty the sun was just saying adios for the day. Jimmy must have settled with the pilots earlier as they thanked them for a safe journey, said goodbye, then walked back to the car.

'There's no need to go back to Terrigal,' said Jimmy, as he did up his seat belt. 'Just go straight back along The Entrance Road and I'll tell you when to turn off.'

'I'll have to stop for some petrol first.'

'Good. While you're doing that, I'll get a torch and a road map.'

Les pulled up at a garage on the other side of the punt bridge, filled the tank and got a packet of Jaffas, while Jimmy got what he needed. Then they got back in the car. Les had only brought one tape with him when they left earlier and, with 'Tube Snake Boogie' by ZZ Top bopping lightly through the car stereo, he set off into the night not having the foggiest idea where Jimmy was taking him.

They drove past Erina and Wamberal then Jimmy told Les to turn left at some roundabout. As they did, Les got a quick glimpse of a sign saying Tumbi Road. It was a long skinny road that curved a bit here and there. Les couldn't make out much in the darkness except trees and houses and other cars going past. They got onto some other road and Les glimpsed a sign saying Berkeley Vale, another one saying Tuggerah, and signs pointing to Newcastle. Then it was all monster roundabouts, more roundabouts, a huge shopping centre, Westfield or something, more roundabouts, more signs pointing to Newcastle, then another one next to another monster roundabout.

'Christ! What the fuck do you call this joint?' said Les, slowing down again as he watched a small truck in the rear-view mirror with its lights on high beam almost run up his arse. 'Land of a thousand fuckin' roundabouts.'

'Not that much further,' replied Jimmy, 'and we should come to the freeway.'

'Terrific,' said Les, as the truck went around him.

They went on further through more roundabouts and

signs pointing to Newcastle when Les saw the traffic slowing down ahead.

'Ohh no. I don't believe it,' he said happily. 'A set of lights for a change. You fuckin' beaut.' Les stopped for the red light and pointed out the window. 'Hey, look over there, Jimmy. A McDonald's. You want to stop for some fries or a chocolate sundae? What about a McFeast?'

'Just keep in this lane, Les,' said Jimmy. 'You got to turn right onto the freeway up ahead.'

'Whoopee. I can't wait.'

When the lights turned green, Les drove on, then took a hairpin kind of turn right and came down onto a long, straight freeway. He kept in the inside lane and stayed right on the speed limit while Jimmy switched his torch on and began shining it over the map. Les still didn't let his curiosity get the better of him. Whatever happened would happen and he had a feeling whatever Jimmy was up to it was only something petty. Though someone had mentioned Newcastle to Les recently, but he couldn't think for the moment where or when. All Les did notice was that they crossed the Wyong River and another sign loomed up on the left saying Morisset.

'Left here,' said Jimmy.

Les drove off the freeway, then pulled up at a set of lights a bit further on. 'Morisset. Isn't that where the rathouse is?'

Jimmy nodded. 'Yeah.'

'You got any relations in there?' Les asked, half jokingly.

Jimmy shook his head and half jokingly replied, 'Not in there.'

201

When they got into Morisset, Les noticed a sign saying Welcome to Lake Macquarie—Australia's Largest Coastal Lake. Then after that it was a complete balls up. Jimmy twisted and turned the map around under the torch and looked at it like it was a Chinese newspaper. Left here. No right here. No, go back there. Left there. Wait on, go right. Les glimpsed a sign saying Sandy Creek, then they got onto some long, straight road and Jimmy said this was it. Les put his foot down, then about four kilometres further on hit the brakes in front of a prime-mover parked across the road with a sign on it saying STOP. ROAD UP FOR REPAIRS. Jimmy cursed, and stared at the map, then it was back the way they came and go right. Or left. They crossed Dora Creek and went through Dora Creek Station, Les kept going as instructed and they finished up at Eraring Power Station. After more cursing and running the light over the map, it was back to Dora Creek Station where they drove round in circles while Jimmy tried to figure out how to get to the other side of the railway lines. As a navigator Jimmy made a good steamroller driver and Les could have come up with some great lines to throw at him and choice amounts of shit to put on him. But it was just as much fun listening to the stereo, eating Jaffas and watching Jimmy flounder around trying to read the map. Finally Jimmy found a way out of the puzzle, they got onto some other straight road and it was now a definite straight ahead. This is it. Les drove on past an old, empty shop and some houses and another sign, this one saying STOP. BRIDGE UP. Then another sign STOP. BRIDGE UP. Then another. On just about every corner they came to was a black-on-yellow sign—STOP. BRIDGE UP. After about the sixth sign Les pointed out the window.

'Jimmy, is it me? Am I seeing things? Or have we just entered the twilight zone?'

'Fuck the signs,' said Jimmy, sweating over the map. 'Keep going. It's just up ahead.'

'Righto.'

They went about another kilometre past one more sign saying STOP. BRIDGE UP. And sure enough. The bridge was up. Les hit the brakes again in front of a huge mound of dirt, stacks of old timber and more prime-movers. There was nothing around but bush, darkness and floating dust caught in the beams from the headlights.

'Well,' said Les, slipping the T-bar into neutral, 'it's not as if there weren't any signs telling us. Would you agree, Jimmy?'

'Fuck! Shit!' Jimmy looked at the map and jerked a thumb behind him. 'Back that way.'

'Back that way, massah. Yes, massah. Ah's doin' mah best, massah.' Les hooked his finger into the wheel and spun the Berlina round. 'Please don't whip these tired old bones no mo', massah. Ah begs yo', massah.'

'For Christ's sake, just drive the car, will you, Les,' said Jimmy, shining the torch on his watch.

'Yes, suh, massah. That's what ah's tryin' to do, massah. Ah swear, massah.'

A sign appeared saying Avondale and somehow Jimmy finally got his shit together; yet Les was sorry in a way. Even though he'd been wasting his time, driving round and round in circles out in the middle of nowhere in the dark, he was getting a funny kick out of watching Jimmy squirm for a change. Jimmy told him to go left and Les came to a V-shaped brick wall with a gate in the middle and a sign saying Avondale Seventh Day Adventists College. Jimmy told him to go left at the gate and another sign saying Cooranbong Aerodrome. Les followed a wide, dusty driveway with a clump of trees in the middle. In the dark he could make out a house on the left, a row of trees further to the right with the college on the other side and in the middle a low, white wooden railing. Behind the railing about half-a-dozen or so light planes were parked in a paddock. Jimmy said to go a bit further to where one railing was missing, open the boot and leave the parking lights on. Les did as he was told and as he flipped the boot catch from inside the glove box Jimmy got out so Les thought he might do the same and stretch his legs. It was quite dark with no one around and at the back of the car Les could make Jimmy out in the tail lights squinting at his watch. Behind him the mainly white planes took on a ghostly sheen in the moonlight.

Les was about to do his jacket up and ask Jimmy just what it was they were waiting for when a low rumbling came from behind the planes. The rumbling got closer, then turned into a muffled, revving roar and two motorbikes with blue tape over the headlights came out of the aerodrome and stopped behind the car. One was a Harley-Davidson, the other an old Indian with a side-car. The Harley stayed back a bit and Les managed to make out a tall man with a Pancho Villa moustache in all black leather with a snug black helmet. Sitting behind the handlebars on the Indian was a barrel-chested man with a blue bandana round his head, wearing a white T-shirt, jeans, biker boots and a thick, black leather vest. Sitting in the side-car wearing the same tracksuit was Louise, the girl Les met at the flat where Jimmy picked up his bag. Resting on her lap was a wooden crate that came to just under her chin. The driver got off, walked round and took the crate by two rope handles at the end, then came over. It was a metre long by about half a metre wide and about the same depth. As the bloke got closer, Les could see he had a couple of teeth missing on the bottom and his T-shirt read Mighty Thunderbirds across the front.

'Christ, Jimmy. Where the fuck have you been?' he said in a deep, rasping kind of voice.

'The bridge was up,' said Jimmy.

'The bridge was up? That's miles down there at fuckin' Stockton Creek. There's eight million bloody signs.'

'Signs?' said Les. 'I didn't see any signs. Did you see any signs, Jimmy?'

'Just put the fuckin' things in the boot, will you, Peirce,' pleaded Jimmy. 'And we can all go home.'

The bloke in the bandana placed the wooden crate in the boot. Les managed to get a fairly good look at it before Jimmy closed the lid and handed the bloke an envelope. Jimmy didn't bother to introduce Les and he didn't wave to or acknowledge the others. Les gave the girl in the side-car half a nod and got half a nod in return.

The stocky bloke in the bandana put the envelope in his vest and patted it down. 'You know about tomorrow,' he said.

Jimmy nodded. 'Yeah.'

'You going?'

Jimmy shrugged. 'Maybe.'

'I think you'd be better off if you didn't.'

'Yeah, well, you know me. I like the band and I like old bikes.'

'Suit yourself.' The bloke had a quick look around, something like a fox sniffing the wind. 'Anyway, I'm gonna fuck off. I don't want to be hanging around any more than I have to.'

'Fair enough. I'll give you a ring.' Jimmy smiled and for a moment its infectiousness was caught in the tail lights. 'But don't worry, everything'll be cool—including all that other shit. I'm telling you.'

'Yeah. Well, you just take care of yourself, Jimmy.' The bloke turned to leave, then stopped. 'Hey, Jimmy, you haven't seen that fuckin' CD of ours have you? The Headhunters.'

Jimmy shook his head. 'No. I thought you had it.'

'Fuck!' The bloke shook his head also. 'They've stopped making the thing, you know.' The bloke shook his head again then got back on the old Indian and they rumbled off the same way they came. Les watched them disappear, then he and Jimmy got in the car and they drove back out past the school.

Jimmy managed to find the right road out this time and somehow he was also able to find a freeway heading south. Ironically, 'Louise' by The Night Hawks was going round for the second time and Les was wondering why they didn't come this way in the first place. He was also starting to wonder what was in the wooden box. It was solidly built pine, roughly smoothed over, with some kind of clumsy, thick military-type stencilling on the sides that could have been anything. German. Italian. French. Yugoslavian. Whatever. With the two rope handles on the side, Les knew an ammunition crate when he saw one. On one hand, it was none of Norton's business to ask what was in it. On the other hand, Les had helped pick it up and if he didn't say something he'd be classed as stupido-numero-uno or Jimmy might think he was getting ideas about stealing it.

'Well, Jimmy,' said Les after he'd just gone round an old, green Torana. 'I've got to ask you—what's in the crate? Though if you don't want to tell me, I suppose that's cool.'

Jimmy took a deep breath, then exhaled. 'Les, I've seen you in action, and what's in that crate wouldn't interest you in the least. It would go straight over your Queensland head. Believe me.'

'Okay, but say you were to tell me anyway?'

Jimmy looked at Les for a moment. Norton's voice was steady. But Jimmy seemed to detect an undertone that even though he didn't have to tell him, if Les wanted to find out, all he had to do was pull over and smash the top off the crate to find out. And there wasn't a great deal Jimmy could do about it.

'All right. What if I was to tell you it was—bottles of wine?'

Les nodded slowly. 'I'd say, fair enough, Jimmy. What kind of wine?'

'What kind of wine?'

'Yeah. What colour? Red or white?'

Jimmy looked curiously at Norton for a moment. 'How about red? Red wine. That do you?'

'Okay. Red wine it is.' Yeah. And I know when some

cunt's pulling my rope, too, thought Les. 'So what would you have with this wine, Jimmy?'

'Have with it? What the fuck are you talking about?'

'Well, you being a food gourmet and all that—what would you have with this fine red wine?'

Jimmy looked at Les for a moment then seemed to smile at some private joke. 'Spaghetti.'

'Spaghetti?' Les couldn't quite believe what he'd just heard.

'Yeah. I'd take it down the No Names in Darling-hurst and have it with spaghetti. That's what I'd do.'

'That'll do me, Jimmy,' nodded Les. 'I believe you 100 per cent.'

'Good. Now why don't we leave it at that.'

'Suits me.'

Jimmy folded his arms and stared through the wind-screen as if he was thinking about something. Les drove on in silence, passing a sign pointing towards Doyalson. But a number of things were starting to clunk together in Norton's mind. So, Jimmy, you shifty little bastard. Like all smarties, you think you're clever, but your big mouth always gives you away. Wine and spaghetti, eh? What's just across that lake from where we were? Newcastle. And what did that cop I bumped into on Thursday night say? They were after a box of machine guns before some bikies in Newcastle got them. And what was in with the machine guns? A thou-sand rounds of spaghetti bullets. That's an ammo crate those bikies have tried to disguise and Jimmy's doing a scam with them. The little cunt. Now I'm driving round with a box of high-tech machine guns in the boot plus the ammo to go with them. Les felt like kicking Jimmy right in the nuts. He had a quick look at the speedo; right on the dot. It all figures, too. They were supposed to bring them round today at a place you can only get to by seaplane or boat. Which makes more sense than two bikies riding round in broad daylight with them sitting in a side-car. The cops'd pull them over just on the strength of it. Bad luck there were water police all over the place today and it would have been the same story. Which is why Jimmy had me drive into Gosford, too, instead of travelling by limo. Good old Les. You wouldn't be interested in what's in that box, Les. It'd go straight over your head. Yeah, like a burst of bullets. As well as kicking Jimmy in the nuts, Les felt like reaching over and grabbing him by the throat as well. Still, thought Norton, it's early days yet. Be cool. Nothing much is going to happen between here and Terrigal and I'm interested to see how this all pans out. And if it looks like getting the least bit heavy I'm on the toe. I can be packed in five minutes and it ain't that long a drive back to my joint. Les chuckled mirthlessly to himself. So much for a quiet holiday on the Central Coast, though.

Before long they were once again approaching the land of a thousand roundabouts.

'So what's on tomorrow, Jimmy? I couldn't help but overhear that bloke saying something earlier.'

'Just a band at a hotel near Kincumber and a vintage bike rally. I'm thinking of going. I'll see how I feel in the morning.'

'Righto.'

They went on a bit further past more roundabouts. 'So what do you feel like doing now, Les?' Jimmy asked.

'Saturday night? I don't know. I can't see us getting into the disco or having a drink at the resort.'

'There's a nice little bar in a restaurant just round from the house. Why don't we put the car in the garage, go up there and I might shout you one because you're such a good bloke.'

'Thanks, Jimmy,' said Les, with an oily smile. 'I was beginning to think you'd never notice.'

Nothing dramatic happened on the way back to Terrigal. They struck a bit of Saturday night traffic along the beachfront and the usual crowd in and around the resort plus a couple of cruising police cars, which gave Les a small twinge of apprehension; but he wasn't drunk or driving too fast. Jimmy told him to take the long way home and on the way he pointed out where they were going for a drink. It was the two-tone brown restaurant called the Silver Conche that Les noticed before; only about five minutes' walk from the house, if that. Next thing they pulled up in the drive-way; Jimmy got out and opened the garage doors, Les drove the Berlina straight in and locked it. Jimmy didn't say anything about stashing the box of machine guns anywhere, all he said when he got his mobile out of Norton's bag as they walked inside was there was no need to get changed.

'I might just run a quick razor over my face and put on a clean T-shirt,' said Les.

'Righto. I'll see you in the kitchen in about ten minutes.' Jimmy went down to his bedroom and Les went to his.

Les put a clean, white Wilderness T-shirt on the bed, then had a quick shave. He was in a better mood now, although finding out what Jimmy's little scam was had certainly put a different spin on things. And I thought it would be something petty, Norton mused, as he squirted his face with shaving gel. What would a box of machine guns get you? Five years. Maybe ten on the top. And what's his next move? Meet up with some more bikies, I suppose. Les raised his chin and scraped the razor underneath. I wonder how Jimmy got mixed up with bikies. He just doesn't seem the type. Money mainly I suppose.

Les finished cleaning up, put his jacket back on and walked out to the kitchen. Jimmy was idly flicking through the paper on the kitchen table. He glanced up as Norton walked in.

'You ready?'

'Seeing you're shouting, Jimmy. I sure am.'

Les locked the house and they began walking. Jimmy was bouncing along in a fairly good sort of mood, so Norton left him to it and they were at the restaurant in no time at all. Les noticed a long, white limo waiting just up from a small parking area next door. There was a step down from the footpath and Jimmy opened the glass door to the restaurant and Les followed him inside.

The restaurant was tastefully appointed with an absolutely stunning view of Terrigal from the window at the end and across the soft lighting Les could make out about thirty or so punters laughing and drinking as they finished off their night. Just on the right was a small, well-stocked bar set behind a wall of wooden slats that looked into the restaurant. There was a table next to it with the menus and fixed to the wooden slats were all the awards for excellence the restaurant had taken out over the years. There were so many that Les was curious why Jimmy hadn't dragged him along there first, seeing it was so handy. A dark-haired man going a bit thin on top, wearing a grey check shirt and neat, black trousers smiled when he saw them.

'Hello, Jimmy,' he said. 'How are you?'

'Real good, thanks, Harry,' Jimmy smiled back. 'We're just going to have a couple of drinks. Okay?'

'Go for your life. In fact, I wouldn't mind joining you. It's been another busy bloody night.'

A waitress came over and said something to the owner. He muttered a quick 'excuse me' to Jimmy then disappeared with her into an alcove between the bar and the kitchen. There were four stools in the bar; Les and Jimmy took the two in the middle and got a smile from a dark-haired girl on the opposite side wearing a crisp white shirt and a black dress.

'Well, what will you have, Les?' asked Jimmy.

Les thought for a moment, then what happened earlier in the day seemed to tickle his fancy. 'I might have a delicious. A JD and Coke.'

'Yeah, me too. Two Jack Daniels and Coke, please.'

'Coming right up.'

Jimmy dropped a twenty on the bar and the drinks arrived in about a minute.

'Well, Jimmy, here's to . . .' Les clinked Jimmy's glass. 'What? You shouted. You propose the toast.'

Jimmy looked at Les for a second. 'To . . . to good old Uncle Price.'

'Yeah, why not,' agreed Norton. 'The dear old chap hasn't shouted us a bad holiday up here so far.'

'I think he can afford it.'

'Can he what.' Les took a good sip of his drink as did Jimmy. 'So how did you get mixed up with bikies, Jimmy?' asked Les, as the bourbon went down.

'Mixed up with bikies? What do you mean?'

'That vest you gave me. What you said round that flat. Those two blokes tonight didn't look like Mormons handing out *The Watch Tower*.'

'Les, every big bloke you see on a fat bike isn't necessarily a gang member, if that's what you're getting at.'

'Well,' shrugged Norton, trying not to sound too nosy. 'I suppose that's what I was getting at.'

'Peirce used to be in a gang. Wade's not. They're just mates of mine I do business with now and again. They're good blokes.'

'Fair enough.'

'To be honest, I try to keep away from the gangs. Most of them are as nutty as fruitcakes, especially when they're on the piss and cranked up on goey.' Jimmy took another sip of his drink. 'You ever had any dealings with bikie gangs, Les?'

'Once, sort of. I actually robbed them and got away with it.' Les smiled over his drink. 'Shit! I hope none of them are up here. I don't think they would have forgotten me in a hurry.'

'There's three gangs up here. The Red Backs, the Mongeroloids and the Tarheels. They're all crazy, they all hate each other and they're all ready to kill each other at the moment over drugs. But the Tarheels are the worst. There wouldn't be a lower bunch of cunts on the planet than them. They're animals.'

213

Jimmy's face suddenly went stone hard and Les had a feeling he'd inadvertently touched an odd kind of nerve by mentioning bikies. It might have been a good idea to drop the subject. But Les was still a little curious, especially considering what Jimmy was up to.

'Tarheels. That's a strange name for a bikie gang. How did they come up with that?' he asked.

'They stick spikes and nails in the heels of their boots,' said Jimmy. 'And when they take off on their bikes, they drag their boots on the road sending showers of sparks everywhere. It looks like their feet are on fire.'

'Like their feet are on fire?' echoed Les.

'Feet, boots, whatever,' said Jimmy. 'I'd like to see more than their fuckin' feet on fire. In fact, if ever . . .' Jimmy's voice trailed off, then the expression seemed to return to his face. 'What are you doing tomorrow, Les?'

Les gave a shrug. 'Nothing in particular. Why?'

'That band I was talking about earlier. They're called Zipper Mushrooms. They're playing over at the Broadwater Resort, not far from that little church we stopped at. We'll go over for sure. I'll get the limo.'

'Righto.'

'And we'll have a look at all the old motorbikes. It'll be a good day, Les. I promise you.'

'Sounds good to me,' said Les, taking another sip of his Jack Daniels.

Jimmy turned away to look at the people in the restaurant. Les stared down at the floor and thought about some of the things Jimmy had just said. Not particularly liking bikies but still doing business with them, that was fair enough. He was pulling some sort of scam right now. But what was it that drunken ratbag said down the beach earlier in the morning? Something about the men with fire in their feet had something to do with Jimmy's mother dying, or some bloody thing. Maybe he was talking about this mob of bikies the Tarheels with hobnail boots dragging on the ground. Maybe Jimmy's mother was an old bikie moll. It could have been drugs. She died from an overdose and they gave it to her. Maybe they pack-raped her right in front of Jimmy when he was very young. Whatever the answer was, there was no love lost between Jimmy and that particular bikie gang. Les swirled the ice round in his glass while a lot of thoughts started swirling around in his head. Jimmy turned round and tapped him vigorously on the shoulder.

'Hey, Les, you're not going to believe who's here.'

'Sorry. What was that?' said Les.

'Over there in the corner, and she knows we're here, too. Shit, she's coming over.'

Les was about to ask Jimmy what he was talking about, when who should sweep into the bar looking very foxy in a tight, blue floral dress tied behind her shoulders, wearing high heels, no stockings and showing plenty of muscle-toned, brown skin but Aunty Megan.

'Hello, Jimmy,' she said excitedly. 'How are you, sweetheart?'

'Real good thanks, Megan. How are you?'

'Great. Especially now that I've seen you.' Megan turned to Norton and smiled. 'Hello, Les. How are you?'

215

'Pretty good thanks, Megan,' replied Les, raising his glass. 'Nice to see you again.' Christ, thought Les, last time I saw her she wouldn't piss on me. Now it's all smiles and hellos. Either she's very forgiving or more than a little schizophrenic.

'So what's happening, Megan, you little fox?' said Jimmy, giving her a quick tickle behind the split in her dress.

'What's happening?' Megan plonked herself down on the stool next to Jimmy. 'Paula and I are stuck with the two most boring pricks God ever put breath into.'

'Even more boring than me and Les?'

Megan placed her hand on Jimmy's knee. 'They're with all these other suits up from Adelaide on a business conference. Toilet duck or cat food or something. We met them at the resort and they took us out to dinner. Now they want to take us to the disco. Oh God.'

'Sounds like a good night,' said Jimmy, taking a delicate sip of his drink. 'Half your luck.'

Megan moved closer to Jimmy and started drooling over him as if she wanted to eat him on the spot. 'You're a proper bastard, Jimmy. You know that, don't you?'

'So people keep telling me.' Jimmy looked right into Megan's eyes. 'How long do you reckon it would take for you to dump these two biro heads and get back to my place for a bit of . . . linedancing?'

Megan looked at her watch. 'Finish your drinks, then leave. And we'll be knocking on your door in about ten minutes. And have a nice cool drink waiting for me, gorgeous. I'm going to need it after such a long walk round.'

Jimmy blew her a kiss from about a foot away that almost steamed off Megan's lipstick. 'One tall, cool drink for one tall, hot woman coming up.'

'Gggrrrhhh.' Megan snarled at Jimmy like a hungry lioness, then went back to her table.

'Well, how about that?' said Jimmy. 'My nude line-dancing partner Megan. And all hot to trot again.'

'Yeah,' said Norton. 'I get the feeling she fancies you a bit.'

'You don't blame her, do you?' winked Jimmy.

'So what's the story?'

'What's the story? The story is. We discreetly finish our drinks like gentlemen. Then stroll home in a leisurely manner, also like gentlemen, and await the arrival of the ladies. Then I'll tip about two thimbles full of drink down Megan's throat and she'll be all over me like a lava flow. Only ten times hotter.'

'And what do I do with the lovely Paula?'

'Paula?' Jimmy got to the last of his Jack Daniels. 'That's your business, Les, not mine. Entertain her in the loungeroom. Recite Plato. Discuss the galactic movements of the constellations into the next millennium. Suck her on her big, wet lamington, then fuck that small piece of brain that accidentally got wedged in her head out of her on the kitchen table for all I care. I honestly don't give a shit, because I'm going to be too busy doing the giant nasty with Aunty Megan.'

Les reflected into his drink for a second or two. 'Jimmy, exactly what are you in the nick for? It's not just for pot, is it?'

Jimmy looked directly at Norton. 'Outboard motors.'

'Outboard motors. What do you mean, outboard motors?'

'I arranged for a bloke to pick up some outboard motors I got hold of.'

'And what went wrong?'

'I hadn't arranged for the bloke with the bloke picking up the outboard motors to be an undercover cop. I got six months.'

Les was tempted to laugh, only he was taken aback by Jimmy's blunt and direct honesty. 'That's okay. At least I know you're not a rotten, low drug dealer.'

'Yeah. I'd like to see the look on your face if I pulled out a big, juicy bag of mull. Come on, let's finish our drinks and go rendezvous with the two lovelies.'

Jimmy led Norton all the way on the short walk home, scampering along like Brer Rabbit in the briar patch. And half his luck, too, thought Les. Megan looked hornier and fitter than ever in her floral dress. Les didn't know what to do about Paula. He was starting to feel a bit tired and he wasn't overenthusiastic about the whole thing, and Les doubted if he rang any of Paula's bells either. Just be polite, have a drink, listen to some music or watch a bit of TV, then hit the sack. She could get a taxi home with Megan after Megan had finished playing out whatever sexual fantasies she had in mind with young Jimmy. Next thing Les opened the front door and they were in the kitchen.

Jimmy got four Bacardis together and put them on the coffee table in the loungeroom. He dimmed the lights, drew the curtain back for a view over the swimming pool and the backyard, put the first tape he found in the stereo and, with 'Two More Bottles of Wine' by Emmy Lou Harris rolling softly out the speakers, everything was set up just fine. Les took a couple of sips of OJ and minutes later there was a knock on the door. Jimmy got up and with a bit of hoo-ha and drunken laughter led Megan and Paula into the lounge-room. Paula was pissed again, only she was wearing a blue shirt over a black mini-dress, black stockings and didn't look too bad. Just drunk.

She gave Norton a boozy smile as she came down the steps. 'Hello, Les.'

'Hello, Paula. How was the dinner?'

'Ohh, about as ordinary as it gets.'

'The food no good?'

'No. The food was fantastic. The company . . .' Paula made a thumbs-down gesture.

'Yeah, well you never know who you're going to meet these days, do you?'

'Come on, make yourself comfortable. Grab a drink.' Jimmy pointed to the Bacardis. Megan took one and sat down on the lounge next to Jimmy. Paula took another and sat down in a loungechair on the opposite side of the room to Les. 'So how did you manage to brush the two Wallies?'

'Just told them we were going to the loo,' said Megan. 'Then did a quick fade out the door and left them with the bill. Christ! Talk about boring. The one Paula was with was that dense light bent around him. The meal and the drinks were lovely, though.'

'Yeah, how come we haven't eaten there yet?' asked Les. 'We've been nearly everywhere else and that's just round the corner.'

'I've been saving that one up,' said Jimmy. 'Just like I've been saving myself for you, Megan. You filthy, fiendish, femme fatale.'

'Bastard,' hissed Megan. She took a huge slurp of Bacardi, then put her glass down and started attacking Jimmy on the spot.

Well, I reckon it's only a matter of time now, thought Les, taking another sip of Bacardi. Minutes at the most. And doesn't time fly when two horny people are having fun? It was closer to seconds when in the soft light Les saw Jimmy take Megan by the hand and they both disappeared, laughing and giggling, down the stairs; leaving Les alone with Paula who didn't seem in the least perturbed. The music played on and not a word passed between them. The only thing Les could think was that it would be more comfortable sitting on the lounge than where he was; it faced the speakers and he could put his feet up on the coffee table. Les took his drink and changed seats. Paula still looked half okay in the soft light, but she was half full of drink and after the low rap Jimmy put on her, Les wasn't all that keen on trying to take her in a passionate embrace. Still, she was probably a good scout underneath or, at least, when she was sober, and it costs nothing to be polite. Les decided he had to say something.

'So what sort of music do you like, Paula?' asked Les as 'Men' by Gina Jeffreys bopped lightly through the stereo.

'Ohh, I reckon this'll do.'

'That's very good, Paula.' Les took a belt of Bacardi. 'Any sort of movies you prefer?'

'Ohh, I reckon Elvis Presley movies are all right.'

'Elvis Presley? Unreal, Paula, I'm impressed. Do you watch much TV?'

Paula shook her head. 'No. But I like "Star Trek".'

' "Star Trek"?'

'Yeah, I always watch "Star Trek". It's me favourite show.'

'You're a trekkie, Paula?'

'Bloody oath!'

'So am I.'

'You? Bullshit!'

'Hey, Paula.' Les made the Vulcan salute. 'Live long and prosper, baby. I went to the convention at Darling Harbour.'

'Onya, Les.'

'Who do you reckon's the coolest dude in Star Fleet Command, Paula?'

'Ohh, DATA. No risk. He's just one big groove.'

'Right on, Paula. Good one, mate.'

'Tell me, Les. Who do you reckon are the lowest dropkicks in the galaxy? The Borg? Or the Kadasians in those 1950s zoot suits with the big shoulder pads?'

'Ohh, no contest,' said Les, making a definitive gesture. 'The Kadasians. They're two-faced, lying bastards. I watched them playing poker with Captain Picard and Lieutenant Worf once and they never stopped cheating all night. And this was on the Holodeck with Dr Crusher bringing them drinks and nibblies. The swines.'

'Beauty, Les,' said Paula. 'I knew there was something good about you.'

'Thanks, Counsellor Troi. I knew you'd pick up my vibe sooner or later.'

Well, there you go, thought Norton. You shouldn't go judging people by appearances. Paula's a trekkie. There's generally some good in all of us. Suddenly Paula seemed to take on a whole new demeanour; her face got prettier, her mini-dress got shorter, her legs got more shapely and the black stockings got blacker. Just as suddenly, Paula got up and sat down on the lounge next to Les.

'You know, Les,' she said, 'I was thinking of going to a fancy dress party once dressed as Counsellor Troi.'

With those maracas you'd sure take out the door prize if they had one, thought Norton. 'Yeah, you'd look a bit like Counsellor Troi if you put some pig-tails in your hair. It's certainly black and shiny enough.'

'Thanks, Les.' Paula took a good sip of Bacardi. 'What about you, Les? If you had to go to a party dressed as someone out of "Star Trek", who would you go as?'

'Me? Well, Paula, being an urbane, debonair, cool sort of swinger, I'd paint my face off-white and go as DATA. Me and DATA are like peas in a pod. Birds of a feather.'

Paula pointed to Norton's face. 'What about the broken nose?'

'If anyone asked, I'd say he got it trying to put his hand up Counsellor Troi's dress.'

'Ooh! Dirty little DATA.'

'What do you reckon'd happen, Paula, if DATA tried to put his dirty android hand on Counsellor Troi's old ring of Saturn, do you reckon he'd get his nose broken?'

Paula smiled and shook her head. 'No, I don't reckon he would.'

222

'Yeah, good old DATA,' Les smiled back. 'You can't help but like him, can you?'

That'll do me, thought Norton. He reached over and put his right arm around Paula's waist. She moved into him and Les took her in a passionate Vulcan embrace, and after giving her a long, lingering kiss was now seriously thinking of doing all sorts of dirty Vulcan things with her. Paula's mouth was warm, moist and sweet and in no time her tongue was out and they were nibbling away at each other's lips. Les started kissing Paula's ears and neck and Paula started doing much the same to Norton. Les undid the front of her shirt, slipped his hand under her white bra strap then eased one massive boob out and started kissing it and licking and sucking the nipple till it swelled up and stuck out like a big, ripe purple grape. Paula started to undo Norton's shirt and stick her fingers beneath his belt as Les slipped her other boob out and started kissing that one too. For her size Paula was in pretty good shape. She wasn't fat at all. Just big. A big, old healthy girl. Les ran his hand up under Paula's dress between her legs and gave her ted a few gentle strokes. Paula spread her legs slightly and Les could feel it start to swell and get moist.

'What do you reckon, Counsellor Troi?' panted Les. 'Here? The holodeck? Or shall I patch through to transporter room two and get us beamed into my bedroom?'

'I reckon your bedroom, captain.'

Norton tapped his fingers on his chest. 'Picard to Enterprise. Two to beam up.'

Les steered Paula towards his bedroom where they

started peeling off their clothes. Norton was as keen as mustard now and so was Mr Wobbly; especially when Paula got down to her black stockings and a pair of skimpy blue knickers with little white stripes across them that sat over her bush and spread across her hips just nicely. She was out of them about the same time Les was out of his, then he placed his hands on her shoulders and they fell back on the bed.

Les kissed Paula on the lips and face, nibbled her neck and rubbed her boobs. Paula slipped her tongue into Norton's ear and took hold of his dick and gently squeezed it. Les pushed her boobs together and started sliding his dick in between them, even sliding it a bit too far and it slipped into Paula's mouth. But she didn't mind in the least and gave the knob a delightfully wet polish that almost sent Norton cross-eyed. He kissed her again, then stroked her clit for a while till he decided that was enough buggerising on the holodeck. It was time to go into warp drive. He eased Paula's legs apart, got between her and slipped Mr Wobbly's evil little head in first, then the rest. Paula was a big solid girl and so was her ted. But it was warm and snug and after a few shoves Les slipped into top gear. Paula didn't buck around or scream out to the world what a great time she was having, but by the smile on her face and the way she kept running her tongue over her lips, Les had an idea she was more than enjoying herself. So was Les. Before long it started to get too enjoyable. Les began pumping away faster and Paula's tongue started flicking faster around from one side of her mouth to the other. Les pushed her knees up and arched his back, Paula pushed up and wiggled her backside around, Les jammed his eyes shut, heard a roaring in his ears, then with a shuddering moan emptied out.

Les flopped down on the bed alongside Paula and put his arm under her head. As well as being a trekkie, Paula was good fun in the sack and Les was keen to see her again before he left if she felt the same way. Les also knew the others would be playing games till all hours yet, so he was keen to see if Paula wanted to go another round or two before she beamed out. Norton was about to get a towel from the bathroom, get cleaned up a bit, then start up some small talk when he heard all this commotion and banging coming from the kitchen and noticed light from the hallway shining beneath the bedroom door. Next thing there was a rapid banging on the bedroom door.

'Paula, are you in there?' It was Megan. Her voice was very shrill and she didn't sound at all happy. 'Paula, how do you open this bloody thing?' The door knob rattled violently, then the door burst open and Les could make out Megan framed in the half light from the hallway. 'Paula, get out here in the kitchen and bloody be quick about it.' Megan left the door ajar and stomped off down the hallway.

'Bloody hell!' exclaimed Les. 'What was that all about?'

'Ohh, I don't know,' said Paula, 'but I reckon I better have a look.'

Paula strapped herself into her bra, got her clothes on somehow, then disappeared out the door. Les waited till he got himself together a bit then climbed into his tracksuit pants and a T-shirt and walked out to the kitchen. The light was on and Paula was standing next to the refrigerator looking noticeably ashen-faced. Megan was standing next to the sink looking awful. Her clothes and hair were a mess, one eye was closing and turning black and she was dabbing a hankie against a fat lip that was trickling blood.

'Shit! What's going on?' asked Les.

'Jimmy just bashed Megan up,' said Paula, 'and she's rung a taxi. We're going home.'

'What?' Les couldn't believe what he was hearing. But he could believe the look on Megan's face. Unlike in the restaurant, where it was all sweetness and light, now it was a mask of pure, black hatred.

'Your bloody little mate did this,' she almost spat. 'Beat me up for no reason at all.'

'He what? Jimmy? I don't believe it.'

'How do you think I got this? Walking into a bloody door? The rotten little bastard. I knew he was no good.'

Les looked at her and felt quite uneasy in the pit of his stomach. 'Shit! I'm sorry, Megan. I mean, I don't know what to say. I just can't believe it. You were both getting on famously the last time I saw you.'

'Yeah, well, you can believe this. I'm getting some photos taken tomorrow when this colour's right up, then I'm going to the police. See how tough your friend Jimmy is when I have him charged with assault. And a few other things too.' Megan cast her eye around the house. 'Nice home he's got here. And I know plenty of nice cops.'

Les stared at her, trying not to believe what he was hearing. 'Are you fair dinkum, Megan?'

'What?' She turned to Paula. 'You saw this, Paula.

226

You know what happened. You too, Les. You saw it. You're both witnesses.'

Paula looked at Les. 'Ohh, I reckon I'm with her, Les.'

Norton looked back at her. 'Yeah, I reckoned you might have been.'

Les didn't for the life of him know what to do. Whether to lend assistance, try to calm Megan down, offer her a Panadol. He wasn't quite in a panic, but this was pretty heavy shit. Megan had definitely been punched in the face. Besides wondering what to do, Les was also wondering where Jimmy was. Norton's questions were answered by the tooting of a horn outside.

'Ohh, I reckon that'll be the taxi,' said Paula.

'Good. Let's get out of here.' Megan dabbed at her lip again and already her black eye seemed to be getting worse. 'Well, come on, Paula. Are you coming?'

Norton made a helpless gesture with his hands. 'Well, goodnight Paula. Shit! I'm sorry about this. I was hoping I might have seen you again.'

'Don't worry, Les,' hissed Megan, 'you'll be seeing her again all right. In court.'

'Goodnight, Les.'

'Yeah, Paula. Goodnight. Goodnight . . .'

Before Les could say Megan, she'd stormed off down the hallway with Paula in tow, slammed the front door behind her and taken off in the taxi, leaving Norton in the kitchen still wondering what was going on and wondering what he was going to do. About the only thing he could do for the moment was have a glass of cold orange juice. Les poured himself one and was about to put the container back in the fridge when he heard a voice near the kitchen door.

'Don't put it away. I'll have one, too.' It was Jimmy, standing behind him in a pair of shorts and a T-shirt. He took the container from Les, poured himself a glass of orange juice and drank nearly half. 'That crazy fuckin' aunty gone?' he said.

'Yeah,' nodded Les. 'She just left in a taxi with Paula.'

'Good.'

'Jimmy, what the fuck's going on? You should have heard what she said before she left. Mate, it wasn't real good.'

'I half-heard her going on about something. I was having a leak.'

Les told Jimmy about Megan raving away in the kitchen and how Paula was backing her up. 'Jimmy, she's going to the cops. If she does, you're in deep shit. Have you see her face?'

'Ahh, fuck her. The silly old moll.' Jimmy drank the rest of his orange juice and refilled his glass.

Norton couldn't quite believe Jimmy's indifferent attitude. But there's always two sides to a story. 'So what happened anyway?'

'She said, "Hit me". So I did.'

'Hit her?'

'Yeah. She's fuckin' mad. She went off her head and got me to do all these weird things with her. Then she asked me to hit her. So I belted her one.'

Les gave Jimmy a double blink. He knew Megan was a little kinky and liked a bit of the bizarre. But Jimmy had completely blown it. 'She probably meant she just wanted a bit of a slap and tickle.'

'Yeah, well I gave her what you gave that bouncer

outside the disco. A left hook, a right uppercut, then another left over the top. And down she went like a bag of shit. She got up all right, but I was too busy lying on the bed laughing.'

Norton slapped his forehead. 'Jimmy, you idiot. You don't hit women.'

'Ahh, who gives a fuck? It'll do her good anyway, the dopey old bat. I'm only sorry I didn't kick her in the ribs.'

Norton shook his head. 'I don't know what to say, Jimmy. I honestly don't know what to say.'

Jimmy raised his orange juice. 'How about "good-night"? I'm knackered and I want to go to bed. I'll see you in the morning.' Jimmy got to the doorway and stopped. 'If I'm not up, will you give us a yell about nine or ten.'

'Yeah, righto.'

'And don't worry about it, Les. It's nothing. Remember, we got a good day on tomorrow.'

'Yeah, terrific. See you in the morning.'

Les finished his orange juice, turned off all the lights, then went back to his room. He stripped off and got under the shower, still not quite believing what had happened. Although he tried to enjoy the nice warm water and soap suds, it was no good. It *had* happened all right and Jimmy was in bad trouble. Even if it was only half his fault, Megan had him bang to rights, and that wasn't even taking into account that Jimmy was already a prisoner out on some sort of leave. Jimmy was up shit creek without a paddle and there was every chance Norton was going to be involved too. Then there was the small matter of a box of machine guns sitting in the boot of the car. It didn't seem to get much better after Les dried off, put on a clean T-shirt and got into bed. Apart from the food and the weather, Norton's holiday in Terrigal was turning into a disaster. In the meantime, though, Megan wouldn't get the photos till her face coloured right up and by the time she got the photos round to the cops and they got their shit together, it'd be late Sunday or early Monday before they'd be banging on the door. Whatever— Norton's holiday was going to be cut short. Very short. For the time being, though, about the only thing Les could do was try and get a good night's sleep. It had been a long and winding day, with not a bad root thrown in at the end.

The following morning Les was up and had his act
together by around eight-thirty. Outside it had clouded
over a little and what wind there was appeared to have
swung round to the north-east. He wasn't feeling all
that hungry as he stood in the kitchen sipping a glass
of orange juice, so rather than have breakfast down the
beach Les decided to get the papers, have something
light at home and watch the 'Sunday' programme on
Channel Nine. Norton zapped down to Terrigal, double-
parked outside the newsagency and was back in the
loungeroom with a cup of coffee and some toast
watching Jim Waley right on nine o'clock. The feature
story was something about the IRA; Les half watched
'Sunday', half read the Sunday papers and mainly
thought things out and planned his next move.

Thanks to Jimmy being a complete little smartarse,
running round with guns and belting women, life on
the beautiful Central Coast had suddenly become
extremely tropical. And Les was more than a bit dirty
because he was starting to enjoy himself. The food was
sensational and some of the girls weren't too bad

either. But the wallopers would be around shortly and as well as Megan and the boot full of machine guns, there was a chance Norton could get pulled in for assaulting those two bouncers, along with the girl, and possibly that mug down the beach with the dog as well. So it was time to split—and the sooner the better. But there was no need to go racing out the door now, thought Les, and let Jimmy think he'd shit himself. No, I'll stick around and act like nothing's happened, let Jimmy think he's Joe Cool. I'll even go and see this band and check out all the old motorbikes with him. That sounds like fun and I want to enjoy my last day up here in Terrigal. Besides, driving into Bondi during the daytime on Sunday is like hell with neverending traffic lights. We should be back by seven or so. That's when I'll depart and miss all the traffic. And as I'm going tell little shitbags exactly what I think of him. See you, mate. You won't be needing this food in the fridge or the booze either. And if you're not back in the nick before Wednesday I'm sure the limo can run you up to the gate, you little prick. I should be back home by around eight-thirty, nine at the latest. I won't tell Price or anyone I'm back. Just go straight home, put my feet up and watch TV. Hello, Warren, nice to see you. Did you miss me? Then after I've filled Price in on what's been happening and told George exactly what I think of his nephew, I'll continue my holiday somewhere else. How about down the South Coast, where I wanted to go in the first place?

Feeling a lot happier now that he knew exactly what he was doing, Norton continued to half read the papers and half watch TV. He finished his coffee and toast and somehow felt that had sharpened his appetite as well. Les was about to go back to the kitchen and organise some more food when Jimmy came up the stairs into the loungeroom, wearing his tracksuit pants and a blue T-shirt.

'G'day, Jimmy,' said Les brightly. 'How are you feeling, mate?'

'Not bad, Les. How's yourself?' Jimmy sounded a little surprised or vague even, as if instead of being all bright and cheery he was expecting Les to have a full-on case of the shits with him.

'Pretty good. There's some fresh coffee in the kitchen. I've been down and got the papers if you want to have a look.' Les kept his eye on the TV while he spoke to Jimmy as if he was concentrating on what was on.

'Yeah, righto.' Jimmy went to the kitchen, came back with a cup of coffee and sat down in one of the loungechairs. 'What's this all about?'

'The IRA and Sinn Fein.'

'Any good?'

'There's plenty of bombs going off.'

They watched the last of 'Sunday' more or less in silence. It ended with a guitarist, then some ads, and Les switched the TV off.

'So what's doing today, Jimmy?' he asked.

'You feeling hungry?'

'Jimmy . . .'

'Yeah, I know, Les, you're always hungry. How would you like lunch down the Galleon?'

'Where's that?'

'Right in Terrigal Haven.'

'Sounds pretty good to me. How're we getting there? You want me to drive?'

'It's not too bad a day outside—I wouldn't mind walking. It's only about fifteen minutes.'

'Righto. I don't mind a bit of exercise.'

'Then about four o'clock we'll get the limo and go over and see the band.'

'Okay. What time do you think we'll be back?'

'Oh, about six. Seven at the latest.'

'Unreal. I like to watch "Sixty Minutes" on Sunday night if I get the chance.'

Jimmy took a couple of sips of coffee and studied Norton over his cup. 'You're in a good mood today, Les.'

Les had started to half glance at the papers again. He looked back up. 'What do you mean, Jimmy?'

'I mean, after last night. You were blowing up the last time I saw you.'

'That?' Les made a dismissive gesture with one hand. 'Forget about it. I thought things over and I reckon that old scrubber's full of shit.'

'That's what I reckon. Fuck her.'

'What's she going to do anyway?' said Les. 'She was pissed and fell down the stairs. It's only her word against yours. And Paula's. Paula didn't see you hit her. I didn't see you hit her. You did hit her, didn't you, Jimmy?'

Jimmy looked shocked. 'Me? No way, man. If anything I was trying to help her up when she fell down drunk.'

'Exactly. You try to do the right thing and some old bitch wants to shaft you.'

234

'Right on, baby.' Jimmy started laughing then settled down and took another sip of coffee while Les continued to scan the paper. 'Hey, Les, you're cool, you know that.'

Les tossed Jimmy a wink and a nod. 'Let's just say, there's worse blokes round than me, Jimmy.'

'Is there what.'

'So what time do you want to head down to this restaurant?'

'Say, about twelve or so. I wouldn't mind having a swim first.'

'Righto. I'll finish reading the papers, then I'll see you—' Les pointed an index finger towards the kitchen, '—back in the office.'

Jimmy finished his coffee, then took his cup out and rinsed it in the sink. Before he went down to his room he stopped at the top of the stairs. 'Hey, Les, how did you go with Paula last night? Did you get into her pants?'

Norton smiled and shook his head. 'Nearly. I was almost there when your girlfriend started banging on the door and stuffed things up. The drunken, rotten moll.'

Jimmy nodded knowingly. 'Right. So that's why you had the shits last night.'

'Well, wouldn't you?'

Jimmy looked at Norton for a moment. 'Over Paula? No.'

Jimmy disappeared down the stairs. Les finished reading the papers, watched him in the pool for a moment or two, then went to his room and started packing his clothes.

There wasn't that much so Les took his time, putting it away neatly so he wouldn't have to iron it again when he got home. He made his bed and gave the room a tidy, then when he was satisfied everything was okay, changed into a pair of jeans and an old white Eumundi Lager T-shirt to wear down to the restaurant. He left his Jamaican T-shirt on the bed to wear over to the hotel along with a light denim shirt to throw over the top. What would he tell Jimmy as he was leaving? How about 'goodbye'? And maybe a toe right up the arse for involving Les in his rotten little scam and a blistering earful of what he could do with his rotten fuckin' machine guns. Les placed his bags by the end of the bed and walked out to the kitchen. Jimmy came in a few minutes later wearing his white tracksuit and Fila trainers.

'You right, Les?' he said.

'Yeah,' replied Les, rubbing his hands together. 'Let's go.'

There was the usual Sunday traffic cruising around, but the walk down was pleasant enough. Jimmy wasn't saying much. He seemed to be thinking about something and taking everything in around him while he skipped along with this cocksure attitude like Brer Rabbit in the briar patch again. Norton left him to himself and let him lead the way. They went past the Silver Conche on the opposite side of the road; Jimmy made some remark about how even though Megan finished with a black eye she still had a better time than being stuck with the two suits from Adelaide. Les laughed like it was one of the funniest things he'd ever heard. See how funny you think it is, you little smarty, when they give you another year, he laughed to himself. They ran out of footpath just past the North Avoca turn-off and crossed the road. On the left was a bowl-shaped valley full of houses and on the right a scrubby rise running along the cliff tops shielded the road from the ocean and the rocks below. They passed a huge house with gables and turrets that looked like it belonged to the Addams Family, then crossed over a bit further on at the turn-off into the Haven.

Les had only glimpsed the Haven going past and didn't realise how big an area it was. A football oval sat in the middle, surrounded by rolling parkland and bush that ran up to the cliffs. On the left was a beach and bay full of boats, pelicans and catamarans, to the right a steep, green rise that Jimmy said was The Skillion towered up over the ocean and further on more scrubby, rugged headlands led round to North Avoca. Cars came and went towing fishing boats or jet-skis, people were kicking balls around the oval, others were either walking about or seated at the picnic tables where a Mr Whippy van was doing brisk business. The Galleon and its surrounding wooden balcony was built over the beach with a dive shop and catamaran club beneath. Les followed Jimmy down some stairs to a carpark and inside the glass doors of the restaurant. At the top of a short set of steps was a wooden counter with a jar of shells sitting on it.

The restaurant was quite spacious and being Sunday lunchtime it was almost full. There was one dining room as you walked in, then another with a line of chairs and tables placed along the balcony overlooking the ocean. The place had a warm, timbered feel about it that welcomed you as you entered. There were indoor plants hanging from the beams and ceiling, paintings and prints mounted on the walls and a number of rope pulleys, old ship pump handles and tiny wooden keels here and there which gave the restaurant a distinctive, nautical ambience. A fair-haired, boyish-faced man in glasses wearing a blue shirt smiled at them from behind the jar of sea shells as they walked in.

'Hello, Jimmy,' he said. 'How's things?'

'Pretty good, Len,' answered Jimmy. 'What about yourself?'

'Busy, but I got a nice one for you,' he added with a wink.

The man led them over to a table on the balcony right above the water. There was a beautiful view across the ocean, a light breeze whispered across the tables and below them Les could hear the gentle, soothing swish of tiny waves lapping against the sand.

'Well, what do you think?' said Jimmy.

'What can I say, Jimmy?' replied Les. 'You've done it again—I'm impressed. If the food's half as good as the view, we're laughing.'

'Have I let you down yet?'

'Not a chance.'

'It's BYO, but I don't feel like drinking much at the moment. And it shouldn't worry you.'

Norton shook his head. 'In fact I'm not having much this afternoon either. I might wait till we get back and have a few watching TV.' You wouldn't like to see me get pinched for drink-driving on my way back to Sydney, would you, Jimmy? thought Les.

'Please yourself.'

A waitress in a blue dress and a white Galleon polo shirt left them with a menu. When she came back, Les had decided to go for the oysters grilled with Thai coconut curry and a Tilo Steak with green peppercorns and garlic gratin potatoes. Jimmy decided on Veal Sweetbreads sautéed in bacon, mushrooms, onion and garlic, and Crispy Skin Honey Sesame Duck with orange and mango compote. For dessert they both chose baked peach cheesecake with chantilly cream all washed down with mineral water, ice and slice, followed by two flat whites. Again the food, the service and the atmosphere were sensational and again Norton didn't leave a great deal on any of the plates. Bad luck this was going to be the last supper because there were probably more restaurants around Terrigal worth sampling. Maybe next time.

'Well, how was that, Les?' asked Jimmy over his cup of coffee.

'Like I said before, Jimmy,' replied Les. 'You've done it again. Fan-fuckin'-tastic.'

'Yeah, not bad. Not bad at all.' Jimmy eased back in his chair, adjusted his sunglasses, then looked around him like he owned the place.

Norton watched him over his coffee for a moment. 'So you got bunged up over some dodgy outboards, eh, Jimmy?'

'Yeah,' replied Jimmy. 'I was a bit stiff.'

'A mover and shaker like you, I'm surprised you couldn't have done a bit of business there.'

'Not on that particular occasion, I couldn't,' said Jimmy. 'Not that you can't up here. Christ! If ever

239

ICAC go through this joint, it'll make Kings Cross look like tea and cakes at Government House.'

'Yeah,' smiled Les, 'I saw one of your local wallopers on TV the other week. Or glimpses of him on video. He was in a brothel getting his bat sucked, snorting coke, watching a porno movie while he tried to buy some ecstasy for his mates. I was talking about it with some cops in Sydney and even they were laughing.'

'The go up here, Les, is to get on the board of some registered club as a director, then wash all the drug money through the club. It's their favourite rort. All ICAC's got to do is find out which cops are directors of clubs up here and go through all their bank statements with a computer. There'd be bent cops going everywhere. I'd love to see it.'

'The way things are going, Jimmy, you probably will.'

'Yeah. So what's Jamaica like again?' said Jimmy, changing the subject.

'Jamaica? All up, Jimmy, I don't think you'd like it very much. Even being an abo.'

Les related a few more things to Jimmy about his time in Montego Bay. He even added a bit about Florida. Jimmy appeared interested and seemed to get a laugh here and there. But when Les told him about Hank and all his guns Jimmy's ears pricked up and he started asking questions about the type, the calibre and the ammunition. Les didn't need any more proof that Jimmy was interested in guns and ammo. On one hand Les was enjoying himself, sitting back amongst the beautiful surroundings telling Jimmy yarns about overseas. On the other hand it seemed somewhat hypo-critical, being sugar sweet and lulling Jimmy into a false sense of security when he was going to give him a good gobful later on and a crisp backhander for being a fuckin' little smartarse. Jimmy would probably think Norton was schizophrenic. Then again, knowing Jimmy, he'd probably take no notice at all, tell Les to get fucked himself and brush it off with his usual sar-donic insouciance. Even now when he was talking, Les felt that though Jimmy was looking at him he was thinking of something else half the time, probably playing him for a mug. A word or two with Jimmy's fat uncle when Les got back to Sydney would definitely be on the cards.

Before long the afternoon had started to slip away and most of the other diners had drifted out of the restaurant. Jimmy looked at his watch and mentioned it to Les. Les paid the bill, left a hefty tip, seeing every-thing was so nice, and they started walking back home the way they came.

Again Norton fell behind and let Jimmy set the pace; Jimmy was stepping along quite smartly and after such a big meal the walk felt good and Les was enjoying it. Nothing much was said. Jimmy seemed to be thinking and was looking around at the trees, the sky, the houses, taking it all in. Now and again Jimmy would turn around, look at Les for a moment as if maybe he was going to say something, then turn away again and keep walking. Les could only guess what was on Jimmy's mind. As they walked past the doors of the Silver Conche Les was expecting Jimmy to make another remark about Megan. But this time he kept quiet. Les was half thinking of being smart himself and speciously suggesting they come there for dinner one night before the holiday ended; then thought why bother? Next thing they were back inside the house.

'I'm going to get changed and sort a few things out,' said Jimmy, glancing at this watch. 'I'll see you at four.'

'Righto,' answered Les.

'What are you going to do?'

'What am I going to do?' The way Jimmy spoke, Norton began to feel as if he was giving him orders or looking down on him. What fuckin' business is it of yours what I do, you little prick, Les thought. 'I might lie on the bed and read my book for a while.'

Jimmy nodded and gave Les a look of grudging approval. 'Yeah, I've done that before today,' he said, then turned and walked down the stairs.

Les went to his bedroom and wondered what he should do. Why not do what he just said? Read his book. After all that food, he'd sink if he had a swim and Sunday afternoon TV is generally *très ordinaire*. Les propped some pillows up at the end of the bed, opened *The Hand that Signed the Paper* and started reading. After twenty or so pages of Stangl, the herr kommandant, organising the killings while Vitaly porked Magda Juskowiak in the hay loft, it was time to make a move. Les placed the book back in his bag, put his shirt on, straightened the bed and went out to the kitchen. Jimmy was standing near the sink sipping a glass of water in his sunglasses. But instead of his usual sartorial elegance, he was wearing black jeans, black Reeboks and a dark green army jacket with angled pockets on the front. At his feet was his overnight bag; it looked full and sticking out one end was the handle of the stockwhip. For a moment Les flashed onto some movie he'd seen on TV lately.

'You know who you remind me of, dressed like that, Jimmy?' he said, half having a little dig at Jimmy about his clothes.

'No. Who?'

'Michael Douglas in *Falling Down*.'

'Yeah? Well, I haven't seen the movie,' he replied, not sounding very interested. 'I've got to see a couple of blokes while I'm over there. Just some business, that's all.' Jimmy took a mouthful of water. He was talking softly, yet he seemed agitated or nervous. Les couldn't see his eyes behind the sunglasses, but he almost looked like he was speeding.

'Whatever.' Les shrugged and before he could say anything else there was a polite knock on the door.

'Righto,' said Jimmy, picking up his overnight bag, 'Let's go to the bike show and see the band.'

'Sounds good to me.'

They walked outside, Jimmy said something to the limo driver and they got in the back.

Not used to being driven around much during the daytime and especially in a nice, comfortable limousine, Les sat back and enjoyed it. Next to him Jimmy still seemed on edge, tapping his foot on the floor, fiddling at his bag sitting on his lap while he stared straight ahead working his jaw muscles. Les watched him out the side of his eye and tried to suss him out. He was going over to this hotel for two reasons besides the band and the old bikes. The stockwhip was just for some friend or whatever, but he also had to see some bikie or bikies about unloading the machine guns and you could bet they'd be as nutty as fruitcakes and a bit unpredictable. So naturally he was nervous. They were just as likely to shoot him and just take the things. Maybe that's why he brought Les along. To look like he had a backup of some description. It was doubtful the swap would be that afternoon. They'd come back in the limo and it would be later that night, when it was quite dark. The bikies would get a surprise when they came round and found Jimmy in the kitchen mopping blood from his face for a change and his red-haired backup nowhere in sight. Les might even piss the fuckin' machine guns off. Price didn't need that sort of shit going down in his house. As for Jimmy's outfit, you could bet the punters at the hotel would be pretty much pie and peas, and getting around looking like a Stuart Membery model, Jimmy would stick out like the proverbial dog's knackers. Yes, mused Norton, these evil webs of deception we weave. Where do they get us? All webbed up and no place to go. He looked at Jimmy and smiled. It was a bit of a buzz watching young master James squirming around, trying to act cool and all the time Les knowing exactly what the little shit was up to.

They cruised along in spacious, air-conditioned silence. Les watched the trees and valleys go past and picked out a couple of places he remembered from when he first got to Terrigal; like a fruit stall on the side of the road and the turn-off to where he and Jimmy went linedancing. Next thing they turned right at a roundabout and Les thought he recognised the corner with the little church on it that they visited when he drove Jimmy down from the gaol. Jimmy had mentioned where they were going, but not being familiar with the area Les had forgotten it was on the way. The limo pulled over in the driveway.

'I won't be long.' Jimmy took his bag and got out as the driver opened the door.

'Take your time,' said Les, not feeling he was invited along this time. 'I'll wait here.'

Les watched Jimmy go through the gate and mellowed out a little towards him. Yes, mused Norton, it's only natural that he'd want to visit his mother's grave. It's on the way and it is Sunday. And I suppose you can't really blame him for a life of crime; he does come from a broken family. That's why I won't break his rotten little neck.

About twenty minutes later Jimmy returned and got back in the limo.

'How are you feeling now, mate?' said Les. 'Everything okay?'

Even from behind his dark glasses, Jimmy's infectious smile seemed to almost light up the back of the car. 'Everything's fine, Les,' he said. 'Everything's just great.'

'That's good, Jimmy.'

Jimmy's smile seemed to radiate a little more. 'In fact, I think it's going to be a fantastic day, Les. I really do.'

'Like I said, Jimmy, that's good. I'm glad.'

The limo eased back in amongst the Sunday afternoon traffic and a few minutes later the driver turned

245

left at another roundabout near a McDonald's and a KFC and they were there.

The hotel was on the right-hand side of a short, sealed road that was all bush and trees on the left before it turned into dirt and disappeared into more bush and trees about two hundred metres or so down the end. It was a single-storey building with a well-kept median strip out the front and two tarred parking areas split in the middle by a driveway that led to an outdoor bottle shop. At the end towards the bush was an Asian restaurant called the China Doll and next to a tree near the median strip was a sign saying Broadwater Hotel Resort. The limo pulled up just before the bottle shop. Les and Jimmy got out, then the driver headed back towards the roundabout. Both parking areas were full of cars with the odd motorbike here and there and a few people walking around who gave them a glance or two as they got out. A short set of steps ran up past the bottle shop into a tiled courtyard with a bistro lounge on the left, an enclosed area full of video machines and a couple of bars on the right. The courtyard was nicely laid out with trees and plants, a barbecue in the middle and palm trees at the far end. Quite a few people were seated or standing around a smattering of white plastic chairs or tables and a flash of chrome amongst some people milling around beyond the palm trees at the end suggested to Les that this was where all the vintage motorbikes were. More people were coming out of the bars on the right carrying drinks and Les was about to say something when Jimmy hoisted his bag over his shoulder and nodded towards the bistro lounge. Les followed him across.

A row of glass windows and doors covered with posters advertising coming bands ran down the side. There was one for Zipper Mushrooms that day from three till six which meant they'd missed the first bracket. Inside it was bright and roomy with a high, white angled ceiling, a colonial brick bistro on the left doing a brisk trade as you entered and on the opposite side a long, wooden bar with brass poles supporting a wooden canopy full of indoor plants and signs for Millers Draught, Big Red and Crown Lager. Behind the bar was a long open verandah and beyond that a large, grassy area that led to a wide bay that Les guessed was the Broadwater. A smattering of chairs, tables and stools led to a dance floor and a low stage at the end with stage lights on scaffolding above and a thick, black curtain for a backdrop. Sitting on the stage were the band's instruments and some kind of rock music was playing softly through the speakers. The hotel in general was bright, clean and modern and looked like quite a pleasant venue to have a drink, a meal or whatever. And as Les had predicted earlier, the punters were dressed pretty casual, mainly jeans, shorts and surfing T-shirts. Some girls wore denim skirts or cotton dresses, but mainly dressed the same as the men. Jimmy appeared to be searching the faces, nodding a hello here and there and getting a hello nodded back in reply. Norton thought he might as well have a beer or two while they were there.

'You want a drink, Jimmy?' he asked.

Jimmy nodded. 'Yeah, get us a delicious, will you.'

The bar was three deep, but it didn't take long and Les was back with a Tooheys long neck and a Jack Daniels and Coke.

'Why don't we go outside and have a look at the old bikes?' said Jimmy, taking a sip of his drink. 'The band doesn't start for a while yet.'

'Good idea.' Les followed Jimmy back into the courtyard and out the end past the palm trees.

Outside was a large, grassy area that led down to the water's edge. A wall of pine logs faced the courtyard and behind that was a tennis court surrounded by trees. Solid wooden tables and benches were spread around another covered barbecue near a pine-log cubbyhouse for the kids to play in and near the log wall was a row of coloured, plastic slippery-dips. People were wandering around everywhere, pennants fluttered in the breeze and a sign above the barbecue saying 'Welcome to the Broadwater Classic Motorbike Rally' added to a carnival atmosphere. Spread around the place were scores of vintage motorbikes and tables surrounded by people selling or swapping parts. Les took a sip of his beer and was about to start looking over the vintage motorcycles, when Jimmy stopped a tall, fair-haired bloke walking past.

'Hey, Stu, have you seen Ian Stanley?'

'Oh, g'day, Jimmy. No, I haven't seen him,' said the bloke.

'Okay. Thanks anyway.' The bloke continued on his way and Jimmy turned to Les. 'Come on, let's go and check out the old bikes.'

They wandered about the mums and dads and kids with their faces painted, checking out the old motorbikes. Norton was impressed—they were absolute classics, beautifully cared for, the paint and chrome sparkling in the balmy, afternoon sun. BSA. Goldstars.

AJSs. Vincents, Indians, old Harley-Davidsons, a 1928 American Excelsior, Vincent Rapides, Triumph Bonnevilles, Matchless G80s, Ariel 500s. There was even a 1927 Cleveland 4. Name a classic bike and it was there looking like it had just come out of the showroom. The owners were just normal people, and it was like Jimmy said, just because you own a powerful bike, you're not necessarily some nutty gang member. Les wandered around taking it all in and thinking about his brother, Murray. He had a couple of old motorbikes and although Les wasn't that mad about them, he used to help Murray with them and take one out for a burble around Dirranbandi now and again. In the course of their wanderings Jimmy would stop and ask people the same question and always get the same answer; they'd shake their head.

'Your contact not here, James?' asked Les, a little derisively.

'No, it doesn't look like it.' Jimmy took another look around, then added quietly, 'I'm not really surprised.'

'What was that?' said Les.

Jimmy shook his head. 'Nothing.' Then looked at his watch. 'Come on, let's go and see the band.'

The bistro lounge was quite crowded by now. Les got another two drinks and they found a spot towards the front where the bar angled off towards the verandah. The music coming out of the speakers stopped and the band got on stage behind their instruments. They looked pretty much your average five-piece band in T-shirts and jeans, except for the singer and the bloke on the keyboards. He was tall and gangly with glasses and black hair and looked like Quentin Tarantino. The singer was just as tall, very surfy, very good-looking, with red hair and a perfect white smile almost as good as Jimmy's. He was wearing a black T-shirt with WEB across a spider web on the front and squinting across the room Les managed to make out Wamberal Express Boardriders. The singer flashed his smile, said a few words to some friends in the audience then the band ripped into a howling version of Counting Crows' 'Mr Jones' and in about two chords the dance floor was almost full of young girls drooling over the singer. The band blitzed that, did a song of their own, then ripped into a hot version of Billy Idol's 'White Wedding'. The band was tight and hot, the singer had a crisp, clear voice that held the notes perfectly and a stage presence all his own. He'd bop across the stage, then do a few rap moves, then bend his knees, put his arms out and surf the music. There were some little kids dancing down the front of the stage. The singer jumped down and started singing to them and dancing with them and the kids loved him along with the crowd. He jumped back on stage and the band cut into The Rolling Stones' 'Mean Disposition' and Norton could have sworn it was Charlie Watts on the drums and the singer was Jimmy Morrison, Mick Jagger and Jesus all rolled into one. They did a couple more of their own then ripped into Confederate Railroad's 'Bill's Honky Tonk Bar and Grill', followed by Gina Jeffreys' 'Girls Night Out' which sent the girls in the audience just about crazy. Next thing the dance floor was honky tonk pickin', linedance kickin' and Norton left Jimmy holding his bag and joined in.

Whatever the band did they could do no wrong and,

like everybody else in the hotel, Les was having the time of his life. He got off the dance floor as the singer handed the mike to the Quentin Tarantino lookalike on keyboards and said, 'Righto, everyone, let's hear it for Gritty.'

Everybody applauded, Les got another two drinks and Gritty cut into a howling, chord-thumping version of AC/DC's 'Gaol Break', jumping all over the stage and rolling around on the dance floor like a man possessed. Les wondered how he was going to top this when Gritty got hold of a tambourine, the singer jumped behind the keyboards and they tore into Sleepy La Beef's 'Standing in the Need of Prayer', complete with the banging tambourine and honky-tonk, pumping piano just like a holy rolling, happy clapping, revivalist meeting. Norton waved his hands in the air, stomped his feet and couldn't ever remember seeing anything like it. They did another two songs of their own, then finished with Hoodoo Gurus' 'Like Wow, Wipeout' and left to thunderous applause. A moment or two later music came through the speakers again and the punters resumed drinking and talking.

'Well, what did you think of the Mushies, Les?' said Jimmy.

'Fuckin' unreal,' said Norton. 'What about Quentin Tarantino on the keyboards?'

'Gritty? He's something else, isn't he?'

'Reckon.' Les looked around and wiped his eyes. 'Shit. They don't mind a cigarette in here, do they?'

'Yeah, it's punishing all right. You want to go outside for a while?'

'Good idea,' nodded Les, and followed Jimmy out to the courtyard.

251

A few other punters had drifted out and were standing around amongst the other people there having a drink and talking, and after the heat and smoke inside it was literally a breath of fresh air. Les shook his shirt and noticed out the back the vintage bike rally appeared to be packing up. He was about to say something to Jimmy when Jimmy turned and stared after some bloke walking past the bottle shop out the front.

'Hey, I think that's Ian,' he said.

With his drink in one hand and his bag over his shoulder, Jimmy started towards the front of the hotel. Curious as to what Jimmy's contact—the mysterious Ian—looked like, Les thought he might tag along and have a look. When he got there Jimmy was standing in the driveway looking around him and obviously whoever he was looking for was nowhere to be seen. The only people around were a few in the bigger carpark on the left and some people standing around an old motorbike parked next to the driveway at the very end of the smaller carpark on their right.

'That's funny,' said Jimmy, 'I'm sure that was him. I wonder where he got to?'

'Maybe he's disappeared into the X-Files,' said Les. 'Maybe he went mad and the police shot him.'

'What?'

Les half laughed at his own joke and looked at his watch. Jimmy's contact didn't look like showing up, the band had finished and Les felt like leaving because that last beer was nice and cold and he was starting to get the taste. 'Anyway,' he said, 'it's all over here. Why don't we finish these and piss off.'

Jimmy looked at Les as if he was about to say

252

something. Before he got a chance to open his mouth a thundering, throbbing roar seemed to come from out of nowhere. It got louder, then suddenly howled round the corner from the direction of McDonald's. It was about twenty or so Harley-Davidsons followed by a Ford towing a box-trailer. As they went past and slowed down, Les got a glimpse of the colours on one bikie's back. A redback spider and Red Backs Motorcycle Club. It was one of the gangs Jimmy had been talking about. They were all wearing various bikie paraphernalia; wraparound sunglasses, metal-studded wristbands, bandanas, heavy boots with chains around them. Some had beards; others had their hair in plaits; one or two wore helmets. The noise as they revved their Harleys and parked them, back wheels to the bush, opposite the hotel was deafening; leaves and branches fell from the trees, dust flew in the air, any birds or other animals around went for their lives. The last time Les had seen anything like this was in Hawaii. But this didn't look like some charity, fluffy-doll ride. They switched off their engines and the road captain ran round, got the sergeant-at-arms and they started to unlock the box-trailer. Les looked at Jimmy, who had this strange smile on his face as if he was enjoying the show. The other few people standing by looked apprehensive. Les was about to ask Jimmy if he knew what was going on when more angry, rolling thunder hung in the air for a second, got closer, then another bikie gang roared around the opposite corner, saw the other gang and gunned their Harleys straight into the bigger carpark. They were all dressed much the same as the others and again the noise was like all hell let loose. Bottles fell from the shelves in the bottle shop, the walls shook and car alarms started going off all over the carpark. As the second gang of bikies revved their huge machines to a halt Les noticed something on the side of the trailer. A skull with eyes and an axe in it and Mongeroloids M.C. Like the others, they switched off their motors and started milling around the trailer.

Les smelled trouble now. He was about to tell Jimmy it was time to make tracks and if Jimmy wanted to hang around he was on his own when several shots rang out from across the road and a volley of shotgun pellets blasted the windows and tail lights from some of the cars parked near the bottle shop. There were loud curses and screams of pain as several Mongeroloids went down, then more shots. The people standing round the old motorbike stopped what they were doing and ran for their lives into the hotel court-yard, along with anybody else who happened to be there. Being almost in the middle of the crossfire, Les thought it might be a good idea, too. He tossed his bottle of beer away and was about to leg it when Jimmy grabbed him from behind and somehow managed to trip him backwards down between the old motorbike and the car parked next to it.

'What the fuck are you doing?' cursed Les, rolling over onto his stomach, his eyes about two inches away from Jimmy's.

'What are you talking about?' said Jimmy, the silly smile still on his face. 'I just saved your life.'

'Saved my life, be fucked,' howled Les, as another volley of shotgun blasts rang out; one shattering the windscreen on the car they were lying next to. 'Now we're fuckin' stuck here.'

'Shut up, you whingeing big sheila and watch this. You won't see anything like this again for a while.'

'Jesus, I don't fuckin' believe it,' howled Les again.

Having a small element of surprise by firing first, the Red Backs began advancing across the street. Some were firing sawn-off shotguns and pistols, others were armed with baseball bats, chains, iron bars, machettes; anything that could smash bones, bust heads or mutilate somebody in general. The Mongeroloids were all armed now, taking cover behind the cars or the walls in front of the bottle shop and firing into the Red Backs. Several Red Backs went down, their faces and chests blown apart from shotgun pellets. A couple of Mongeroloids fell amongst the parked cars, oozing blood, as more shotgun pellets shattered windscreens and tail lights, raked door panels, ricocheted and tore posters off the wall in front of the bottle shop. Next thing it was like one murderous mosh pit of howling, screaming men as they converged on each other, shooting, cursing, hacking, stabbing and bashing in a wild free-for-all.

Les looked up and couldn't believe it; they seemed to be all around him, either in groups or on their own. Men were going down with their heads bashed in, throats cut, their faces shot off, limbs broken or blown away. Norton watched as one bikie came up behind another, swung a blood-stained baseball bat across the side of his face, smashing his jaw and shattering his teeth. He hit the ground just as another bikie brought a machette down across his assailant's head, splitting it open like a rockmelon. He went down next to the other one and two other bikies started bashing them on the ground till one got shot in the ribs and the other got a chain wrapped round his face. The screams and curses and the sounds of gunshots and the steady whack and thump of baseball bats smashing heads and breaking bones was horrendous.

Jimmy nudged Norton in the ribs. 'Unreal or what, Les?' he said, the stupid smile still on his face.

'Unreal?' yelled Les. 'You fuckin' idiot. I just hope we get out of this alive.'

If Les hadn't have been trying to climb underneath the carpark and pull the tar surface over the top of him, he would have belted Jimmy one right there on the spot. In the meantime, all he could do was watch the frenzy going on around him, hope a stray bullet or shotgun blast didn't hit him or a bunch of nutters with knives and baseball bats didn't come across him, and try to stay alive. Just as Les was praying things wouldn't get any worse, another wall of rumbling, reverberating thunder approached, somehow sounding louder and more sinister than before. Les looked up as another bikie gang came storming up the short street from across the other side of the main road. They didn't bother about the other traffic or anything else, but roared straight over the roundabout and back onto the road, a huge shower of sparks flying in their wake coming from the soles of their boots. From where Norton was it looked like twenty or more fiery chariots from hell. Les didn't have to be told it was the Tarheels. They didn't have a trailer; just axes hanging from chains round their necks and shotguns in scabbards across the handlebars of their Harleys. In what looked like one rehearsed movement, they parked their motorbikes, switched off the engines and, like a mob of wild animals, charged straight into the Mongeroloids and the Red Backs, shooting and hacking.

If it was bad before, now, with the arrival of a third gang even more vicious than the others if that was possible, it was pure, insane bloody carnage and made the Milperra bikie massacre look like a Buddhist picnic.

Les turned round to find Jimmy smiling at him. 'Right on time,' said Jimmy, 'and so nice to see them, too.'

Les stared back at Jimmy, both in disbelief and horror. 'You knew this was going to be on, didn't you? That's why you came over.'

'I had half an idea,' shrugged Jimmy. 'But I still had to bring Ian his whip.'

More shots rang out and more bikies went down screaming and covered in blood as the battle intensified around them. Ignoring Les, Jimmy calmly got up on his knees, unzipped his overnight bag and took out a small, bundled-up black towel. Carefully he placed it on the ground and opened it to reveal a chunky pistol with a squared-over barrel and a fat-looking handle and three clips of bullets. Les had seen one at Eddie's. It was a Glock 9 mm.

Norton's eyes widened like soup bowls. 'Jimmy, what the fuck . . .?'

Jimmy slapped a clip of bullets into the Glock, working a round into the chamber, placed the other two clips in the front pocket of his jacket, then stood up and smiled at Norton. 'They had some fun with my mother,

Les. Now it's my turn to have some fun with them.'

Norton shook his head. 'Jimmy, you're . . .'

Les watched dumbfounded at first, then absolutely amazed, as Jimmy stepped across to the grass behind the old motorbike, got into a combat stance and took out four Tarheels with five shots. Two got it square in the chest, the other two got it in the head. The fifth shot tore through the throat of a Red Back who didn't get out of the way quickly enough. Like Jimmy said on the beach, he couldn't fight, but give him a weapon of some sort and he was pretty sweet. He certainly knew how to use a gun. Jimmy crouched a little lower and took out another two Tarheels with two bullets to the chest. A Tarheel raised a sawn-off shotgun at Jimmy, fired and missed. Jimmy shot him in the face from about four metres away, then shot a Mongeroloid standing behind him through the heart.

Suddenly, instead of anger, Les felt a sense of jubilation for Jimmy and, temporarily unaware of the danger around him, sat up. Yeah, go, Jimmy, go, he thought. Have a get-square with these cunts. And he began mentally cheering Jimmy on. Maybe Jimmy tuned into Norton's thoughts or maybe he was trying to show off a little, but he turned round and flashed Norton one of his magical smiles. Les smiled back, nodded, winked and gave Jimmy a thumbs-up. Jimmy turned back to the battle, emptied the last of the clip into a Tarheel, almost blowing his chest apart, jammed another clip into the Glock then shot another Tarheel through the eye and a Red Back holding a chain with two bullets in the stomach. Whether he was speeding, brave or plain impervious to the melee around him,

Jimmy was dropping baddies like Clint Eastwood in *The Outlaw Josey Wales* and, at the rate he was going, looked like taking out every Tarheel left standing. Les watched him empty another clip into them and their Harleys. Then, as Jimmy reloaded, Les saw a movement near the front of the bottle shop. A Mongeroloid with blood streaming down his face and dripping from his beard raised a shotgun and aimed it at Jimmy.

Despite the danger, Les leapt to his feet. 'Jimmy, behind you,' he yelled out.

Jimmy didn't hear Les. He had his arms out in front of him holding the Glock and the blast took him under his left armpit. He shuddered with pain and shock, raised his arms over his head, still holding the gun, as the Mongeroloid reloaded and fired again. The next one half missed, but a few pellets hit Jimmy in the side of the face, sending his sunglasses flying. He spun slightly to his right and Les saw another movement in front of him as a Red Back raised his shotgun and shot Jimmy in his young, handsome face, blowing most of it away. Jimmy slowly sank to his backside, the Glock fell on the ground and the Red Back reloaded and shot him once more in the chest. What was left of Jimmy Rosewater's lifeless body slumped to the driveway, oozing blood everywhere, literally shot to pieces.

'Jimmy. No! Ohh, fuckin' no!' Les stared down at Jimmy and punched one hand into another with grief and frustration. Whatever Jimmy was, he didn't deserve that.

Even though Jimmy had thinned the ranks of fighters, the battle was still raging around Les. He looked away from Jimmy and saw the two bikies who had just shot Jimmy aim their guns at him. Les hit the deck as they both fired at once. One blast hit the wall of the hotel, the other blew the back windows out of the car next to him. Les looked up and saw the two bikies advancing towards where he was lying, waiting to get a good shot at him. For some reason they'd got a fixation on killing him instead of each other; for the time being anyway. Les felt his mouth go dry and it was like the last seconds of his life were ticking away and there wasn't much he could do. If he stayed there he'd get shot, if he stood up he'd get shot, if he got up and made a run for it he'd still get shot. He looked across at Jimmy's body, crumpled and bleeding on the driveway, and thought, it won't be long before I'll be joining you in the Dreamtime.

Then Les noticed Jimmy's bag still open where he'd left it. In one movement he grabbed the handle of the stockwhip and flipped the bag up in the air. The Red Back saw it, fired and missed. The Mongeroloid pulled the trigger on his shotgun and blew Jimmy's bag to pieces. This gave Norton just enough time to jump up, whirl the whip round his head and crack it across the Mongeroloid's already bleeding face, slicing his lips open through his beard, making him drop the gun and yelp with pain. Les spun the whip round again and in a backhand movement lashed the Red Back across the eyes. He screamed, clutched at his face and dropped his shotgun also.

The stockwhip was beautifully crafted and balanced and just about anyone could make it work. But in Norton's powerful hands it was a cruel and deadly weapon. He turned back to the Mongeroloid, still clutching at his face, and lashed him across the neck. He went down on his knees and Les lashed him again and again, ripping his jacket and his colours to pieces. He rolled up in a ball and Les lashed him in the groin from behind; even above the noise going on around them the Mongeroloid's scream hung in the air as Les almost castrated him. Then Norton turned to the Red Back and started to mercilessly flog him, ripping bloodied strips of flesh from his hands and scalp and tearing off one of his ears. The Red Back screamed with pain and tried to roll up in a ball also as Les kept lashing him. After what they did to Jimmy, Les could quite happily have flogged both bikies to death. Then it all left him. Norton's rage and adrenalin settled down and reason mixed with self-preservation took over. Shit, he thought, his chest still heaving, this is madness. I've got to get out of here. *Now*. But bloody how?

With the screams and curses of wounded and fighting men hanging in the air along with gun shots and the whiz of shotgun pellets flying around the carpark, Les crouched back down between the old motorbike and the car next to it and looked for an escape route. He didn't fancy running into the hotel and being stuck inside with all the screaming patrons; even then he'd have to sprint through a perimeter of fighting bikies and there was a chance he'd walk into a baseball bat, stop a knife or get shot in the back. Forget trying to find a cab. No taxi would come within cooee of the place at the moment. What about the limo? Hah! Even if he knew the number, Jimmy's mobile, along with his bag, had been blown all over the carpark. And the limo driver would be thinking the same as the cab drivers. It looked like a long walk or run back to Terrigal. *If* he could get out. Then Les noticed whoever owned the old motorbike had left the keys in it when they ran off. That'll do. I haven't ridden one for a while, but I can learn again. What kind is it? The old bike was all sparkling chrome and shiny black leather and paint, and when Les saw what was written along the side in gold paint he couldn't believe his eyes. NORTON 850 COMMANDO. He looked up at the sky. It was truly the prophecy. He curled the stockwhip round his neck, straddled the Norton and looked for the ignition. There wasn't one. It was a true man's bike. He flipped the jets, turned on the ignition, kicked the stand back and jumped on the kick start. Nothing. Just a cough and he felt as if he'd dislocated his knee. Then Les remembered—you don't jump all over these old sweethearts. You tickle them more with your toes. He hit the starter a bit softer with the ball of his foot and bingo! The old Norton roared into life with a sweet, even note that crackled straight out the twin exhausts running along the sides. Les gave it a couple of revs, backed it out a bit, kicked it into what he was certain was first gear and hit it. Not ready for so much power, Les thought he was riding a Saturn space rocket and skidded and slewed across the grassy median strip, nearly losing it and scattering several bikies in the process. One Red Back was a bit slow, so Les went straight over him, breaking both his legs. He thumped the bike over a couple of dead bodies, then ducked under a swinging baseball bat as he heard a couple of shots behind him and a whizzing sound go past his head. But whether Les had been shot or not, he didn't know. He was

262

going that fast he'd probably outrun the buckshot and in barely seconds he'd grabbed the brakes and skidded to a halt before the roundabout at the end of the street. There wasn't that much traffic. Everybody was probably still in a log jam at the back of the hotel or too frightened to go to their cars. Les eased the throttle this time, took a right at the roundabout and, with the wind streaming through his hair, the stockwhip jammed against his chest and his shirt flapping behind him in the breeze, high-tailed it towards Terrigal as the first motorbike burst into flames outside the hotel.

Only that he'd just got one of the biggest frights of his life and on top of seeing what happened to poor little Jimmy, Les would have enjoyed the ride home. The old Norton had a ton of grunt and handled like a charm once you got used to it. Losing his sunglasses in the melee and not being able to protect his eyes didn't help much either. Les slewed his head from one side to the other as the wind whipped at his face and hair. He switched the lights on just as a police wagon screamed past in the opposite direction, its siren howling and lights flashing. Les hit the throttle and easily went past an old Kombi wagon. After that it was just a few more bends and he took the right turn to Price's house. Just back from the corner, he switched off the lights, cut the engine and coasted quietly up to the garage. He kicked the stand out, opened the garage door, then pushed the Norton inside and closed it again behind him. After standing the bike up again at one end of the garage, Les threw the whip over the handlebars and went inside.

Norton's adrenalin was still pumping and his hands

263

were shaking slightly when he stood in the kitchen and poured himself a glass of water. It was the same glass Jimmy had been using before they left. Even though his face felt like it had been sand-blasted, his hair was plastered against his scalp and his eyes were red and sore, Les still couldn't quite believe what he'd just seen and been through. He went into the bathroom, switched on the light and looked at himself in the mirror and was surprised to find flecks of dried blood across his cheeks and tiny nicks in his ears. Either shards of flying glass had cut him or some stray shotgun pellets had just grazed him and in the madness going on around him, he hadn't felt it. Whatever it was, he'd certainly been lucky again. The face staring back at Norton looked shocked, strained and grainy, not a good look at all, and inside, Norton's stomach and chest were a volcano of heaving emotions, almost making him physically sick. However, Les didn't need a beautician or an Alka-Seltzer. What Les wanted was to get out of there and back home. And the sooner the better. He finished the glass of water and started gathering his things.

The food in the fridge could stay there, along with whatever was in Jimmy's room; Price could sort that out through the week and the old motorbike in the garage too. The booze went with him because Les knew as soon as he got back to Bondi he was going to have the one; and one more and another one after that.

He turned off all the lights, made sure the house was secure then went out to the garage and slung his bags on the back seat of the car along with the whip. That was definitely going with him. The stockwhip had probably saved his life. Trying to be as cool as he could, Les opened the garage door, quietly backed the Berlina out and locked the garage door behind him. After one last look at the house, Les slipped the T-bar into drive and split for Sydney. He was going past the high school and almost at Terrigal Drive when he remembered the box of machine guns was still in the boot. Shit, Les cursed to himself. What should he do with the fuckin' things? If he took them back to the house he'd have to stuff around finding a place to hide them and if the cops came round they still might find them. If they pulled him over . . . Pulled him over? Any cops in the area, on or off-duty, would only have one thing on their mind at the moment. A quiet gentleman driving a nice new sedan in the correct manner wouldn't get a second look. It turned out Les was right about cops. As he went past the Avoca turn-off there were heaps of them; along with ambulances, fire engines and media crews, and all heading in the one direction. Les settled back a little and motored on past Brisbane Water. He climbed the hill out of Gosford and was going past the turn-off to Kurrirong Juvenile Justice Centre, where the whole sorry saga started, when Les switched the radio on, pushed some buttons and somehow managed to find 2GB.

The brawl was news all right. It was news, more news, world news and news in between the news. There were on-the-spot interviews with police, ambulance drivers, paramedics, firemen, eye-witnesses. Already the press was calling it 'the Broadwater Bikie Massacre'. The further Les drove, the higher the body count rose. By the time he got to Jolls Bridge it was 27 dead and 31 injured. All gang members except for one innocent bystander; an unidentified male standing by the bottle shop. Police had cordonned off the area and made 100 arrests. I know who the unidentified bystander was, thought Norton. And with the wallopers running around arresting everyone in sight, you can bet that's where I'd be now if I hadn't got away. Les switched the radio off and went to slip on a tape, but found he couldn't handle any music. His nerves were on edge, he still felt sick, and every time a police car or ambulance would go screaming past he'd get a knot in his stomach. He kicked the Berlina back to overtake a car towing a boat and, although his mind was going every which way at once, he tried to kick a few things over in his head.

Bloody Jimmy. He'd been psyching himself up ever since Les had mentioned bikies on Saturday night. Whatever those Tarheels did to his mother, he sure wanted to get square. All the time he was walking around the hotel with the whip, he had that gun in his bag. And as soon as he saw them he jumped up and started blazing away. And he wanted Les to see it too. Maybe he was on a death wish? Maybe the Jack Daniels sent him off. Every time he had a JD and Coke he went a bit spare; bashing and abusing women. Well, he got square, all right. And where did it get him, in his Kirk Douglas, *Falling Down* outfit? Dead. Blown to pieces on a hotel driveway. Norton shuddered at the memory. Kirk Douglas. Michael Douglas. Whatever. Like father, like son. Stuffed if I know. Anyway, he's gone now, poor bastard. And I'm only lucky I didn't go with him. Then as Norton drove on in silence, his runaway mind took another tack. A slightly more suspicious one. It's funny how Uncle Price and Uncle George never mentioned nephew Jimmy to me before. And how they told me he was only in the nick over a bit of pot when really it was for outboard motors. That's no big deal, I suppose, but I only found out when I offhandedly asked Jimmy. And it just seems a bit of a coincidence all this going down the same time they got him out. Jimmy could have been doing it on his own, but I just wonder if Price had something to do with it? Him and Eddie. Eddie doesn't mind dealing in guns. And they both like a shifty earn now and again. Shit, we all do. It wouldn't surprise me in the least.

Norton caught his face in the rear-vision mirror as he watched a car's headlights coming up behind him. I'm getting a feeling there's more to this than meets the eye. I'm also getting that feeling I've been had—again. Norton's eyes narrowed as he slowed down for the lights at the Hornsby turn-off and he started thinking about some of the people he'd met at Terrigal and some of the things they said. The lights turned green and Les was still thinking as he joined the other traffic on the Pacific Highway. By the time he was approaching the Harbour Bridge, Les thought he might make one stop before Bondi and catch up with a few old friends.

A few doors up from the Kelly Club was a driveway with a sign across the shutters saying STRICTLY NO PARKING. 24 HOURS A DAY. OFFENDERS WILL BE PROSECUTED. Les drove straight up to the sign, turned off the motor, and got out of the car. After having a quick look around while he stretched his legs, he opened the boot, took the wooden crate out and laid it on the ground.

For its size, it wasn't as heavy as Les thought and how many guns and whatever were in it, he could only guess. He locked his bags along with the whip in the boot, took the crate by the two rope handles, then walked up to the Kelly Club and knocked on the door. Billy opened it. Standing behind him eating a sandwich was Danny McCormack.

'Les, what are you doing back already? Shit, what's in the box?'

'Chocolate Surprises,' replied Les, as Billy closed the door behind him. 'Is Price here?'

'Yeah, they're all up in the office. Kerry's keeping an eye on things.'

'Good.' Les walked across to the stairs. 'Hello, Danny.'

'G'day, Les. I thought you weren't working tonight.'

'I'm not. I just stopped by for a sandwich.'

'Yeah, I don't blame you,' Danny nodded enthusiastically. 'The smoked salmon and onion chutney's unreal.'

'If you've got a minute later, Billy, come upstairs.'

'Yeah . . . all right.'

Norton manhandled the wooden crate up the stairs and into the casino. Being early it wasn't very crowded. A couple of punters looked up momentarily, saw who it was, then went back to their cards. Kerry, the dark-haired hostess, wearing a smart green dress, smiled over from the other side of the room; Les smiled back then walked across to the office, knocked on the door, carried the crate inside and closed the door behind him.

George was seated to the right of Price's desk, Eddie was sitting on the lounge, Price was standing in the middle showing Eddie something in the Sunday paper. George was wearing a dark blue double-breasted jacket, Eddie his favourite black leather jacket, Price looked his usual immaculate self in a light grey suit and matching silk tie. They all looked up at Norton's knock, then gave a double blink when he walked in and placed the wooden crate on Price's desk.

'Les, how are you, mate?' said Price. 'What are you doing back so soon?'

'I had to cut the holiday short. Hello, George. G'day, Eddie.'

George looked as surprised as Price. 'Les, what a pleasant surprise.'

'Christ,' said Eddie. 'What happened to you? You look like you've just been bashed and raped by Aeon Flux.'

'What happened? I'm glad you asked, Eddie.' Before Les could start to come up with some sarcastic answer, Price threw the Sunday paper on the lounge and started jumping up and down excitedly, yelling out to George.

'He got them. He got them. Les, you're a bloody genius.' Price threw his arms around Norton's shoulders and kissed him on top of the head. 'What a guy. What a bloody guy.'

Les pushed Price away—not roughly, but firm enough to make him sit down on the lounge next to Eddie. 'I got them, eh?' Les said through clenched teeth. '*I got them*? You were in on this.'

'Well, yeah.' Price looked at George and Eddie. 'I mean, we all—'

'You were all in on it.' Norton's anger was starting

to rise. 'You low bastards. I should have known. You bastards.'

Eddie looked puzzled. 'Les, what's—?'

Les ignored him. 'All right, let's just see what you got for your fuckin' blood money.' Before any of the others could say or do anything, Les went to a closet in the office corner that held some tools and other odds and ends. He found a hammer, dropped it and picked up a small pinch bar. Still grim-faced, he walked back to the crate and jammed the pinch bar under one of the pine boards.

'Les, what the fuck are you doing?' yelled Price. 'Christ, take it easy.'

'He's gone mad,' said George.

'Shut up. The fuckin' lot of you.'

Eddie, Price and George sat there looking at Les and looking at each other. They'd seen the big Queenslander throw the odd wobbly now and again, but this was a strange one. Best to let him run. If the worst came to the worst Eddie could shoot him in the leg. There was a knock on the door and Billy walked in. Not quite knowing what was going on, but sensing something odd was in the air, he sat down on a seat alongside Eddie and joined the others staring at Les. Les continued to jemmy the wooden crate. It creaked and groaned and the nails popped with a rasping, dry screech and it was obvious they'd been in there a long time. He jemmied some more wooden boards away till there was enough room to get his hand through; inside, the crate was packed with old wood shavings, pieces of greasy wool clippings and yellowed newspapers. Norton put the pinch bar on the desk, reached in and

270

pulled out the first thing he got his hand on. It was a bottle of wine.

'Wine?'

'Yeah. Wine,' said Price. 'What did you think was in there, you fuckin' big hillbilly? Chocolate Surprises?'

'I thought it was guns.'

'Guns? Are you off your dopey bloody head?'

'I . . . I'm starting to think I am.'

Les looked at the dusty bottle. It was clear, chunky in shape with a fine, elongated neck and a delicate lace pattern on the glass. The cork was sealed with wax and whatever was inside was a beautiful, rich pink. On the front was a white label with a little pink rose in the corner. Les wiped the dust off and written on the label in old, Germanic print was 'Father Gunther-Otto Eindhoven. Avondale Muscat Rosé. '38. Lot 2'.

'Anyway, give me that.' Price snatched the bottle of wine out of Norton's hand and sat back down on the lounge, cradling it like it was a newborn baby.

Suddenly, as well as being angry and confused, Les felt lost; deflated. 'Price,' he said, 'would you mind telling me what's going on?'

Price looked at George for a second as if they both thought it might be best to get it over with as quickly as possible. 'All right,' he said. 'I'll admit we weren't quite fair dinkum with you first up.' Price's voice was calm and soothing, almost fatherly towards Les as he spoke. 'Jimmy is a bit of a villain. A bit. But all that trouble he was in, in the nick, is true, and it wasn't his fault. So, anyway, he got in touch with me and George and said if I could get him leave for a week and sort all this Elliott out he'd do something for me. He knew I

271

liked to collect wine and he said he knew where this special crate of wine was from when he worked up the Hunter Valley and how he could get it. So I pulled a few strings. Shit! Did I have to pull a few strings! Spread a heap of bloody money around. And here it is.' Price gave the bottle a little kiss. 'Jimmy was telling the truth.'

'But why go to all that trouble?' said Les. 'I mean, what's so special about a few bottles of plonk?'

'It's worth about twenty-five grand a bottle,' said George. 'Is that special enough?'

'It's more than that,' said Price. 'This is like having a Rembrandt. It was made by an old German monk who came out here just before the Second World War. He was about the first person to start a winery in the Hunter Valley when there was nothing up there but trees and kangaroos. He made some other wines, then he made this Avondale Rosé from some unique grapes he brought out with him from Germany. He only made four batches and a horse kicked the poor old bludger in the face. Where one case is, nobody knows. One got opened somehow and that's how the wine buffs got to know how good it is. Some bloke was hoarding another crate and it all got smashed during the Newcastle earthquake. And Uncle Price has now got the other one. I know talking about wine shits you a bit, Les, but you've delivered me the holy grail of Australian wine. Thanks, mate, I owe you another one.'

Norton shook his head. 'I don't believe it.'

'That's all it was, mate,' said Price. 'Vintage wine. Very expensive vintage wine. But just vintage wine.

The bloke Jimmy stole it off stole it in the first place. So it's doubtful if he's going to do anything. And the reason I didn't say anything at first was because I thought you might have got the wrong idea and in case Jimmy might have been half full of shit. Eddie was coming up in the morning to get the crate and have a bit of lunch with you. Then you and Jimmy could continue spending all my money and having a good time in Terrigal, doing whatever it is you were doing.'

'Didn't Jimmy tell you, you big goose?' asked George.

'Yeah, what have you done with Jimmy anyway?' asked Price.

'Jimmy's dead.'

'Dead?' All four voices seemed to echo round the office at once. Price and Eddie sat up on the lounge. George's face almost hit the floor.

'I've just been caught in that bikie massacre at Broadwater. Jimmy got shot. I nearly got shot myself.'

'Shot? Ohh, no,' said George. 'Don't fuckin' say that.'

'I saw that on TV before I got here,' said Eddie. 'It's all over the news. Were you there?' Not that Eddie needed to know when Les was telling the truth.

Neither did Billy. 'Shit! I saw some of it, too. What happened, Les?'

'It was a horror show,' said Les. 'I can tell you that.'

Les gave them a quick rundown on what happened at the hotel and how they happened to be there. Jimmy pulling out the gun, the whip, picking up his bag at the massacre house, the two bikies shooting him. Getting away on the Norton, the vintage bike show. It was a bit

273

of a jumble and Les was letting it all hang out, but somehow the others managed to understand what he was talking about. Yet at the same time Les was talking and watching their astonished faces; in between sentences, he kept thinking about Jimmy. Jimmy had been telling the truth all along. When Les asked him what was in the box, Jimmy told him. Bottles of wine. Red wine. He just didn't elaborate at the time because he was still probably feeling uptight about getting lost and keeping the other two waiting. And like he said, it would go straight over Norton's head. Then, when Les was trying to be clever and asked Jimmy what he'd have with the wine, and Jimmy said spaghetti at the No Names, that was just Jimmy's cynical sense of humour. The No Names would be just the place you'd take a $25,000 bottle of wine to eat with a $6 plate of spaghetti on a laminex table. Although Jimmy probably would have explained it all to him when Eddie arrived, he couldn't be bothered at the time, so he had a loan of Les. Which wasn't hard for Jimmy. And Norton, in his usual, untrusting, bull-at-a-gate style of thinking, had got his bowels in a great, big, screaming knot again over nothing. There was no gun deal going down with any bikies. Jimmy took the whip to the hotel for that bloke Ian and one of his mates who might have wanted one too. Jimmy was just hell-bent on revenge with that bikie gang, and when the chance came he took it. Maybe he thought he could get away with it in all the confusion. Maybe he was speeding. Who knows what was going through his mind half the time. Bloody Jimmy. You could say what you liked about him, but he had style and he had balls. And it was like that crazy bloke said—he could certainly arrange things if he had to. Maybe he shouldn't have belted poor silly Megan, but she was a disaster waiting to happen and in a way she was lucky she only got it off a lightweight. One thing for sure, wherever Jimmy was now, he'd be having the last laugh on Norton. Try not to look like a Queenslander, Les. Whoops. Too late, you've done it again.

'There's heaps more happened than that up there,' said Les, 'but honestly, I wouldn't know where to begin.'

'Christ! That's not bad for a start,' said Eddie.

'What about the escape from the hotel?' said Billy. 'Indiana Jones, eat your heart out.'

'I'll tell you what you need, Les,' said Price. 'A drink. In fact after that, I might even get you one myself.'

'Not a bad idea,' said Les, feeling a lot lighter and happier, now that he'd sorted things out a bit and got things off his chest. Then Norton got that look in his eye again. He snatched the bottle of wine out of Price's hands. 'What's this taste like?'

'Taste like?' howled Price. 'You don't drink that, you fuckin' hillbilly. It's a collector's item.'

'What do you mean, you don't drink it? It's piss, ain't it?'

Before Price or anyone else had a chance to do anything, Les got a bottle opener from the bar, scraped away the wax seal and uncorked the bottle of wine with a gentle pop. He placed five whisky tumblers on Price's desk, filled them, then offered them around. Everybody took one except George.

Les raised his glass. 'Well, here's to Jimmy.'

'To Jimmy,' said Eddie.

'Jimmy,' nodded Billy solemnly.

'Yeah, bloody nephew Jimmy,' said Price, staring mournfully at the opened twenty-five thousand dollar bottle of rosé sitting next to the old wooden crate on his desk.

Les watched Price for a moment, then took a sip. Whether he appreciated good wine or not, it was the best Norton had ever tasted; or any liquor for that matter. It had a sweet, gentle fragrance, was silky smooth and slid down your throat with an exquisite taste that was almost heavenly. Slightly chilled, it would have been like drinking honeyed sunshine. Even sitting in the thick whisky glass, the wine's delicate beauty seemed to capture the light in the room and sparkle like a handful of tiny, pink diamonds. Nevertheless, Norton had to show his crass ignorance.

'Yeah, not bad,' he said, licking his lips, 'but there's no way it's worth twenty-five grand a bottle. It's not sweet enough.' So Les got some ice cubes from the bar fridge and dropped them in his glass, then opened a small bottle of lemonade and pretended to add that as well. He stirred the ice cubes around with his index finger, licked it, then took a sip. 'Yeah, that's better. It just needed a bit of sugar.'

Price buried his face in one hand. 'I don't believe it,' he said, shaking his head with despair.

'Tastes pretty good to me,' said Billy.

'Beautiful,' agreed Eddie. 'I've never tasted anything like it.'

'Yeah, you're probably right,' said Les, 'but what

would you expect from a poor, hillbilly Queenslander that hangs around with Mafia types and assassins that go round burying people.'

George was still staring silently into space, his glass of wine where Norton had left it on Price's desk, untouched. Les reached over and gave the glass a gentle clink.

'Well, come on, George. Don't look so sad. Drink up. Have one for Jimmy. I mean, he was only your nephew. It's not as if you lost a son or something, is it—Kirk Douglas?'

George turned slowly to Norton. 'What are you talking about, Les?'

Norton shook his head. 'Nothing. Nothing at all, dancing man. Nothing at all.'